WYN1

The Wyndspelle Trilogy
Book One

Aola Vandergriff

SAPERE
BOOKS

WYNDSPELLE

Published by Sapere Books.

24 Trafalgar Road, Ilkley, LS29 8HH

saperebooks.com

ISBN: 978-0-85495-577-0

For Mother and Dad
Whom I have loved the longest

For Noel and Sean
My latest loves

And for Bill
— eternally —

PROLOGUE

Winter held back, giving the grim rock-bound coast one more blue day.

To the Puritan folk in their inland settlement, it was only another Sabbath, to be spent in Meeting. The scattering of cabins and cottages stood deserted in the Sunday stillness. Nothing moved on the common. Even the colt in the far pasture was quiet, seeming to sense the strictures of the Puritan religion.

It was only near the spring on the forest path that a bird dared to sing and the leaves flaunt their colors.

Down the coast, much farther, there was life. Portuguese fishermen in their small village watched the reaches of the sea, seeing the gray rim along the horizon that sped them to secure their gear for what they knew was to come.

Between the Puritan colony and the fisherfolk was Wyndspelle. High on a promontory above a rocky beach and an unpredictable sea, it bridged a chasm in the face of the crag; a rift that was widest where it touched the water, forming a natural landing for small craft. Below it now, the waves purred like a kitten at a saucer of milk as they lapped gently at the cleft in the rock.

And while the Puritans prayed in Meeting and the Portuguese fishermen hastened to secure their gear against the coming storm, the house waited. Wyndspelle waited for the wind to come, and the waves to rise.

For when the sea thundered below it, exploding into white plumes against the stone in anger, spume flying on the screaming wind, the house would come to life —

And begin to breathe —

CHAPTER 1

The floors had been scrubbed and now the small cabin reeked with the odor of wet wood. Adria looked toward the caulked wooden buckets which were on a low shelf against the wall. They were almost empty, and a trip to the spring was forbidden on a Sabbath Day.

Well, they were all in Meeting. Who would know? Besides, scrubbing floors was forbidden, too, on this day of rest and worship. Yet that was exactly what Reverend Potts, her adoptive father, had ordered her to do. And all because young Tim Tyson had looked on her, Adria, with favor, rather than the Reverend's lumpy daughter, Naomi.

"The devil is in you, girl!" he had thundered. "You are not fit to sit in the house of God. You will remain home this day!"

Adria suppressed a smile. He had considered making her remain here a punishment. Scrubbing floors was a small price to pay for freedom. How she dreaded Sundays! Forced to sit quietly, the sound of Reverend Potts' voice droning in her ears, knowing she would be questioned as to the sermon's content later.

She had even feared that Mistress Potts, the minister's namby-pamby wife, might put in a word in her defense, suggesting that it was the Lord's Day, and Adria should attend the Meeting. Thankfully, the woman did not. She, too, had her nose out of joint because Tim shunned Naomi. Besides, a clean house helped to alleviate her worry over Adria's soul; Adria was sure of that.

And now, the water pails were near-empty. While outside, freedom beckoned, the forest called...

Dared she?

She dared!

Adria picked up the buckets, one for drinking, one for washing, and stepped through the cabin door. There, leaning against the wall, was the wooden yoke used for water-carrying. Hanging the empty buckets from it, she slipped it over her shoulders, then glanced toward the square, weathered building that was the Meeting House. They would be praying in there. Perhaps for her.

Why was it her the devil had chosen for his own? She, Adria, who brought in the armful of golden flowers that made Reverend Potts sneeze all through his sermon last Sabbath Day; she, for whom the cow would not give down her milk, for whom, sometimes, the butter would not come?

She shivered a little, then tossed her head and raced across the common, skirts flying, buckets jangling, to arrive, cheeks stained a deep rose, at the entrance to the forest path that led to the spring.

It had felt good to run, she thought, sighing and pushing back a tendril of hair that had escaped from her cap. Though running through the forest at her age was considered unseemly. If Reverend Potts went through with his plans to wed her to the aging widower, Joseph Shanks, next spring, there would be no freedom ever. She would cook and sew, care for a sick old man with grown children of his own. Maybe — the thought was repellent — bear him more.

She would not think of that now. Putting the buckets down, she breathed in deeply, savoring the late autumn day. Most of the leaves had already fallen to the ground, but the few that still clung to the trees, dancing in a faint breeze, were incredible shades of red and gold. Adria reached for one, holding it in slim brown fingers, admiring its color. She would like to have a gown in that shade. But that would be a sinful vanity, according to Reverend Potts.

"My mother wore such colors," she had told him. "She had a scarlet petticoat for best."

"Then your mother is doomed to everlasting hell," was his answer.

Tears trembled on her lashes as she thought of her mother and father. Her parents had hidden her away when the natives came to their home, a distance to the north. And they had died in their burning house. Another family of settlers, fleeing the massacre, had found her and brought her here. Adria had been placed in the care of Reverend Ephraim Potts, now determined to save her soul. She could not manage to feel properly grateful, which was another sign of the devil's hold. How *did* one learn meekness and humility, she wondered...

A bird, scolding from its perch above her, brought her back to the present with a jolt. Dusk was falling. She must get back to the cabin before the other members of the family returned. They would not question the filled pails as long as they did not catch her in the act.

Smiling upward, she answered the bird, saucily, with a clear, warbling imitation. Then she compressed her lips, remembering Reverend Potts' admonition. *"Whistling woman, crowing hen, always come to some bad end."* Turning, she filled the pails, lifting the yoke again to her shoulders.

Her progress as she returned along the path was slow. The yoke was heavy, but no heavier than her heart at the thought of having to return to the minister's cabin. Though she was lucky to have a roof over her head, sometimes she felt like a caged wild bird — and thought she would die of it. There could not be too many days like this left in the year. Soon the cold would come, and the snows. And Adria would be shut in … shut in…

At the edge of the clearing, she stopped. There was something eerie about the late-evening Sabbath stillness. Before her, the scattering of cabins bulked ominously in the approaching dusk. The Meeting House, with its closed doors and windows, seemed to hold no life. And to the left —

To the left, at a great distance, silhouetted where it stood on its promontory overlooking the sea, was the house of the devil. The place they called Wyndspelle. The place of the witch!

It looked frightening enough now, starkly outlined against the sky. But in a little while, the mists would begin to rise around it. The house would float there on a misty sea, seemingly rootless, ethereal…

Adria's heart gave a little bump, as it always did when she looked toward that distant scene. It was as if the structure were a magnet, drawing her to it. Was it more than her lively curiosity which the minister had deplored so often? Or could it be that there was a devil in her? Something that pulled her toward the forbidden, the unknown? She felt a sudden urge to run toward the cabin, but now she must walk carefully. The water would spill. In addition to disobeying the Sabbath laws, she would add the crime of being wasteful.

Cautiously making her way down the path, she stopped, frozen in fear, as a figure stepped in front of her.

A man! But such a man as she had never seen. His fair hair was tied back with a ribbon, and his clothes would be those a prince would wear! A prince, or — the devil.

Gasping, Adria shrank away.

"Your pardon, lass," the stranger said in a soft voice. "Did I frighten you?"

"N — Nay," she managed to stammer.

"Then might I have a drink of water to quench my thirst?"

Adria lifted the yoke from her shoulders, set the pails down, and tipped one of them to fill his cupped hands, noting the lace at his wrists, the fair head that seemed to glow in the dusk.

At last, taking a bit of linen from his sleeve, the man touched his hands and lips. "Now," he said, "Perhaps you can aid me. I am here on an errand, and there seems to be no one about. I seek a good woman to do service in a house where the mistress lies ill. Someone with a knowledge of herbs and healing —"

As he spoke, Adria felt a surge of hope. She had such knowledge, and here was escape. Escape from Reverend Potts and from Joseph Shanks! She opened her lips to volunteer, then remembered that there was no great house near. Nothing but —!

"Where is this place?" she asked.

He indicated Wyndspelle, with a gracious wave of his hand, and she was not surprised.

"You will find no one here. No one," she whispered. "You must look elsewhere. This is a Puritan community. It would be forbidden."

"Puritan?" He studied her sober dress. "Yes, I see." Then his gaze moved to her kerchiefed shoulders, finally to the bright face surrounded by tendrils of dark hair that had escaped from her cap. His hand went out to cup itself under her chin.

"God's teeth!" he said, with a little hiss of indrawn breath. "If you're the spawn of those long-faced sober-sides, then I'm King George!" Laughing, he kissed her cheek.

Stumbling backward, Adria snatched up her burden, placed it across her shoulders, and hurried toward the cabin, spilling water as she went. And after her, the stranger called, "Keep your eyes open, lass. See if there are any among you not too holy to aid a dying woman!"

Once inside the cottage, the pails back on their shelf, door closed behind her, Adria stood with her hand pressed to her cheek. She had been kissed by a stranger. Shamed! The Reverend Potts must never know she had been bussed like a common woman. Perhaps by the devil himself!

What was worse, she had enjoyed it! The vanity she'd been accused of had come to the fore. She'd felt only pleased that he found her fair.

At last, forcing herself to move, she added a few dippers of water to the stew that simmered in a black iron pot in the hearth, and fed sticks of wood to the fire below, poking it into flame. But she could still feel the impact of the stranger's eyes upon her.

She wondered what those eyes had seen as she remembered a bit of mirror-glass her mother had. A glass that was probably now in native hands. Two things had Adria salvaged from that burnt-out cabin: the locket she wore hidden beneath her gown, concealed from Puritan eyes, and the crystal bowl wrapped in an old apron in the loft, beneath her bedding straw. Else her early life might have been a dream.

Her mother was beautiful. Once Adria remembered catching sight of her own face in a clear pool of water and daring to believe she might resemble her.

A pool of water…

Adria caught up her skirts and scurried up the ladder to the loft. Scrabbling in the straw, she found the bowl and carried it down. The family wouldn't return until it was full dark. She would have time…

Heart hammering with excitement, she looked around for the things she would need. A black cloth. The Reverend Potts' old black cloak hung on a nail beside the door. Taking it down, she spread it across the table. Placing the crystal bowl in the middle of it, she carried several dippers of water to fill it to the brim. Then, holding a candle beside her face, she looked down into the water.

It mirrored back her face. Too thin and brown for prettiness, its only beauty lay in her huge, long-lashed eyes. Still searching for a resemblance to the mother she loved, Adria removed her cap, releasing her hair to fall in raven wings. At last, she removed the kerchief that covered her shoulders and unbuttoned the buttons at her throat to let the locket swing and sway. So absorbed was she that she did not notice she was no longer alone.

It was the breathing that caught her attention, a harsh, heavy sound intruding into her dream. She jerked up her head to see Josiah, the Reverend Potts' married son. His eyes looked strange, and his mouth was wet and open as he came toward her, hands reaching out…

"Nay!" she whispered as his hand closed on her arm. "What — what are you doing here? You — you're supposed to be in Meeting!"

"But I'm not." He pulled her toward him. "I'm here. I saw what you did out there! I saw that popinjay kiss you! But you just might be able to persuade me not to tell Papa."

She tried to jerk away, frantic eyes seeking the door. Then his arms were around her and she was struggling, twisting her face away from him, terrified, calling for help.

And help came. It came in the form of a thundering voice from the doorway, a voice that shouted, not *Josiah,* but *Mistress Adria!*

The hands that bruised Adria's arms dropped away and Josiah turned, his mouth agape. In the doorway stood the Reverend Potts, his face suffused with rage. "What does this mean?" he roared.

There was a moment's silence, then Josiah took a step toward his father. Adria held her breath. He was going to tell! Tell about seeing her with the stranger on the common. And the Reverend Potts would believe him. She would be beaten again…

But the words that Josiah brought forth in a choking voice portended more than a beating. "The girl's a *witch*," he said, licking his lips. His eyes shifted away from Adria's startled ones. "A witch! She put a spell on me, sir. I could not help myself!" With one hand, he gestured toward the bowl; the cloak serving as a black cloth beneath it. The candle.

"A witch!" The words hissed from the clergyman's teeth. "May God help us!" Reaching out one thin, black-clad arm, he drew his son behind him. "'Tis not your fault, son. 'Tis mine, for bringing this she-devil into my home!"

"It — it is not as it appears to be! I was only…" Adria started toward the two men, palms outstretched to show her innocence.

"Silence, woman!" Turning to Josiah, the man said, more gently, "We must seek guidance, boy. We must go to the Meeting House and you will testify as to what you have seen here. Then we will decide what must be done."

And they were gone, leaving Adria stunned and shaken. This was the year 1720. They didn't burn witches anymore, did they? If she were accused, she would be found guilty, that she knew. Though she had been here some years, she was still an outsider, a strange bird in the Puritan flock, no matter how she tried to fit in with them. But what would they do to her?

Ducking, like Goody Tillie Frame? *She* had been proven innocent, having sunk like a stone, for whatever good that did her. Or maybe the stocks, like drunken Ben Woolford. But, please God, not burning. She had a horror of fire.

She stared at the table before her, at the crystal bowl on the black cloak, evidence of her guilt. But she didn't see it. Before her eyes was the memory of the burning cabin in which her parents had died. The recollection of their screaming rang in her ears.

She must escape! But where could she run? She had no idea what lay beyond the forest behind the settlement. There would be wild animals, that was a certainty, and this too-warm day had presaged a weather change. She would either die of exposure or be torn to bits.

The coast! If she could make her way along the rocky shore, there was a Portuguese fishing village about two days distant. The Puritans had no truck with those people because of their Popish ways, and there she might be safe. But to get there, she must cross Wyndspelle lands.

Wyndspelle. Though she was terrified at the thought of the place, the stranger she had met on the path had surely been a fair and gentle man. He was no more a devil than she, Adria, was a witch! And they needed someone there to nurse a sick woman. She would go to Wyndspelle and throw herself upon the mercy of whoever — or whatever — lived there. If, as Reverend Potts claimed, it was the home of the devil, was the prospect of hell more frightening than the fate she was facing now?

Besides, she could be of service to the sick woman. She would be needed. No matter what her other crimes had been, she was young, healthy, and not afraid of work. Her small calloused hands were proof of that. Best of all, she would be far from Joseph Shanks, though there would be no question of his wanting to marry her now.

She would go, but not like this. Not like a beggar in the drab gown she stood in. It was stained with scrubbing and soot from the fireplace, the hem soaked with the water she had spilled. Her Sunday gown, and her one pair of rough, hand-cobbled shoes, were in the loft. It would only take a moment to get them.

She started toward the steps that led upward, then stopped short at the sound of the Meeting House bell. The dull, lead-throated bell that rang once for church, thrice to call forth an emergency session to the faithful. People would be returning to the building, calling out to each other excitedly, wondering why they had been summoned so.

She counted the off-key chimes. *One:* they were being called to a session. *Two:* At which Adria Anne Turner would be — *Three:* — tried, judged, and sentenced as a witch.

They would accuse her to her face. They would send someone to fetch her. A wave of terror rose within her. This was happening. It was real! Her very life might be at stake. There was no time to spare —

She would have to go as she was, barefoot and in her soiled gray gown. She would take only her precious possessions that were at hand — the locket she still wore about her throat, and the crystal dish.

She snatched at the bowl and it slipped through her fingers, smashing into shards on the scrubbed plank floor. The object that was once her mother's prized possession, which had survived a trip across the seas and a massacre, now lay scattered on the bleached wood, splintered beyond repair. The broken pieces looked like tears.

Adria shed tears to match them as she gave the debris one last long look before she turned away. It was a sorrowing, frightened girl who slipped from the cabin door to run away into the night.

CHAPTER 2

Hours later, Adria crouched behind a rock, her heart struggling like a frightened rabbit in her breast. For the first time, she dared to think she had really escaped. Would they have the courage to follow her here, on Wyndspelle land?

The door to the Meeting House had opened as she ran from the cabin. And there, silhouetted against the yellow glow of oil lamps used to illuminate the building, she had seen two dark figures. Men. And she knew they had been sent to fetch her to be tried. To be found guilty before a room filled with unsmiling, disapproving faces.

She had run, thankful that she'd left the white cap and kerchief behind, as they would mark her in the darkness. She ran on bare feet, silent as a shadow, first through the briars that tore her skirts, shredding them, then, nearing the sea, cutting her bare brown feet on the stony path. In her desperation, she had forgotten the need for silence or concealment. All she could do was run, run toward the sea and the haven of Wyndspelle — the unknown.

The fog had moved in from the waters now, surrounding gray granite boulders on the beach, turning them into Druid-like structures. Things seemed different here, Adria thought, not realizing that she, too, had undergone a transformation. With her black hair tumbling about her shoulders, she bore no resemblance to the adoptive daughter of a Puritan clergyman.

With the instincts of a small animal, she cringed, her face against the cool stone as she listened. Nothing. Either she had shaken her pursuers, or they had not dared to follow her here.

But to be sure, she would walk along the edge of the water where the incoming tide would sweep her footprints away. And in order to do that, she would have to pass the haunted place. The place that gave Wyndspelle its name. The spot where Elizabeth Miller, witch, was bound to a stake, faggots placed at her feet, and set ablaze.

Adria, closing her eyes, could imagine the scene as it was that day, some years before she was born. Black boiling clouds out to sea, waves beginning to run before the wind, the bound girl, the flames. The story, as it was told in Meeting. She could hear Reverend Potts' words in her ears as he ranted from the pulpit.

"And then she cried out, the smoke rising around her. She called to the spirits of the wind and the sea. A wind came, and a great wave. And when it was gone, it had taken her and those who stood on the sand. Jemmie Wheeler. Jenkin Haymes. And John Cooper, her accuser. Those who watched from the promontory above saw a gull rise against the black sky as the fires of hell crackled around them, and they smelled the fumes of the netherworld, of fire and brimstone, of evil…"

It was one of his favorite sermons, both at home and in Meeting. Designed to strike fear into the hearts of his parishioners and keep them in the paths of righteousness, and to serve as an example to the young girl he had taken under his roof. Cotton Mather had even come out, pleading the cause of justice for those thus accused. But not the Reverend Potts.

Nightly Adria, forced to her knees as that goodly man wrestled with Satan for her soul, had wondered if his religious zeal might not mask something else. Something dark and cruel…

She shivered. Whether it was from the memory of those nights or the creeping fog, she did not know. Her frayed skirts were wet from her headlong flight. Beneath the long dress, one knee was bruised and bleeding. But she had to go on. If evil awaited here, it might be preferable to the goodness she'd left behind.

She stood up, shaking down her skirts, brushing at the wet sand that clung to the tattered hem, then moved on, stepping carefully, just out of reach of the waves that sucked greedily at the shoreline. Out there, somewhere in the grayness, she heard the waters booming against the offshore rocks like the voice of God. A plume of spray struck her and she turned inland, tripping in her panic. Her hands felt the roundness of stones beneath them. The cairn!

The cairn of stones that marked the place where the stake to which Elizabeth Miller was tied had stood. The stake was gone now. It was said the Devil took it from the sand and it now formed the lintel for the fireplace in the big house. But the cairn remained, shrouded now in curling mist, but still with its memory of evil.

Frozen for a moment, Adria forced herself to relax. If the spirit of Elizabeth Miller still lingered here, she, herself, should have nothing to fear. For after all, hadn't she, Adria, been accused of the same transgressions? Elizabeth Miller had tempted a man, through the use of trickery and artifice. A sober, married member of the Meeting. It was he who accused her when they were caught. It was she who was punished.

And was it not for attempting to seduce Josiah, her adoptive brother, that Adria Anne Turner, aged seventeen, was denounced this very night in Meeting?

"I didn't do anything wrong," she told herself as she made her way across the beach. "I didn't!" But her voice lacked the surety required to ease the conscience Reverend Potts had inflicted upon her. Perhaps she *was* guilty of using tricks and artifice, but not for the reasons that were being used against her. And perhaps she had been wicked. Maybe the man she met this afternoon, a member of the very household toward which she was now heading, had been an emissary of the devil.

Her cheeks grew warm as she thought of how he'd stopped her on her way back from the spring, the way he had kissed her so boldly. And he would surely be here, at Wyndspelle.

Standing waist-deep in fog now, she looked up at the great house on the promontory. It seemed to float in the air, without foundation, since the lower story was built of the same granite as the stone on which it stood, the frame part of the structure overhanging it in the English style.

The place was dark. Only the cold wisp of moon reflecting in its windows like spirit candles. Adria was suddenly afraid, shivering.

Perhaps the Reverend Potts was right about this place. Maybe it was empty of humanity and only spirits lived here, the spirits of evil and wickedness. The very crag the house was built upon had a fault, a rift that ran down to the sea. The house bridged the chasm where it narrowed at the top of the promontory. Though it wasn't visible from where she stood, Adria knew that it was there. It was part of the story. "A staircase to hell," her adoptive father had explained, "to allow access to the demons of the deep."

His theory was borne out by those with tales of witnessing strange lights dancing at the base of the cliff on certain nights. There were some who said it was Elizabeth Miller coming home…

Stories to frighten children with, Adria thought. To keep them out of mischief and send them early to their beds with the doors barred against the unknown. Afraid or not, she must present herself at Wyndspelle. She had no other choice.

Moving toward the rocky cliff, she felt her way through the fog until she found the steps that were hewn into the stone many years before. They had crumbled in spots and she moved slowly, carefully, making sure of her footing at each step. Perhaps it would have been better to come the back way, across the bitter lands of Wyndspelle, blighted by the great wave. But then they might have caught her.

Her hand slipped and she caught herself, pressing against the stone, weak for a moment with fright. Then, telling herself it would be better to go crashing to the rocks and the sea below than to face the wrath of the Puritan community, she took a deep breath and began to inch upward again, slowly, slowly…

When she reached the top at last, the fog had moved with her. Below her was a sea of white that muffled the surf sounds, making the place seem dreamlike, unreal. Before her, tendrils of mist twined about a set of stone steps that arched to a landing above and was matched by another set leading downward on the other side. A narrow walkway led beneath the arching stairs to a plain wooden door set into the granite wall of the lower house. Here, there was no glass, only the familiar shuttered openings Adria was accustomed to seeing. This would be the servant's quarters, the kitchens, she thought. And the wooden door would be the entrance at which she should present herself.

She hurried down the steps, grateful for a brief shelter from the cold that seemed to intensify on this promontory above the sea. There, she paused for a moment, trying to tidy her tangled hair, brushing at her stained dress. At last, she tapped at the door, timorously at first, then harder. Surely there was someone here! She pressed against the door, but it didn't move. Barred from the inside.

With a twinge of horror, it dawned on her that the house might be empty. That whoever — or *whatever* — lived here, had gone away. But the stranger on the path had said there was a sick woman here! A woman in need of help!

Tears of helplessness streaked her cheeks as she huddled against the door wondering what to do next. Maybe she could find a sheltered place in the rocks and wait until morning. They might open the door then. She wrapped her arms around herself to warm her shivering body. She could freeze to death out here with no one to know — or care.

As if to taunt her, the fog began to move, twisting before a rising wind in ragged wraithlike wisps. Adria knew the sea wind by now. How it could rise in the night and scream around the rocky projections on the shore. Above her, the timbers of the great house creaked in a sudden gust.

She would have to get in some way, she thought, or go back down. Down the slippery rock steps to the beach with its treacherous tides. She could not stay where she was. The wind would grow stronger through the night. It would not let her stay and live.

Moving from one window to another, she tried the shutters. There would be other doors and windows at the back of the building, but she was uncertain of the terrain. One step taken the wrong way, and she could plunge to her death.

At last, she eyed the great stairs arching to the upper floor. Taking her courage in hand, she ascended them, the wind plastering her wet skirts against her body, lashing her hair across her eyes, screaming like a woman in agony.

There, she faced an arched door with a fanlight of colored glass. Here again, she tapped. Then, shuddering with cold, she knocked boldly. Finally, in desperation, she turned the brass knob. Smoothly, the door slid open.

Adria stepped inside, pulling it shut behind her. Her eyes, wind-whipped, were streaming tears and she could not control the shivering of her body. She found herself in a huge, vaulted room, cold, wrapped in darkness, and there was a harsh sound of labored, measured breathing in her ears.

Breathing? She held her breath. It was not her own. There was something inhuman about the sound. It was as if the house, itself, were breathing. Her knees went weak.

"Is — is anyone here?"

There was no answer. The room was empty of life, but at least someone had been here: ahead of her, at the far end of the great hall, were candles placed wide apart as though at the ends of a long table of some kind. The candles danced and flickered, illuminating a cavernous dark fireplace just beyond.

Again Adria thought of the stake to which Elizabeth Miller had been bound, and the tale that the devil had taken it to use as the lintel above his fire.

Suppressing a desire to turn and run, she forced herself to walk toward the candlelight. The breathing sound seemed to come from the walls around her, emanating from the shadows, keeping time with her reluctant steps until she entered the circle of light. Then the room seemed to echo with a choking gasp that ended on a sigh.

Adria stopped short, her spine paralyzed in an icy grip of horror that held her frozen to the spot.

For what she had thought to be a table flanked by candles was a bier. And on it lay a woman, smiling contemptuously into the darkness that hovered above, features set in a grimacing mask of death.

Adria stood, unable to move, to breathe. Then, from somewhere in the enshrouding darkness, she heard an eerie wailing sound — like the voice of a lost soul, crying out from hell.

The fear that closed her throat released its grip as she stepped backward, blind with revulsion and terror. She screamed. A shriek that rose to the topmost floor of Wyndspelle, sounding above the shrilling wind and the sleet that had now begun to hurl itself against the windows of the house on the crag above the sea.

CHAPTER 3

As the echo of her scream died away, Adria clasped her hands over her mouth and shrank, backing toward the doorway. Above her, in the gloom that the candles could not penetrate, she heard the sound of running footsteps. Mind alive with imagined demons, her only thought was to leave this house and run…

A thing brushed her skirt in the darkness. Her bare bruised foot trod on something and she leaped away. The thing, whatever it was, shot away from her with a screech that made her blood run cold and sent her clawing at the door, searching for escape. Then she heard a voice above her. A woman's voice, raised in a kind of lament.

"Cor!" it said. "It's 'er! It's 'er! The witch! The witch!" The voice rose to a high keening sound as Adria lifted her eyes to see two white faces that seemed to float above the lamps they carried like spectral moons. They stood, looking down at her from a balcony, apparently too frightened to move.

"Please," Adria said in a small voice, "I just —" But the keening sound went on until it was interrupted by a voice from the other side of the hall above her.

"Silence, girl! Your noise is fit to wake the dead!"

Adria cast a hasty glance toward the body on the bier, then raised her eyes to the man who stood at the other side of the balcony that traversed three sides of the great room. He, too, held a lamp, and by its light, she recognized a familiar face. That of the stranger who had kissed her on the path back from the spring. She went limp with relief.

"Now," he said, "Let's see what we have here!"

He moved down the steps that led from the balcony to Adria's side, holding the lamp before him. In spite of his brave words, she could see that his face was white with shock. Then he said, "It's all right, Dorrie. It's all right, Mistress Murchison. 'Tis only a lass. And from the looks of her, she's met up with some of our bully boys who guard the back."

Then to Adria, "You've been mishandled, lass? Our lads gave you rough treatment?"

"N — Nay," Adria stammered. "I met no one."

"Then how came ye here?"

"By way of the shore. Up the side of the crag —"

"You lie! It is not possible! Who are you? Who sent you?" He grasped her shoulder, and she trembled beneath his hand, feeling faint and dizzy as he thrust the lamp closer to her face.

"*God's teeth!* 'Tis the little Puritan! Don't tell me you were cozened here with a kiss!" The pressure on her arm lessened. It was gentle now, like a caress, as he smiled down on her with a kind of royal assurance.

Adria felt the blush that stained her cheeks. "You were seeking someone to care for a sick woman. I am well versed in herbs and the like —"

"As you can see, the need for such service has passed." He indicated the bier. "I must say I am sorry, I would be well pleased with your presence in this house."

"Then let me stay!" Adria fell to her knees, clutching the hem of the fur-trimmed velvet robe he wore around his shoulders. "I beg you, let me stay! I have no place to go!"

Her shoulders were shaking, her face wet with tears. Those hated tears that Reverend Potts seemed to take such a delight in provoking. She had learned to swallow them and stand with shoulders straight and erect as he hammered at her for her sins. Now she was cold, frightened, and beyond pride.

The man took her elbows in his hands and lifted her, studying her face. "Well," he said, "Perhaps —"

"It will not do!"

Adria turned to face the woman who spoke so decisively. The two women who had appeared on the balcony at her scream had descended the stairs that led down at the other side. One, a dull-looking girl, stood farther back, but the speaker seemed angry. "You know what the situation is, Mark! We've got to get her out of here before Sir Anthony sees her —"

"Sees her?" The man she called Mark laughed, a little mockingly. "You know he won't *see* her! We can keep her out of his way. Tell him she's just a kitchen drab, a dullwit, to help Mother Moseby in her labors — when *they* come. Leave it to me."

"No!" The woman glared at Adria inimically. "There are enough loose tongues here, spying. 'Tis dangerous as it is. And you heard the master at table tonight! If he thought this girl would do —"

"But she's chilled through," the man said, "and terrified! See how she trembles! A night's rest, and Vincente can return her to her home." At the woman's implacable expression, he shrugged. "I suppose you are right."

"You know I am. You can dally with your pleasures later." She turned to Adria. "Go."

"Please," Adria pleaded, "I cannot go back!"

"You can! And by the way you came."

Taking Adria's arm, she pressed her toward the door. Adria looked back at the slender blond man, seeking some sign of compassion, then turned toward the creature called Dorrie who only stared at her, mouth slack and open.

Then Adria gathered up the remnants of her pride. Stiffening her shoulders, she said, "I thank you. I am sorry to have put you to trouble, since there was no need for my services."

She turned toward the door. Out there was the wind that would tear at her, numbing her hands as she clung to the rocks on her way down to the sand. Below, the Druid stones waited to catch her body as she fell, and then the hungry sea would reach in to draw her into its wet mouth.

Hand on the door, she braced herself to open it. Then another voice intruded. A voice from the stair.

"What the bleeding hell is going on?" a deep voice thundered. "Mark! Mistress Murchison! Dorrie! What is the meaning of this uproar in the night?"

Adria turned to see the three beside her exchange glances. Then Mistress Murchison said smoothly, "All is well, milord. We are only here keeping watch with poor Emma, as you directed. Your pardon, if we have disturbed you."

"But there is someone here," he said, irritably. "I heard another voice. A woman —"

Again the three exchanged glances. And finally, Mistress Murchison said, flatly, "Yes, there is someone. A young chit from the settlement. She had the effrontery to follow Mark here, and he will have none of her. We are sending her back where she came from. It is not worthy disturbing your rest over."

"I'll judge this for myself." The man came down the stairs, moving slowly and carefully. As he neared the light, Adria could see that, in contrast to the elegant Mark, this man wore his dark hair clubbed back in simple fashion. His white silk shirt was partially unbuttoned, revealing a brown, muscular chest. His face was somber, with harsh lines around the mouth, and a scar creased his forehead.

There was something about him that made Adria's heart pound in her chest as he came toward the light. Something in his eyes. A dark, fixed expression as he looked at her. Then she saw that he carried a cane in one hand. This man was blind, or nearly so.

"Who are you?" he said, harshly. "Well, speak up, girl?"

"A — Adria. Adria Anne Turner," she said, hating the childishness in her voice. "I heard you needed someone to care for a sick woman."

He nodded. "My wife. But as you can see, it is no longer necessary. How old are you, child?"

"S — Seventeen."

"Young," he mused, "but soft-spoken." He put his hand beneath Adria's chin, tilting her face upward. "A white blur with two great eyes. That's all I can see," he said, sadly. "But she is attractive, isn't she, Mark?"

Mark's face wore a peculiar expression. "No more than most, sir," he said, stiffly.

"Well, she has youth. And the Lady Jane would be how old now, Mark? Her late twenties? Nearing thirty? How she must hate growing old!"

"Please, sir," Adria whispered, "Let me stay here. I have no place to go. I'll do anything. Anything!"

The eyebrows above the strange eyes quirked. "*Would* you?" Again that close inspection. He might not be able to see her face, Adria thought, shivering, but it was as if he could look into the depths of her very soul. And again she remembered how the Reverend Potts had proclaimed that the devil, himself, lived here.

His eyes finally releasing her, he turned to the others. "It would seem that all is in order then," he said, with a harsh laugh that held no humor. "Now it can be as I have planned when my esteemed stepmother and the Lady Jane arrive. As you see, the lady is willing —"

"For the love of God," Mark burst out, "you can't do this, Anthony!"

"Can I not?" The blind man drew himself up haughtily, directing the stare of those dreadful commanding eyes at Mark, who wilted and spread his hands as if in defeat.

"It need not be done immediately," Mistress Murchison interposed. "With Emma just dead, 'tis not decent!"

"There's nothing decent in this world," the blind man said wearily. "Take her to the rose room, Mistress Murchison. Get her bathed and suitably dressed for the ceremony. I will have Mother Moseby prepare her a hot potion for her chills. Mark, call Vincente and one of his lads. We have work to do here."

He was still issuing orders when the women led Adria toward the stairs. The girl's knees were still shaking from shock and fatigue and she was too dazed to take note of her surroundings as they went. All she knew was that, for some reason, she had gained a temporary respite. And that she could still hear that tortured, demonic breathing that had frightened her so.

"What — what is that sound?" she stammered.

"I hear nothing." Mistress Murchison did not seem disposed to be friendly, and Adria subsided.

At the top of the stairs there seemed to be many doors, and she was led to the first of these. As the women escorted her inside, she came alive with a new fear.

Why had she been brought here? This was no servant's room! Dazed, Adria looked toward the great bed. Its curtains were drawn back, revealing pillows and tumbled silken sheets.

It looked as if it had been recently occupied. By whom? Surely not the man called Anthony, the blind master of Wyndspelle! He would not think that she —! Adria's cheeks flamed. As if sensing the question in the girl's mind, Mistress Murchison scowled at her.

"'Tain't decent, like I said," she said to Dorrie. "My poor sister hardly cold. Not even time to air the bed and change the linens. And here's a new one in Emma's place!"

Adria breathed again. At least it was not what she'd thought. These had been a woman's chambers. But it was no pleasant prospect, either, to think of occupying a bed in which a woman had just died. It need only be for the night, however. On the morrow, she would plead her case before the blind man. Perhaps he would help her find a way to some other, more populated area. Perhaps an inn, where she might work for her keep.

"What — what ailed the lady?" she asked Mistress Murchison."

"Could be she caught a chill in her bones. Could be somebody wished her dead!"

What was the woman saying? That her sister, the former mistress of this house, had been *murdered*? Adria was shocked into silence as the woman turned her back on her, deliberately, and drew curtains that revealed a hip bath. "I'll go down and send Vincente up with some water," she grumbled. "Dorrie, you do what needs be done. I want no part of it. Emma's red velvet, I think. The rubies. Do something with that mop of hair!"

"Wait," Adria said, a note of desperation in her voice. "I don't understand this! Any of it! Why have I been given this room? I would be content with a pallet of straw off the kitchens! I came here to go into service —"

"Ask him. He'll tell you. It's not my place. Just remember, I tried to get you to go." And she was gone.

Adria turned to Dorrie, a question in her eyes. The girl grinned at her good-naturedly. "I dunno what's up. 'Is ludship's a queer cove, 'e is. I was you, I'd take advantage, 'im sayin' treat you like a lydy."

"But I'm not a lady," Adria cried. "I'm a human being! 'Tis wrong for a person to set himself above another. The Good Book says —" She stopped, reddening. She had sounded like the Reverend Potts, and Dorrie was staring at her, openmouthed.

"I'm sorry," she continued, contritely. "I didn't mean to preach. 'Tis just that," she waved a hand at the ornate surroundings, "I'm not accustomed to this. I seem to be treated as an honored guest, and I do not know why. I don't even know the name of my host."

"It be Sir Anthony Mordelle."

"And — the other young man? Who is he?" Adria blushed again, recalling Mistress Murchison's statement that she had followed that gentleman here, seeking his favor. Apparently it had been his opinion, also.

"'E be Master Welles. Mark Welles. 'E was cap'n of is ludship's vessel when 'e got is 'urt." The information was given grudgingly. It was clear the girl had no liking for Mark Welles. "'Tis Master Welles what runs things 'ere," Dorrie went on, "save for Murchison, the 'ousekeeper."

That, thought Adria, explained the girl's aversion. She seemed good-natured, but none too bright and a little lazy. Traits that were bound to bring down the wrath of one responsible for the household upon occasion. But all that was beside the point. The blond man did not need Adria to defend him. The important thing was to discover exactly what she had got herself into. The horror that had greeted her upon her entry into this house hung over her mind like a dark cloud.

"You're in the devil's house," the voice of Reverend Potts spoke in her ear. *"Look about you! Fripperies, baubles, gee-gaws! Do you need further proof? Do you really think you are in this room for some good purpose?"*

"Dorrie,' she said, faintly, "Dorrie — Mistress Murchison was right. I cannot stay here. I must go down and thank them and tell them —"

"The morrow be soon enough for that," the girl said. "Now you can do with a bit of a wash and a rest. Sit you 'ere." She pulled out a low bench, placing it in front of a mirror. "Let's get some of them tangles out of yer 'air while we wait for the 'ot water." Taking up a bejeweled brush, she attacked Adria's dark locks with vigor, not stopping until they fell in a shining stream.

"Cor," the girl said. "That be some better. All frowsy like you was, small wonder I took you for *'er!*"

Her tone startled Adria, who had been studying the face that was her own, yet was as unfamiliar as that of a stranger, with the dark eyes and tawny complexion. "Who?" she asked.

"The witch, that's 'oo!" Dorrie darted a fearful glance toward the corners of the room as if she feared calling up an apparition. "I've saw 'er there afore, y'know. All in black, like, there afore the fire where you was standing."

"Well, I'm no witch!" Adria tried for a light touch, but her voice sounded thin in her own ears as she thought of the accusations that had been hurled at her earlier this day.

"Didn't think you be, luv. Now, 'ere's Vincente with the 'ot water. Just sit you still."

There was something in the way the girl said the name that made Adria look at her, wonderingly. Dorrie's face had turned a dull, ugly pink and the smile she gave the young man at the door was almost a grimace. It was obvious that she was in love with him. It was equally plain that the boy was not interested. Slender and dark, he stepped inside the door with his two steaming pails.

"Senhora," he said, bowing.

He poured the contents of the buckets in the bath, then bowed his way out again, the moon-eyed Dorrie staring after him.

"He — he's foreign, isn't he?" Adria guessed.

"Portygee," Dorrie said, with a deep sigh. Then, turning to Adria, "Well, luv, let's get them rags off."

Rags? The girl meant her clothing! Surely she didn't think she would allow her to undress her? To assist her in bathing? Modesty had been a key word in the Potts' household. One undressed in the darkness, sliding one garment off by degrees while donning another. The thought of removing her clothing before another person was shocking.

"Nay," Adria said, backing away. "I can manage by myself. If you'll just leave me —"

There was another tap at the door. This time, it opened to admit the housekeeper, Mistress Murchison. One hand kept her long black skirts swept back. The other held a goblet.

"The master sent it for the girl," the woman said to Dorrie. "See that she drinks it."

Dorrie took the goblet, sniffed at it, then looked at Adria strangely. "Do this be wot I think it be?" she asked the housekeeper. The woman nodded and retreated to the hall. Dorrie followed her, the goblet in her hand, closing the door behind her. Adria could hear only a mumble of voices: Dorrie questioning, Mistress Murchison answering. Then the girl's awed exclamation. "Cor!"

When Dorrie re-entered, her casual, friendly attitude was gone. She dipped a little curtsy. "'Ere, milady. This be good for you. You maun drink it down."

"What is it? I — I've never tasted spirits."

"It don't be spirits, mum. It be summat 'e brought from the Indies. Fix you up right proper, that will. No 'arm in it."

Adria tasted it. It had an odd flavor, but it wasn't too unpleasant. A delightful warmth began to seep through her chilled bones, and with it, a feeling of euphoria. Around her, the gaudy silks and satins shimmered. She felt Dorrie's roughened fingers at the fastenings of her gown, but lacked the will to insist upon her privacy. Only when the girl tried to remove her locket did she find strength to dissent. Dorrie, obsequious now, and servile, left it in place as she helped Adria into the warm bath.

What's the matter with me? Adria wondered. *I can't think!* She kept talking in an effort to keep her incoherent thoughts together. "The master," she mumbled, "what sort of man is he?"

"'E's a good man," Dorrie said, staunchly. "'E'll be good to you, 'e will. Nobbut a good man 'ud a took us from gaol like 'e done. And 'im a' but 'anged by the neck 'isself!"

"Hanged? What do you mean? Did he commit some crime?"

"Lots on 'em, I vow," Dorrie laughed, "in *'is* trade. But that time, it be murder. Kilt 'is own brother, 'e did!"

I will go from this house on the morrow, Adria thought, dazedly. Reverend Potts' voice rang in her mind. *"And Cain slew Abel,"* it said. Perhaps that scar the lord of Wyndspelle wore was the mark of Cain. His blindness God's punishment, visited upon him for his sins.

She would go back to the settlement in the sanity of sunlight and throw herself upon the mercy of the people there. She could not stay in this house of wickedness. Tonight, she would pray…

But her thoughts refused to hang together. The candle flames were turning into bright colored bubbles that floated toward the ceiling. Dorrie's voice came to her only as a soothing murmur. It had something to do with the potion, Adria thought fuzzily. The drink —

Helped from the bath, she was led toward the bed where a queen's finery was laid out. Her drugged senses were drowned in scents and colors as she obediently followed Dorrie's direction. It was only when she was laced into the red velvet gown that she regained any mind of her own.

"Cor!" Dorrie breathed, "Look at you!" She led her to the mirror, and Adria looked at the vision she presented through blurred eyes. She imagined the Reverend Potts standing before her, a scandalized expression on his austere face, shaking a bony finger at her. This could not be she, herself, in this immodest garb. *"Jezebel!"* the Reverend's voice rang in her ears. *"Harlot! Witch!"*

"Nay," she moaned, retreating from her reflection. "Nay!" What was she doing here, dressed like this? How had she come here, to this room, to a murderer's house?

Now someone was trying to take her locket from her!

"Wear these 'ere," Dorrie's voice coaxed. "These be real jools, mum. 'Ere, let Dorrie 'elp you." The ruby necklace swung and glittered before Adria's fascinated gaze, its jewels glittering like red eyes. Evil eyes. She shrank away.

The door opened and closed behind her, and Mistress Murchison's voice broke in. "They're ready for the ceremony."

"She won't leave go of 'er locket," Dorrie's voice was near to tears. "Won't 'urt to 'ave 'er own way in one thing, now will it?"

"I suppose not. Come on." Dorrie on one side, Mistress Murchison at the other, Adria was propelled toward the stairs, the carpet pattern beneath her feet seeming to crawl and writhe before her drugged eyes.

Ceremony? she thought. Mistress Murchison had said something about a ceremony. Was that why she had been dressed in this manner? Perhaps it was a funeral for the dead woman. But this was no funeral garb.

With a sudden chill, she remembered a dissertation Reverend Potts had given on the devil's Mass. The eerie rites, the sacrifice of virgins… Surely this was not what the strange inhabitants of Wyndspelle had in mind!

She turned her face to look at Dorrie, who met her eyes only for a moment with an expression of pity and fear, then ducked her head. There was something wrong here.

If she could only break away from the two women who held her! If she could run! Falling to her death on the rocks below Wyndspelle would be preferable to this. But she was powerless. That potion —

Though her mind protested, her body was helpless as the women led her down the stairs. As they reached the base of the steps and came out into the great hall, it was glittering with light. In the center of the enormous room hung a chandelier, dripping tears of crystal beneath a hundred lighted candles. Adria's eyes went fearfully toward the table as they entered. The body of the dead woman was gone. Behind the table, a fire burned high on the hearth. On the object that had served as a bier stood a candelabra. To one side, the face of the master of Wyndspelle was satanic in the flickering light. At the other, Mark Welles looked oddly stern and serious. It was plain, as he avoided her pleading gaze, that whatever happened, he had no intention of interfering.

"Please," Adria whispered. "Please."

Her plea fell on deaf ears and she was drawn forward, toward whatever fate held in store for her. *'Tis a dream,* she thought. *'Tis only a dream. After a while, I'll awaken* — But hadn't she followed that manner of thinking before? Had she not lain in the straw in the loft of Reverend Potts' cabin and pretended she was in the midst of some cruel nightmare? That she would wake and discover herself to be back in her own home, with her mother and father still alive? And each morning, she had risen to the grim reality that it was not a dream.

She whimpered a little, as the women dragged her toward the fire and the men who waited silently. They reached the table, Adria, numb, hypnotized by the flames dancing on the hearth beyond. A log shifted, and for an instant, thrust upward into the flame like a reaching, blackened hand. And with an eerie cry that seemed an echo of the one Adria had heard upon entering this house, a black cat sprang to the table to seat itself beside the candelabra, green eyes fastened on Adria's face, mesmerizing her.

Swaying between the two women in her drug-induced trance, Adria was lost, drowning in the green depths of the animal's gaze until Mistress Murchison's fingers bit cruelly into her arm. Someone had said something in a droning mumble and she was evidently expected to answer.

"Say 'I will'!" the woman hissed.

"I will," Adria repeated, obediently. Then she thought, *What have I agreed to?* She stared at Mark, realizing he had been speaking for some time, reading from a book he held in his hand and which he now closed. It looked like —

"It is done," said Anthony Mordelle with satisfaction. "Dorrie, Mistress Murchison, you may take my wife to her room."

Adria gave a little cry, her body turning to ice as she faced this new horror. Dear God, what kind of unholy alliance had she entered into?

The two women, one at either side, led her toward the stair. Behind her, the fireplace spat and crackled as the great log shifted in the flames.

The house began to breathe again.

CHAPTER 4

It was the sound of breathing that woke Adria in the morning. There was a feel of silken sheets beneath her body as, not daring to open her eyes, she listened. *Let it be a dream,* she prayed. *Please, God, let me wake on my pallet in the loft! Let it be a dream!*

No, it was real. Too terribly real. She fastened on the last words she remembered from the night. *"Take my wife to her room."*

Last night, in the great hall where a body had lain in state only a short time before, she had been wedded to a stranger. A frightening blind man of whom she knew nothing, except that he lived in the devil's house.

Turning her head, fearfully, she opened her eyes at last. The pillow beside her seemed untouched. She had slept alone. Now, her only hope was to escape before the day's end. Surely, that mockery of a marriage would not stand before God!

Sitting up in the canopied bed, she pushed the draperies aside, her muscles tensed, ready for flight, if need be. Dorrie, who had entered with a pitcher of warm water, jumped with a nervous squeal. Then she apologized, bobbing a curtsy.

"I thought you 'ud still be sleepin', mum." She poured the water into a bowl and dampened a soft cloth. "'Ere's for a bit of a wash, like." Bending to open a door to the stand beneath the bowl, she said, "'Ere's the slops. I'll be fetchin' yer tray now, mum."

Adria looked down at the filmy gown covering her body and pulled the sheet beneath her chin. "Where is my clothing?"

"In the wardrobe, mum. I'll lay them out arfter you've breakfasted. Summat pretty, I'd say. 'Is ludship wishes to 'ave a talk with you."

There was a silence as Adria sought for words. Except for the breathing that sighed in and out, in and out. Dorrie did not seem to hear it. Adria clasped her hands over her ears, then removed them. The sound was still there, not rasping as it had been the night before, but sighing, whispering.

"That sound — there *is* a sound! Isn't there?"

"Oh, yes, mum. 'Tis the 'ouse. You'll grow used to it, mum."

"The *house*?"

"The way 'twas built, mum. O'er a 'ole, like, that runs down to the sea. The wind, and all. Master Welles can tell you 'ow it comes to 'appen so."

Adria studied the girl's face thoughtfully. What she said made a kind of sense. It was possible there might be some type of pressures from the rift in the rock; the waves coming in and out to produce the strange sound. But why did the girl pale as she offered the explanation? And she was avoiding Adria's eyes. Either she had concocted some story, or she did not believe what she, herself, had been told of the sound's source...

No matter. The important thing was to find some means of getting away, and Dorrie might help her.

"Dorrie, can I consider you a friend?"

"Oh, indeed, mum!" The servant looked shocked. "That is, so far as to be *proper*," she amended.

"You knew that I was given some kind of drug last night? That I was tricked into marriage?"

"Yes, mum." Dorrie hung her head.

"I'm not blaming you, Dorrie. I know you only did as you were told. 'Tis just — I've got to get away, and I beg you to help me." When the girl's face remained blank, she said, desperately, "At least give me my own clothing —"

"They be burned, mum. They was nobbut rags. You be the mistress now, mum. E's rich, the master is!"

"But I don't want to be the mistress! I — I could not be with a man who was not of my own choosing!"

To Adria's surprise, the girl laughed. "If *that* be wot's a-worriting you, 'e won't bother you none. 'E but wants 'im a wife. 'E never come in to Mistress Emma. All you 'ave to do is run the 'ouse and look pretty, like."

What was the girl trying to say? That she was safe from Anthony Mordelle's advances? A wife in name only? "Then why did he wed me in such a strange fashion? Is he — deranged?"

The girl shrugged. "Guess 'e's got 'is reasons. 'Ave to ask 'im wot they be. Now I maun bring you up a bit of breakfast, mum."

Bobbing cheerfully, she left the room. Adria rose and hurried to the wardrobe, one thought in her mind. There would not be a repetition of last night when she'd been dressed by a stranger's hands. She intended to be clothed when Dorrie returned, and then she would ponder on the next step. Escape.

She rummaged through the gowns crowded into the wardrobe's interior, shocked at the style and cut of the garments. These were not appropriate for a Puritan lass! She would not appear in front of a man dressed in this fashion, even if he *was* blind. Still, she must find something to replace the silken gown she was wearing now. Her night shift at home had been made of heavy unbleached muslin. This was indecent!

At last, she settled on a gown of russet. Just the color of the leaf she'd found by the spring. Was it only yesterday?

Yesterday that she'd wished for a dress of this shade? Well, now she'd had that wish. She would retract it if she could.

Getting into the gown, exhausted by the struggle to reach impossible hooks, she turned to the mirror, heart sinking. This would never do! Finally, rummaging through a chest that stood against the wall, she found a shawl which she put around her shoulders like a kerchief, pinning it at the throat with a brooch from the jewel box. At least she had covered her nakedness. Pulling her long hair into a loose bun, she studied the soft white cloth with which Dorrie had patted her face dry. It was only a little damp. With a little effort, she contrived it into a cap.

Dressed at last, she sat herself down, hands clasped in her lap, to wait Dorrie's return, finally able to take a good look at her surroundings. There were two of the handmade chairs, such as several of the wealthier villagers owned, but they were artfully concealed with velvet cushions. The spindly gilt chair by the window, however, could never have been made in the colonies. The mirror, too, was framed in gilt, the walls papered in cloth with a stripe of rose that was velvet to the touch. Adria had never seen anything like it, even in her dreams.

Perhaps Anthony Mordelle was not the devil, as the Reverend Potts had said, but he was surely doomed to hell. He was a rich man. Far too rich to be allowed into heaven.

She stood, moving to the gilt chair, touching its fragility with reverent fingers, appreciating its beauty. What a shame that such an object was considered a frippery, and sinful! Why did things that were lovely, or happy, have to be a crime against Godliness? She felt an instant's rebellion, then jerked her hand away as if it had been burned. She was being tempted! She looked guiltily about, then remembered that, according to Reverend Potts, God sees everything.

She must leave this house before she lost her immortal soul.

Going to the window, she drew the drapes aside. The leaded glass window was coated with ice, indicative of the temperature of the night before. Finally discovering a way to open it, she stepped back with an indrawn breath. For she was looking straight down into the sea. Cold and gray, it seemed to be lashing at her very feet. She had forgotten how the house was positioned on its rock.

Leaning out a little, the bitter air chilling her cheeks, she could see the beach from which she'd climbed last night. A white ribbon of sand studded with stones now sheeted with ice. How had she managed to scale the crag to Wyndspelle? It seemed an impossible feat.

Now, with everything glazed and slippery, it would be suicide to return in the manner in which she'd come. She knew she couldn't manage that perilous descent. She would have to go the back way, across the blighted land. She closed the window.

There was a thump at the door and Dorrie backed in, her arms laden. Turning, she set the tray down and stared at Adria in shocked disapproval.

"Cor, you can't wear that, mum! 'E wouldn't like it — not 'arf. Now, let Dorrie find you summat proper —"

"This is what I've chosen to wear," Adria said stiffly, staring the servant girl down.

"But, mum!"

"That will be enough, Dorrie!"

"Yes, mum."

Adria couldn't believe her ears. She had taken a page from Reverend Potts' book. How many times he had said it to her, just that way! *That will be enough, Adria!* And it had reduced her to blind obedience. She would have to remember this tactic in the future. Not, *"Dorrie, will you help me to escape?"* but, *"Dorrie, you will help me!"*

The flustered servant set the tray on a table near the window, drawing the small gilt chair to face it. Adria stared at the tray, which seemed to consist of a silver teapot and a number of silver bowls turned upside down.

Dorrie removed the covers, revealing food such as Adria had not seen before. And except for her mother's crystal bowl, she had not seen such dishes. Translucent china, flanked by silver utensils she did not know how to use. In her own home and that of Reverend Potts, she had been accustomed to eating from hollowed wooden trenchers, using a pewter spoon.

Suddenly, she realized she was starving, not having eaten since the day before. But she didn't want to shame herself before Dorrie, who would surely know how to handle these eating tools properly. The smell of the food drifted up to her, making her feel hollow and empty. There were slices of hot bread, browned over coals, and a kind of fruit paste. And in one saucer, eggs that had been stirred in butter. Dorrie poured a cup of steaming tea and Adria swayed, a little faint.

"You may go, Dorrie," she said, with all the command she could muster. "You may come back in a little while."

When the door closed behind the servant, Adria attacked the food voraciously, with both fingers and spoon. It didn't matter how she ate, she told herself, it was important only that she eat enough to last for a while. Taking the last slice of bread, she spread it with the paste and folded it over, wrapping it inside a handkerchief, tucking it in her bosom below the shawl. This, she would take with her, provender for the trip to the Portuguese village down the coast.

Finished, she wiped her sticky fingers on a cloth that seemed to have been provided for that purpose. She felt embarrassed and ashamed. True gentlefolk would have been appalled at her manners, she thought. Mark Welles, for instance. She wondered if she would see him before she left this house.

Did she want to see him? Why hadn't he protected her last night? The memory of his face, solemn and disapproving, brought the scene to her mind, making her shiver. But though he had not approved, Mark Welles himself had performed the ceremony. By what right? Surely, he was not a minister of any faith! A minister would not have performed a marriage based upon trickery.

She seemed to sense, again, the intense cold she'd felt as she stood before that blazing fire last night. And as if in response to her chill, a wind rose, its keening note sounding above the boom of the waves at the base of the promontory. Perhaps she hadn't closed the window tightly enough.

Rising, she started toward it, then stopped with an eerie sensation. Against one wall, a tapestry, woven in threads of crimson and gold, seemed to billow in and sway toward her.

It was only the draught, she thought, uneasily, but she made herself move toward the tapestry, lifting it. Behind it was a door. Forcing herself to turn the knob, she pushed it open a little way. Here was a vast chamber with masculine furnishings. On the wall, directly opposite, hung a pair of dueling pistols. A cloak was thrown casually over a chair, a cane leaning against it.

Her heart beating in her throat, Adria closed the door softly, letting the tapestry fall back in place. There was no time to lose. In spite of Dorrie's reassurance, she must leave this house at once.

Hurrying to the wardrobe, she snatched down a long cloak, then headed toward the door, stopping guiltily as someone rapped upon it. "Yes, Dorrie," she said, shakily, "I'm finished. Come in."

The door opened to admit, not Dorrie, but Mistress Murchison. "You've finished your breakfast, milady? Your husband wishes to see you." Her eyes scanned the girl, taking in her attempts at creating a subdued costume. "You look lovely," she said, surprisingly kind. "However, you won't need the cloak. He's in the tower room."

The housekeeper led her to the last door, where the balcony formed an ell. Opened, it revealed another staircase that led sharply upward, into a T-shaped hall. "The smaller rooms are up here," Mistress Murchison said, "Linen closets and the like. And here," she paused at the foot of a ship's ladder at the base of the T, "are the steps to the upper room. After climbing those rocks last night, I shouldn't think you'll have any trouble."

Adria studied the woman's face. Last night, she had attempted to drive her out into the darkness; seemingly a cold, cruel person. Perhaps it was only because the housekeeper knew what was in store for her. She may have been trying to protect Adria after all.

"I must talk to you, Mistress Murchison," Adria whispered. "You must help me. I cannot —"

"Later," the woman said, "He's waiting."

Waiting?

Waking this morning to find herself unmolested; hearing Dorrie bustling about and speaking of Sir Anthony in human terms, Adria's fears had been somewhat diminished. Now, with the knowledge that the dark man with a devil's face was awaiting her, that in a few moments she would be closeted with him alone, her terror intensified. Turning to Mistress

Murchison, she gave the woman one last look of frantic appeal. The housekeeper showed no signs of compassion.

Trembling, Adria mounted the ladder-like stair.

The door at the top had been propped open and Adria emerged into a room of windows. The sleet that frosted them glittered with diffused light, letting in a kind of lemony glow and a chill stiff breeze from a pane that stood open. There, beside a telescope pointed out to sea, stood Anthony Mordelle.

Adria went weak with relief. What had she expected? A dark and gloomy attic room where a ravening monster waited to destroy her? The lord of Wyndspelle was no devil, but a man. An ordinary man, such as any other…

And then he turned.

The shock of his presence struck her like a blow as those blind eyes found her; the pale sun turning his face into a mask of copper planes, coloring the scar that slashed across it with the red of a freshly opened wound. He moved toward her, his head high and arrogant, sightless eyes burning into hers.

"Ah," he said, "My *wife*."

The way he said the word, giving it a contemptuous twist, made anger flare inside her, sufficient to counteract her fear.

"I do not count myself your wife, sir," she said. "The marriage was performed through trickery —"

"But a marriage, nonetheless."

"Not to me. It was not a religious ceremony. I am of the Puritan persuasion, as you may know."

"A Puritan lass." He nodded, his mouth lifting in a sardonic smile. "A Puritan lass, but with something to fear, eh? A fear so mighty as to bring you crawling up a rock to a forbidden place in the middle of the night. Fear of being burned as a witch, mayhap?"

How could he know this? Was it possible he possessed the power to see into her mind?

"The Reverend Potts says you are the devil himself!" Adria whispered.

"And the good Reverend just might possibly be right." The man, if man he was, turned his back and was staring out of the window once more. He remained there so long she began to fear he had forgotten her presence.

"Please," she said, "'tis true I was accused of witchcraft, and that I ran from the settlement to come here. But I am no witch. I had intended to work for my keep, but since the lady to whom I intended to offer my services is dead, I should like to go down the coast to the fisheries. Surely someone there will take me in —"

He laughed, a harsh barking sound without humor. "No, milady. I have no intention of allowing you to go. You are my wife and you will remain so as long as I have need of one. If you recall, 'twas a bargain between us. You asked for shelter here, saying you would do anything to be allowed to stay. Is a Puritan maiden's promise so easily broken? Come here!"

Adria obeyed, unable to resist the strength of his will. His hand grasped her wrist and she cowered beneath his touch. Dear God, what did he intend to do?

"I can see only a blur," he growled, "but what is *this*?" He pulled the makeshift cap from her head, tossing it to the floor. "And *this*?"

Anthony Mordelle's hand slid up her arm, tugging at the shawl that covered her shoulders, groping until he reached the brooch that held it fast. Unpinning it, he pulled the shawl free from her dress, the jam-sodden concoction she'd hidden for her journey coming with it.

His face registered surprise, shock, distaste. "And *this?*" he asked in a strange voice. He touched his sticky hand to his lips, identifying the object for what it was, then wiped it with his handkerchief. "Good God, girl! You don't have to store food away like a squirrel! There is more where that came from."

"It — it was for my journey," she said in a small voice.

"And there will be no journey. What's more, you will not be a Puritan lass nor a country wench in this house! You will dress in the manner of a great lady befitting your station. And you will not — er — store food upon your person. Is that clear?"

When she stood mutinously silent, not answering, he continued, "A wife's duty is to obey her husband's wishes. In return for such behavior, you will receive shelter and protection. It will be necessary for you to take over your role as mistress of Wyndspelle as soon as possible, since we will have guests arriving from England. Mistress Murchison will instruct you as to household duties. And in order that you will not shame me, Mark Welles will teach you your manners."

He was quiet for a long moment, staring at her. Adria stood silent, not even daring to breathe beneath that awful scrutiny. "Are you still there?" he asked abruptly. "I do not hear you."

When she did not speak, he came toward her, his hand outstretched, and she finally found her tongue. "Do not touch me!" she said in a voice of icy rage. *"Don't you dare touch me!"*

He raised his brows in surprise. "But I had no intention of doing so, milady. In fact, our first — and only — contact was quite offensive to me." He spread his fingers, as though remembering the stickiness he had encountered, and turned away to the window. "You may go," he said. "Mistress Murchison is waiting. She has her instructions."

Shaking with fury, Adria let herself down the ladder. She had never been so humiliated in her life — not even when her waywardness was discussed in Meeting and they had prayed over her!

Her hair had been loosened when Anthony pulled the cap from her head, and was hanging down her back like a child's. Her bared neck and shoulders felt indecent, exposed. Her face burned as she thought of how the man had put his hands upon her. And finding the food she'd tucked away to stay her on her journey. No wonder he thought her an ill-bred country lass!

And Mark Welles was to teach her manners. Manners!

Reaching the foot of the steps, Adria turned to face Mistress Murchison, who, she was certain, had heard the whole thing and knew the reason for her flaming, tear-stained face.

"Come," the woman said, as if there were nothing amiss. "I will show you the rest of the house."

CHAPTER 5

Adria, in her hurt and anger, remembered little of the tour that followed. First she was shown the upper story with its small rooms opening off a T-shaped hall, five gables overlooking the sea.

"This is my room," the housekeeper said. "And here is Dorrie's. These closets are where the linens are kept. You need not concern yourself with the details of the household, mum. All is in good order."

After the opening of many doors, she led the dazed girl down to the balcony that overlooked the hall below, forming three sides of a square. Here, the rooms were luxurious, the bedchambers similar to Adria's, except for the colors. Anthony's, she could see now that the curtains were drawn, was papered in a deep dark red. A devil's room. She shuddered as she recalled Reverend Potts' warnings about the house of the devil.

Adria spoke for the first time since her descent from the upper room. "Is there a key to the door that connects my room and my — husband's?" she asked, flinging caution to the winds. Let Mistress Murchison think what she would!

"Nay," the woman said, "there is no key."

Adria felt faint. "I — I don't think I feel up to seeing the rest of the house this morning." Suddenly it seemed imperative that she be alone, to think on her conversation with the master of Wyndspelle, to plan…

"I'm sorry," the housekeeper said, stubbornly, "but you must. 'Tis the master's orders."

For a moment, Adria considered mutiny; the woman could hardly drag her kicking and screaming down the stairs! But such behavior would only bear out Sir Anthony's opinion that she was a crude, untutored child, and it would solve nothing to hide away in her room. If she were to attempt an escape, it would be best to know the layout of the house.

Silently, she followed Mistress Murchison, retracing her trip to the altar the night before, down into the great hall.

Today, it did not seem so ominous. The draperies had been opened, and enough light filtered through the sleet-coated windows to dispel the shadows. The table before the fireplace was draped with a fine lace cloth, and thronelike chairs were drawn up to it. Still, Adria did not feel a sense of warmth or welcome, despite the fire blazing on the hearth, the rich velvet of chairs and draperies. The room was too large, the only concession to decoration being crossed sabers on a wall, and a suit of armor at one side of the staircase they had descended. At the other side, a scale model of a ship was set into a recess. A ship that flew a pirate's black flag. She longed to stop and study it, but the housekeeper hurried her along.

"You are expected to dine with the master, tonight," the woman said as they passed the table.

"Here?" Adria asked, feeling sick.

The woman nodded, though her brows were raised in a question. Adria was silent, remembering the use to which that table was put last night. A body had lain in state there! Then the table that served as a bier became the setting for a marriage in which she had replaced the newly dead woman.

And here she was expected to dine! Dear God, what kind of a place was this to which she had come?

She wanted to ask what had happened to the corpse. Had there been a burial ceremony as she slept? Skirting the fireplace on Mistress Murchison's heels, she felt again that sense of chill, even though the fire was burning high.

At one side of the fireplace, set in behind it, was a man's study. There were bookshelves around the walls and a desk piled high with charts. Adria looked at the leather-bound books in awe, wanting to take one down — to turn the pages. In Reverend Potts' home, there were no such treasures. Only the Bible.

She was still lagging, looking backward, when the housekeeper reminded her, sharply, that there was more to be seen.

Leaving the study, they crossed in front of the hearth again. At the other side, a door led to a lady's parlor. The room contained a spinet, dainty velvet-cushioned chairs, several gilt tables, and an embroidery frame, with a needle thrust through the cloth as if the artist would return to her handiwork at any moment. It had belonged to Emma, Adria knew. To Sir Anthony's dead wife.

"Here is where you will be expected to spend much of your time," Mistress Murchison said.

Adria felt the walls of the room closing around her. She could not endure this, she who loved the forests, flowers, the outdoors. A half-opened drapery revealed shuttered windows and she fought a smothering sensation. Even with Joseph Shanks, she would have had more freedom than this. Here, she felt like an intruder. As if the dead woman resented her presence.

Well, she vowed to herself, *I shall not be here long!* Yet, in the tour of the house, she had only seen one door — one at the front of the house where the crag dropped steeply at both sides. She would not be eager to retrace her precipitous climb.

"Is there not a back entrance somewhere?" she asked carefully. "One that leads into the grounds?"

"From the kitchens. But 'twould not be wise to venture in that direction, milady. Sir Anthony employs a pack of ruffians to guard the rear. Should you attempt to cross the lands without his direction, you would be returned post haste."

Adria's face fell, then she tried to smile as she saw that the woman was studying her closely. With a quick glance about to make certain they were alone, the housekeeper leaned near and whispered.

"You want to leave here, don't you, lass?"

At the woman's sudden understanding, the girl's tears began to fall like rain. "Yes," she sobbed, wiping them away. "Oh, yes!"

The housekeeper nodded. "I thought as much. And I wish to apologize. I misjudged you at first, thinking you to be an opportunist, coming here at just the right time. It was wrong, what Sir Anthony did. Forcing a young maid like you into such a situation." Her mouth tightened. "Though it be not the worst thing the man's done, by any means. Still, 'tis not for me to judge —"

"Will you help me?" Adria pleaded. "Can you get me past those men?"

The woman shook her head. "They are loyal to the master only. Even Mark Welles has no control over them. But 'tis not the only way. I can leave the front door unlocked this night. I still say, if you came up those rocks, you can go down." Adria's face blanched and the housekeeper hurried on. "'Tis safer than remaining here, believe me, lass. Unless you want to meet the same end poor Emma did, when he's through with you."

"You are my wife," Anthony had said, *"and you will remain so long as I have need of one."*

The girl's blood ran cold. What was the measure of his need?

"Why has he put me in this position?" she asked the woman. "No one will tell me what his reasons are. I — I'm frightened."

"And well you should be. But 'tis not for me to speak of the master's business. I am only the housekeeper. I can see to it that the door is left open, if you wish me to."

"Let me think on it."

"You do that." Mistress Murchison returned briskly to the business at hand. "Now, these stairs from the parlor lead down to the kitchens."

The kitchens, Adria remembered, where a back door led to freedom, if she could only find a way. She was small and fleet. Perhaps if she wore something dark, she might slip into the night and evade the watchers behind the house.

Now, she followed Mistress Murchison down the steps that terminated in a huge room with stone walls that dripped water as steam from boiling kettles condensed upon them.

Squatting over a cauldron, stirring at its contents, was a white-haired old crone. She looked so like a witch that Adria caught her breath. The image was enhanced when the woman stood and turned, ladle in hand, to be introduced. She was crook-backed and wall-eyed, seeming to look in two directions at the same time.

"This is the new mistress, Mother Moseby," the housekeeper said.

The old woman cackled and reached a claw-like hand to touch Adria's hair. "'Er be a pritty thing," she mumbled.

"Watch your locket," came a laughing warning from behind them. Adria whirled to see Mark Welles standing at an open door that gave a view of another flight of narrow steps leading down.

"Mother Moseby just happens to be the most proficient thief to ever escape the London gaol. If you miss anything, milady, you'll know where to find it."

The old woman cackled again, as though she'd received a compliment, and turned back to her stirring.

Mark Welles stepped up into the kitchen and tipped his blond head in a graceful bow. "And how is your health this morning, milady? I trust you have had no ill effects from your adventures last night? You have seen Sir Anthony this morning?"

"I have just come from him," she said, her fists tightening at her sides in memory of that visit.

"Indeed? And now what are you about?"

"I am giving *Lady Mordelle*," the housekeeper interrupted, sullenly, "a tour of the household. At the master's instruction. So if you will excuse us —"

"I shall do better than that! I will take your place so that you may attend to your other duties. Have you seen the wine cellars yet, milady? Nay? Good! You may return to your chores, Mistress Murchison."

The housekeeper looked furious, and Adria wondered at her anger. Perhaps the woman had no more liking for Master Welles than she had for Sir Anthony. She did not wish to anger the woman who was her only ally, yet she might find a friend in Master Welles. She wavered until Mark took her arm, leading her toward the narrow stairs. It seemed dark down there, and she had no desire to be alone with the man. Yet he drew her forward, closing the door to the kitchens behind them.

"You will learn," he said by way of explanation, "that Mistress Murchison has a very long nose!"

The cellar they entered was cavernous and irregular, filled with shadows that flickered and danced in a candle's single flame. The very eeriness of the place made Adria draw close to her companion as she studied the roof, fearfully, visions of bats and spiders in her mind. Then his arm went about her and she experienced a thrill of something that was not entirely fear. She pulled away.

"'Tis a rather frightening place, is it not?" she said quickly.

"Not as frightening as it appears," he told her. "'Tis a natural cave, left just as it was when the house was built above it. Perfect for the keeping of wines." Picking up a dusty bottle, he blew on it, then rubbed the glass to show her the ruby red of its content.

There was silence for a moment, and Adria wondered if the sound she heard was the thundering of the surf below, or the beating of her own heart. She was not accustomed to a man's nearness. To cover her confusion, she said, "I have always been told of a rift below this house, supposed to lead into the sea. Is this a part of it?"

He looked at her, speculatively, for a moment, then shrugged. "It is, indeed. And since you're the new mistress, I see no harm in showing you the rest of your domain."

Leading Adria to a corner of the cavern, Mark lifted a trapdoor. And Adria stepped back, crying aloud at the view that lay before her.

Far below, the sea boiled and churned, sending up plumes of icy spray. From where Adria stood with Mark, a flight of steps was roughly hewn into the granite of the promontory. They led downward, black where they were wet, flecked with flying foam as waves crashed against them and receded.

Part way up those chiseled stairs, a small boat lay at an angle. It was just out of reach of the raging waters; a canvas covering it. Here at the top of the steps, the air was still. Below, it whistled and moaned at the mouth of the rift as if trying to force its way inside.

It was an awesome sight. Adria stood immobilized by the wild beauty of the scene before her. Truly, she could believe the tales she'd heard of this place now. Its violence and mystery seemed to match the personality of its master. She trembled with the same strange fascination she'd felt in his presence. And as she marveled, Mark skipped lightly down several steps and looked up at her, his face alive with laughter and excitement.

"The best sight of all is down here, lass," he called over the crying of the wind. "Come and see it — if you dare!"

Dared she? Adria looked down at the wildness below her; the chasm, reputed to be a pathway for the demons of the deep.

If there is a way in, she thought, *there is a way out!* Her heart began to beat a little faster.

If she could only manage to loosen the knot that fastened the boat to an iron ring; if she could get it launched and around the promontory, would the waves not wash it in toward the shore? Perhaps farther down the coast, in the direction of the fishing village?

Tearing her eyes from the boat at its mooring, she forced herself to smile at Mark Welles. It would be easy to forget that he had not protected her last night and that, therefore, he should be considered an enemy.

"Of course I dare," she said.

He reached up a hand to her and led her down the narrow stairway. Suddenly, surprisingly, the rift widened at one side, making a sort of sheltered room. Adria caught her breath at the sight of the room's contents.

It was a treasure trove. There were chests, some of them open, spilling jewels that glittered in the light of a torch implanted in the stone. She saw countless bales and bundles that, as Mark threw back their protective coverings, proved to be silks, velvets, Chinese brocades. Adria stood silent as Mark roved through it all, pointing out objects of particular beauty: a gem-studded sword, a golden cup, a painting. Examining the contents of one chest, he seemed to forget her presence.

Her own moment of bedazzlement over, she looked toward the boat. The boat that could carry her to freedom. Taking one silent step downward, she paused to see if it had caught his attention. Then she was running, slipping on the iced steps, regaining her footing, slipping again...

She had reached the dory and was working on the frozen knot that held it fast when Mark Welles called from above her.

"God's teeth! What the devil are you doing, girl! Come back here!" Then he was coming toward her, swearing as he, too, slipped on the icy stairs.

He regained his balance and came on. With his coming, a wave lashed in, rocking the boat, sending Adria flat against the wall for cover. With the wave came a wind that folded the canvas over, folding it back against itself, revealing the grisly thing that lay beneath it.

Adria began to shiver, uncontrollably, as she looked down into Emma Mordelle's dead face.

She was still trembling when Mark Welles took her in his arms.

CHAPTER 6

"Lass, lass! Don't!" Mark said, cajolingly, as Adria sobbed against his shoulder. "'Tis not what it looks to be —"

"Is it not?" She pulled herself free of him, eyes blank with horror. "'Tis monstrous! Monstrous! Wedding me while his wife lies below — dead — cast off like so much rubbish!" Her voice rose, verging on hysteria.

"Nay, lass! Listen! Listen to me!" He shook her. "As I said, 'tis not what it appears to be. At her own wish, the lady is to be buried at sea. And to do so, we must wait until the waters calm. Would you have us keep a dead body in a warm house? Be sensible, girl!"

"I — I am trying." Adria bit her lip, trying to still her chattering teeth, then gave it up. "How can I be sensible," she wailed, "when everything about me seems so *insane?* No one will explain my situation. 'Tis a nightmare!"

"I'm sorry, girl. God's teeth! 'Tis all my fault in bringing you down here! I had but thought to give you pleasure in seeing those gems. I had no idea you would venture further. What were you trying to do?"

"I wanted nothing but to get away," she sobbed. "I thought perhaps I might be able to launch the boat and — and escape. Oh, I hate him! Hate him!"

He stared at her. "Has Anthony done anything to injure you?"

"Nay," she said stiffly. "Except that I am a prisoner in a most frightening house — a house of strangers — wedded to a man I fear and dislike for no seeming reason, save 'twas his whim!"

Mark sighed. "I suppose it does appear that you've been badly used."

"Is that what you call it?" She was indignant. "Drugged? Forced into a false marriage, through trickery?"

"I do not believe that was in Anthony's mind. You did say that you would do anything in order to remain beneath this roof, did you not?"

"Yes," she faltered, "but the drug —"

"The drug was used for the purpose which Anthony intended. You were in a nervous state, chilled, nearly mad with fear. It has excellent medicinal properties, though it robs one of one's powers to a certain extent."

"To the extent that I was married against my own wishes," Adria said, bitterly. "And you did not come to my aid!"

Mark bowed his head, then raised his eyes to meet hers again. "Lass, I could not. Anthony had no intention of doing you harm. And at the time, I owed you nothing. I owe him much. He is blind because he risked his life to save my own. But that is in the past. Now, I do feel I have contributed to your unhappiness, and I would like to help you —"

"Then help me get away!" Her eyes went to the boat, and she shuddered a little at the thought of what it contained. Still, it was a way.

Mark shook his head, reading her thoughts in her face. "Nay, 'twould never work. 'Twould smash on these rocks like a cockle shell in inexperienced hands."

"Then through the back, across the grounds?"

He shook his head again. "'Tis well guarded, lass."

She shut her lips tightly. She would not mention the front way, down the rocks, the way she came. There, if Mistress

Murchison left the door open as she promised, she would need no one's help but God's. "What would you have me do?" she asked, instead.

"Just wait. Have patience. And when the time comes, I will help you go free." His voice held such assurance that she could almost believe him. "And perhaps I can ease your mind in regard to your husband."

"He is not my husband!"

"Well," Mark laughed, "On the basis of Anthony Mordelle, then. He is a bitter man. A little mad, perhaps, but not the devil he is claimed to be. Would it help to know of his background? What made him as he is today?"

Adria looked toward the boat, seeing the dead woman's face, the waves lapping upward, making the boat move a little as though the burden it carried were still alive. "Not here," she said, faintly, wanting only to leave the grisly scene.

Mark studied her white face with concern. "Of course," he said with compassion. "This is no place for a conversation!" Replacing the canvas cover over the woman's body, he led Adria upward, into the wine cellar, locking the trapdoor behind him. Then they mounted the stairs to the kitchens where Mark instructed Mother Moseby to prepare a pot of tea.

"The mistress caught a chill in the cellars," he explained.

"Eeee," the old crone agreed. "She do look peaky, like." With surprising haste for such an old bag of bones, she had a tray fixed in a trice. Mark carried it up into the parlor, Adria on his heels.

Placing the service on a low table, he poured a cup for Adria. She was still shivering, but the warmth of the liquid and Mark's solicitous behavior were beginning to calm her.

"Now," Mark smiled down at her, "I have promised to tell you something of Anthony's background. Perhaps explain your situation in a way, which I am certain Anthony, himself, is too proud to do. But it is a long story, and I hardly know where to begin." He pinched at his lower lip, frowning slightly.

"Perhaps a course in English history is in order. You do know George the First is now King of England?"

She nodded, though she did not. Reverend Potts did not believe in education for the feminine sex. A woman's duty was to listen to the Bible as read and interpreted by a man; to cook, clean, bear children, tend the sick. Mark smiled and went on with his tale.

He and Anthony Mordelle had grown up on neighboring estates, Mark having a hero-worship for the older boy, who was handsome, his father's heir, and slated to wed the loveliest girl in all of England — the Lady Jane.

But when George was about to be crowned king, many of his subjects rebelled. For one thing, German George could not even speak the English language; for another, he was ignorant of English custom. Those rebels had a preference for James, son of James II. Ready to fight for their beliefs, they followed Lord Bolingbroke to France, and an expedition was set up to invade Great Britain.

Among the followers of Bolingbroke were Anthony Mordelle and Mark Welles.

"We did hold Scotland for a time," Mark said, "but our invasion failed. Bolingbroke — Bolingbroke deserted the cause, returning to England to work for a pardon, leaving us leaderless. We had no recourse but to return home."

He stopped. "I can see this means nothing to you, but I am leading up to other events — events which were spawned during our absence. My father, who had fought the coronation of George openly, was imprisoned, our wealth confiscated. But Anthony was in even worse condition.

"His father, at the insistence of his second wife, Anthony's stepmother, had declared Anthony legally dead. The younger son, Anthony's half-brother, had inherited everything, since the father died before Anthony's return. To further complicate matters, the younger brother had married Jane, the girl who was to have been Anthony's wife."

"And then?" Adria asked, remembering the story that Dorrie had told her, fearing what his answer would be.

"He killed his brother."

There it was. The truth, at last. She was joined in wedlock to a murderer. Adria swayed a little, her face going pale.

"Wait, lass! Did I put it too bluntly? There is more. It was not wanton murder, but a duel, fair-fought. The lad died, and Anthony was imprisoned, since his stepmother and Jane swore he was an imposter. He was sentenced to be hanged, but rescued through the efforts of friends who proved him who he claimed to be. 'Twas then he set London on its ear, marrying himself a prison drab to show Jane he cared not a fig for her. As for his wealth, he threw it back to the ladies in a public gesture, save for enough to outfit a ship, and took to the seas — eventually being wounded and coming here —"

It was a sad tale, in truth. The man had known much grief and misery in his lifetime. It was enough to make any man bitter. Still, Mark's story did not explain Anthony's treatment of her, nor his own part in that mockery of a marriage.

"Why are you telling me this?" she asked, in a low voice. "Are you asking me to pity him?"

"I am asking you to understand him."

"Understand him? Violence begets violence! What has happened to the man, he has brought upon himself! But how do you explain what he has done to *me*? Taking me in marriage as he did! Making me little more than a prisoner in this house!"

"It is very simple. Jane is coming here."

Adria stared at him in disbelief. "His brother's widow? The girl he was to have wed? Who — who would have seen him *hanged*?"

Mark nodded. "The same. Anthony's stepmother and Lady Jane are no longer wealthy. They were soon fleeced of their properties, and Anthony received word that they were destitute. He sent his vessel for them at once, offering his hospitality. It has been months since, and the ship is due to return at any time, so haste was necessary."

"But I do not understand! Why is it important he have a wife to greet them?"

"Because he still loves the lady," Mark said, "And because he has an odd, twisted kind of pride. He cannot, in all conscience, marry the widow of the brother he killed, yet he has no resistance to her charms, despite her ill-treatment of him. In this way, he is free to offer her his hospitality, to watch over her, and there will be nothing more, since you are there between them."

She was being used! Adria stood up, her cheeks pink and her eyes shooting sparks. "I do not like it," she said, flatly. "It puts me in an impossible situation! Suppose the girl arrives and Anthony decides he has made a mistake in judgment? He wishes to marry her, after all?"

"We will cross that bridge when we come to it, lass."

"And what of *my* pride?" Adria cried, close to tears. "Does it count for nothing? Since I came to this house, I have been tricked, shouted at, humiliated, treated like a child! And now, I'm supposed to play the fool while the man makes up his mind? And then what will he do? Put me safely away — like Emma? To lie in the chasm — dead — while he takes a new bride?"

"I will not let you come to danger, lass."

"I am leaving," she said, dully. "Mistress Murchison has promised to aid me —"

"That meddling old biddy!" Mark came toward her, his face concerned. "Don't run away, lass. There's nothing to be gained by running. Have a little patience —"

"Patience!" All the resentment that had been brewing since her interview with Anthony echoed in the word. "I have been forced into a marriage, held here against my will, treated most shamefully, and you suggest patience!" She glared at Mark, loosing her pent-up fury. "And now, after finding that — that thing in the boat below! How can I stay?" She shut her eyes as if the dreadful scene were still with her.

"I understand your feelings. But you know what will happen if you return to the settlement. Do you wish to be burned as a witch-girl?"

Adria's eyes opened wide. "How did you know?"

"One of our lads meets with a Puritan maid under cover of darkness. Your fate has already been decided. 'Tis said you were seen at the spring, consorting with the devil, himself."

"But — 'twas you!"

"They will not believe it. Once a tale as wild as this is started, you will find yourself accused of all that goes wrong here, from a sick cow to the pox."

What he said was true. It would be foolish to let her anger and pride drive her back into danger. And it was true that Mark, with his story, had set some of her fears at rest. Anthony, in spite of his brooding presence and gloomy countenance, was not the devil Reverend Potts proclaimed him to be — no more than she, Adria, was a witch. He was just a man, a human being. A man with a scar on his soul as well as his face — a man who had suffered.

And Wyndspelle was only a house. Grander, finer than any other she had seen, but a house…

As if he could read her thoughts, Mark's face lit up. "You do see! 'Tis best to let things ride as they do for now, believe me. And, though I do not wish to talk of it yet, I have a plan. A plan that must wait until the ship arrives. Perhaps, when Anthony and his lady are reconciled, I can find a way to take you to safety. If you trust me." Putting his hands on her shoulders, he pulled her against him. "You do trust me, don't you?"

"Yes," she whispered, "I do —"

Then, beyond him in the doorway, she saw Mistress Murchison. The woman's arms were folded, her face set and hard as she looked on. It was obvious the woman had come to her own conclusions about the scene she had happened upon.

Cheeks flaming, Adria drew away. Mark looked discomfited for a moment, then laughed. "Well, Mistress Murchison, do you seek something here?"

"I thought Lady Mordelle might wish to rest before dinner, sir." Then, to Adria, "I will go up with you, mum, if you are ready."

"Yes," said Adria.

She needed to be alone for a while, to think over what she'd learned this afternoon. Mark Welles had been most convincing in his arguments — too convincing, perhaps. For her every instinct seemed to be telling her to go, to run as far and as fast from this house as she possibly could. And there was still the alternative of climbing down the side of the promontory — Mistress Murchison's open door.

Mind whirling, she followed the black-clad housekeeper up the stairs and to her room. Mistress Murchison entered on the

pretext of laying out a fresh gown, and Adria wandered
nervously toward the window.

Only to be deafened by a blast that shook the room, making
the walls shimmer before her eyes, the floor quake underfoot
—

She stood frozen for a moment, eyes blank with shock, then
drew in a shuddering breath. And with it, the scent of
brimstone.

CHAPTER 7

A sound of movement behind her brought Adria to her senses. Turning, she saw the housekeeper. The woman calmly shook out a dress and placed it on the bed.

"Did — did you not hear it?" she asked, her voice trembling a little.

"The explosion? Yes, I did." Mistress Murchison inspected a ruffle, pleating it with her fingers. "There, mum, will this gown suit you?"

"But what was it? It seemed to shake the very house!"

"Blasting, mum. Black powder. 'Twas done at Sir Anthony's orders. He's been quite upset, having learned 'twas possible to reach the house from the beach below. He values his privacy. So —" Leaving her sentence unfinished, she searched the bottom of the clothes press for slippers to match the gown.

Adria stood for a moment, chilled by the implication in the woman's words, then went to the window, opening it, leaning far out. The beach below and to the side was sprinkled with a rubble of new stone. And the side of the promontory was no longer an incline with a step here, a handhold there, but a sheer drop, falling cleanly away to the rock-studded sands below.

Her one avenue of escape had been closed. Now she must rely on Mark Welles. Yet Mark had lied to her. The blind man who held her prisoner was not the poor beleaguered soul Mark had represented him to be, but a monster — a devil in human form!

"There," Mistress Murchison said with satisfaction. "'Tis done. I must see to things below, if you have no other needs." Then, after a pause, "Milady?"

"Yes?" Adria looked at her, dully, not quite seeing her, her mind still filled with bewilderment and confusion.

"I would like to give you a warning," the woman said carefully, "concerning a member of the household. Some people are not to be trusted, mum. There is one I could mention, who is immoral, a womanizer —"

"Please," Adria said. Her head ached and the woman's voice rasped at her nerves. She could not allow her to erode the delicate trust she was beginning to have, which she was *forced* to have, in Mark Welles. "Please go," she said more firmly. "Please go!"

Mistress Murchison left without another word and Adria sank down upon the bed, the woman's words still ringing in her ears. Immoral! A womanizer! It could not be true! Yet there was something in the way he looked at her, something in his touch…

Perhaps Anthony Mordelle was the devil and Mark Welles was his emissary! The one fair and smiling, the other dark and brooding, both possessed of a kind of magnetism.

And she was a prisoner in this house!

With trembling fingers, she opened the locket at her throat. Within it were two locks of hair, twined into a love-knot. A bit of her father's heavy dark hair, and a soft blond curl from her mother's head. A surge of homesickness tugged at her as she touched them.

"Help me," she prayed, her eyes welling with tears. "Mama, Papa! I need you so! Help me!"

So intent was she that she did not hear the door open. Her first knowledge that someone was in the room came when she heard Dorrie's small whimper. She turned to see the girl, white-faced, backed against the door that had closed behind her.

"Why, Dorrie," she said, uncertainly. "What —"

But Dorrie was staring at the love-knot in Adria's hand, her eyes popping with terror. And the girl was not alone. The black cat had entered with her.

With feline grace, it bounded across the room and leaped to Adria's side. Oddly enough, it broke Dorrie's trance-like state. With another small sound of fear, the servant turned and fumbled at the door, unable to open it in her frantic haste.

"Dorrie, wait! What is it? Surely, you're not afraid of a cat!"

The girl turned back, her eyes rolling a little, and Adria realized what had happened. Evidently, the story of her exposure as a witch had run through the house like wildfire. Dorrie, entering unheard, had believed her to be muttering some kind of spell over an amulet.

"Dorrie, come here! What *is* the matter with you?"

"Nothing, mum."

"Is this what frightened you?" Adria held up the love-knot. "What did you think it was?"

"'Air, mum." The coarse lips trembled.

"That's exactly what it is. A keepsake. A lock of my mother's hair, entwined with my father's." At the look of disbelief on Dorrie's face, she said, "Don't you believe me?"

"Looks like the master's 'air to me, mum. An' a bit of Lady Emma's."

"Well, 'tis not!" Adria spoke sharply as she considered what was in the girl's mind. Did she think she, Adria, had used witchcraft to bring about Emma's death and install herself as mistress of the house? "Dorrie," she said, finally, "has someone been talking to you? Telling you that I might be a witch? 'Tis not true. There is no such creature, believe me —"

"That cat, 'e don't take up with no one," the girl said obliquely.

"And what does that prove?" Adria was angry now. "I know you've heard the story; how I ran away from the settlement because I was accused of witchcraft. Do you honestly think I could be guilty of a thing like that? Dorrie, I'm your friend! You *do* believe me?"

"Yes, mum." The two words held a world of doubt. Then, the whites of her eyes showing, mouth twitching with fright, the servant stammered, "If — if you be my friend, mum, mayhap you'd 'elp me? 'Tis Vincente, mum. I 'ear there be things — a potion, summat to put in 'is tea — to get 'is attention, like —"

What was the girl saying? She had still not managed to convince her. She hadn't got through to her at all! "Dorrie," she said angrily, reaching out a hand to her. "Dorrie!"

With a rabbit-like shriek, the girl fled. Adria stood, paralyzed, looking after her. As the door slammed, she looked down at her hand. She had thrust it out in a detaining motion, fingers crooked.

The terrified Dorrie had seen her action as a witch's curse.

Adria sank down on her bed. She would never be able to convince the dull-witted girl of her innocence. Ignorant and superstitious as Dorrie was, she had been a cheerful companion. She felt she had lost a friend.

If she could only turn time back, she thought wistfully, she would listen to the Reverend Potts' teachings. She would be the quiet, submissive creature his God dictated that she be. No more sidelong glances at Tim Tyson to tease Naomi Potts; no more yearning to run in the sunlight like a child. She would cook, scrub, churn, and spin without complaint.

But she could not go back, not ever. They would not let her now, even if she could. She was trapped here, her one avenue of escape blasted out of existence. Why had Anthony Mordelle done this, she wondered forlornly? To keep the members of this household in — or to keep the world outside?

Tears on her lashes, Adria lifted the purring cat and held it close for a long time.

The animal was curled on her bed when Mistress Murchison came to fetch her downstairs. Adria had heard a bell but, not understanding its import, had remained where she was until the housekeeper came. She followed the woman, embarrassed at the cut of her taffeta gown. At least, there would be no reason for Anthony Mordelle to be contemptuous of her.

She held her head high as she entered the great hall, concentrating on proving she was not the crude country maid he deemed her to be. Perhaps Mark Welles would be kind enough to remark upon her ladylike appearance. Surely that glow in his eyes was one of appreciation.

She forgot Mark as Anthony turned toward her. As before, Adria sensed he saw right through her to her very soul, and found her lacking. Her confidence ebbed and her steps slowed. This approach was too reminiscent of the night before. She could shut her eyes and imagine the scene as it was then: the dead fireplace, candles flickering in a shadowed room. A corpse smiling into the darkness. The same dead face that now smiled in the chasm below —

True, the setting was different tonight. A fire blazed cheerfully on the hearth; the candles in the fixture overhead glowed, the dangling prisms catching their reflections, casting them forth in shimmering rainbows of light. But the feeling in the room was much the same. A heavy feeling, as if some dreadful thing was about to happen.

Despite the great fire, she felt cold.

"Come along, mum." The housekeeper's voice was tart as she turned back for her. Adria realized she had stopped dead still. The men were still standing, possibly wondering if she lacked good sense. She was as imaginative as Dorrie! It was only the memory of her fright last night, and the grisly use to which this table had been put. Now, with the candles in the chandelier above and the shadows dispelled, it looked less ominous. Yet here she stood, gaping like a country bumpkin. She made herself move forward, smiling at Mark Welles, who smiled back at her.

"Allow me," he said gallantly, moving to assist her in seating herself. She caught her foot in the hem of her gown and sat down hard, blushing, knowing she had handled herself awkwardly. Then she bowed her head and waited for a blessing that never came.

Raising her eyes at last, she was conscious that Mark was attempting to conceal the laughter in his face. Her cheeks burned again. It was a natural mistake! She had assumed that meals in every household began with a prayer of thankfulness.

But of course at Wyndspelle, it would be unthought of. Here, where the master was said to be the devil.

As Dorrie and Mistress Murchison served the dinner, Adria studied Anthony covertly. He dominated the table in a throne-like chair, its high back carved of some exotic wood and inset with jewels. Though he leaned back, surveying the table with his brooding blind eyes, there was something tense about him. As if he might explode into violence at a word.

He seemed to sense her gaze upon him, and the saturnine face turned toward her. "Milady," he said, raising his goblet, "A toast. A toast to my bride."

The words were a mockery! Adria was livid with fury and embarrassment as Anthony lifted the wine to his lips, drinking deeply before he set the goblet down. Then he drummed on the table with his dark, nervous fingers. "Unless my ears deceive me," he said, "our food is before us. We are waiting for you, milady."

Adria jumped a little and looked at him in confusion, then at Mark. Mark's eyes signaled that she was expected to begin her meal. Apparently the gentlemen would then follow suit. She stared down at her plate, stricken at the sight of those unfamiliar utensils.

Why hadn't she asked Dorrie to instruct her in their use this morning? She twisted her hands in her lap as the others waited, thankful when Mark, his eyes suddenly understanding, rested his hand on a piece of silver.

At the sound of it against her plate, Anthony began his meal, Mark following. She watched them closely, trying to emulate their actions. The blind man used his tools deftly and silently. Hers clanged against her dish. She dropped food into her lap, staining the taffeta gown beyond redemption, food sticking in her throat as the others conversed politely.

"And you, milady, are your chambers comfortable?"

As Anthony addressed the question to her, Adria choked on a bit of bread. Reaching for her goblet, she knocked it over in her nervousness. Helplessly, she watched a stream of wine pour across the table and into Anthony's lap. He flinched a little and blotted his damp trousers with a napkin as she stammered an apology.

"No matter," he said coolly. "No harm done. 'Tis what one might expect." Then, turning to Mark, he said, "I must ask you to instruct the lady in social graces before our guests arrive, so that she will be accustomed to our ways —"

Adria waited to hear no more. Jumping to her feet, she fled to her room, only reaching the foot of the stair before she burst into tears of anger and humiliation.

Reaching the safety of her own quarters, she slammed the door and threw herself across the bed, hating the man downstairs. What a trial both of Anthony's wives must have been to his high and mighty lordship! First a London drab and now a colonial savage! A crude, ill-mannered colonial savage!

The black cat prowled around her, purring, making little anxious mewing cries, and at last she drew it close, her tears wetting its sleek fur. Her friend. Her only true friend in this hateful house!

Hours later, she heard the sounds that announced Anthony Mordelle's presence on the balcony. His hesitant footsteps, the tapping of his cane.

The sound seemed to pause at her door.

She sat up, her heart beating a little too fast, her hand pressed tightly against the thin silk that covered it. What did he want with her? Had he come to deliver an apology for his cruel words of the evening? Or a further lecture? Or even — the thought shook her — *something else?* Her eyes were fastened on the door as she drew the coverlet to her throat, waiting with the stillness of a small bird hypnotized by a snake…

And the steps moved on. She heard the door to the next room open — and close.

Sinking back against her pillows, she went weak with relief. She wanted no part of the master of Wyndspelle. No apologies, no lectures — nothing! Then she had another thought, one even more frightening. She remembered the tapestry that covered a door that had no key. She watched the tapestry for a long time, the embroidered figures on it seeming to move, to come alive in the light of her candle. She watched, waiting for something, man or demon she did not know, to enter.

It was now far too late. He did not intend to come. Not this night, at any rate. But how many nights would she have to lie like this, in mortal terror? For no reason, she began to cry again. Holding the black cat close, she sobbed herself to sleep.

CHAPTER 8

In the morning, a new Adria rose from the big canopied bed, her soft face now firm and set with resolve. During the night, she had made a few decisions for herself. She had been as namby-pamby as Mistress Potts since her arrival here, letting herself be bullied, humiliated, frightened out of her wits — but no more!

First, Anthony Mordelle was only a man. A human being like herself. He had no right to treat her in the fashion he had done yesterday. She did not intend to allow such treatment to continue. Her eyes flashed sparks at the thought of his mocking face. He was a sadist, that was what he was! And he had enjoyed embarrassing her. In running from the table last night, she'd done exactly what he'd expected of her.

No more!

It was true that she was in need of his protection at this time, but she did not intend to be indebted to him. She would repay him by being exactly what he wished — the mistress of Wyndspelle. As such, she would insist upon respect. In return for the shelter of his roof, she would live up to what was expected of her, fulfilling the duties he'd outlined to the best of her ability.

Until she could escape, Anthony Mordelle would have no cause to complain of her behavior! She would be mistress of the house in word and deed.

Uneasily, she thought of Mark and the scene the housekeeper had happened upon in the parlor. Such a thing must not occur again. Not until she was free to go. Until the

ship came and Anthony was re-united with his true love —
And she is welcome to him, Adria thought grimly — she must
regard Mark, not as a friend, not as an attractive man, but as a
member of the household. When she left this house, she would
owe Anthony nothing!

Eyes burning, she turned to ready herself for the day. A
pitcher of cold water sat upon her table. Adria had visions of
Dorrie slipping in with it, frightened of the 'witch', relieved to
see that Adria still slept.

Still, the cool water was balm to her swollen eyes and mouth,
still bruised from her anger of the night before. She was ready
for the day when Mistress Murchison entered.

"Don't know where that fool Dorrie's got to," the woman
said. She set down the tray and picked up the cat, which hissed
and clawed at her as she tossed it out into the hall. "I'll have a
word to say to that girl," she went on, grimly. "She knew she
was supposed to bring your breakfast!"

"I'm glad you brought it," Adria said. "I wanted to tell you
I'm ready to begin taking charge of the household today. I'd
like to go into the housekeeping details a little more fully. Take
a look at the laundry rooms and check the quality of the
linens."

The woman looked astounded, then angry. "There's no need
for you to handle these things, milady. I've managed quite well
heretofore! Emma —"

"The Lady Emma is dead, and I have my own way of doing
things. I would like the keys." Adria held out her hand.

"I'm sure there is a spare set," the woman began. "I'll send
them up to you, after I've spoken to the master."

"It would be simpler to give me those," Adria said, her voice
firm and eyes steady. "You may take the other set for
yourself."

With a murderous expression, the woman handed over the ring at her waist, then turned and marched out, her back stiff with fury.

I've made an enemy, Adria thought, sitting down to her breakfast, trembling a little at her own bravado. Then she began to laugh. Check the linens, indeed! She who had felt lucky to have a scratchy patchwork quilt to cover her in her bed of straw at night, the mistress of Wyndspelle! This was quite a task she had set for herself. And without help; that was one thing she could be certain of. For a fleeting moment, she thought wistfully of Dorrie, wishing she could regain the girl's trust and affection. Then she picked up a piece of silver from the tray. Last night, she had seen Mark hold it *this* way. Awkwardly, at first, then with increasing dexterity, she began to eat.

She had finished, noting with satisfaction that there had been few spills, when Mistress Murchison returned. "I've come for the tray, mum," the woman said. Then, almost triumphantly, "And the master wishes to see you."

She had got to him so soon? Adria rose, sighing a little. "Where is he? The tower room, I suppose?"

"No, mum. He's confined to his bed. Another one of his spells."

"Spells?" Adria stared at the housekeeper, a question in her eyes.

"From his injury. His head pains him at times. Puts him in a proper temper, too." It sounded like a warning.

"Perhaps I can help him, then," Adria said with more assurance than she felt. "I have some knowledge of medicines." She crumpled her napkin and dropped it on the tray, nodding to indicate that the woman was dismissed and the conversation at an end.

After the housekeeper had gone, Adria stood for a moment, trying to summon her courage. She looked at the tapestry covering the connecting door between her room and Anthony's. Should she use that entrance? No, it would be better for that door to remain closed forever!

She went out onto the balcony and tapped at the door to the next room, knowing full well that Mistress Murchison was standing at the far corner of the great hall below, watching.

At Anthony's muffled command, she entered. The shades were drawn and the room was in semi-darkness. Adria's heart beat a little too fast as she tried to orient herself to the absence of light, looking fearfully toward the huge bed. She gasped as the head on the pillow turned slowly toward her.

On the scarred side of Anthony's face, there seemed to be a dark hole, in lieu of an eye.

"Mistress Murchison?"

"Nay," Adria said faintly. "'Tis I."

"And who might *I* be? You do have a name, milady!"

"Adria." The dark face still wore a look of impatience, as if her title had not been complete. "Adria — Anne — Turner," she faltered.

"Allow me to correct you," he said. "'Tis Adria Anne Mordelle, is it not? Mistress Mordelle. I suggest you keep it in mind, milady."

Adria shut her mouth tightly, holding back the furious words that threatened to escape. *I am not your wife,* she wanted to scream. *I will not use your name!* She remembered her new resolutions just in time: to assume her role as mistress of Wyndspelle; to maintain her personal dignity; to allow herself to be frightened and humiliated no more.

"Yes, milord," she said, coolly, "Was there anything more?"

A moment of silence, then he said, "Come closer. My head pains me less when I lie flat."

Swallowing her dread of him, she approached the bed. To her relief, she saw that his eye was intact, but that he wore a dark patch over it. "You are in much pain?"

"Some," he admitted. "A chronic thing, of little importance. 'Tis you I am concerned about."

"Concerned, sir?"

"First, I have had word from Dorrie that you are a witch, and that my present condition is possibly the result of a curse you placed upon me. Some spell you work from your room."

She stopped short, ready with a hot denial. Surely he did not believe the girl's story! Then the corner of the lips below the black patch twitched. He was trying not to laugh. But was he laughing at her, or at Dorrie?

"Then I shall have to work another spell, sir, to make you well. Is there anything else?"

"It would seem from another source, that you are disrupting my household, exceeding your authority, and forgetting your place."

Mistress Murchison! Adria forced herself to speak calmly. "And what is my place, sir? Since we are expecting guests, I assumed 'twould be best to assume my wifely duties prior to their arrival. I would suggest the complainer may have exceeded *her* authority. Forgotten *her* place."

"'Twould not be wise to make an enemy of the woman."

"I'm sure we can manage to reach agreement in most things." Adria's knees were trembling now, beneath the checked gown, but her tone was still level. "And now, milord, I would like to know more of your health. Why do you wear the covering over your eye? Does the light pain you? Is it inflamed?"

He turned his face from her, wincing as he moved. "Yes, to both counts," he said harshly. "But 'tis none of your concern."

"If I am to serve as mistress of Wyndspelle," she said, "then 'tis my duty to nurse the sick. I shall be back soon." Before he could protest, she was out of the room and gone.

First, she went to her room, where she cut two small squares from a fine linen petticoat. She sewed them into small bags with tiny stitches, wondering at her temerity as she did so. Sir Anthony had been no less fearsome lying stricken, like a fallen tree, his dark features stormy, brooding, forbidding. Yet she had been able to speak without stammering. It was the role she was playing. She might not be able to survive this household as Adria Anne Turner, but as mistress of Wyndspelle, she could — and would!

The bags completed, Adria hurried down to the kitchen where she requested tea leaves from Mother Moseby. Shaking them into the containers from a paper spill, she stitched the tops shut with a needle, making small packets.

"Eh," the old crone asked, "you do be making charms?"

Adria shook her head, though it was obvious the woman disbelieved her. Then, taking a pitcher of hot water, she carried the materials to Anthony's room. She rapped, entered, and put the bags to steep in the wash bowl beside his bed, without speaking.

When she removed the patch from his eye, he said nothing, though she saw his jaw clench as he grimaced with pain. He swore a little as she placed one of the warm, damp bags over each eye. Waiting until his fists curled against the sheet and his face relaxed, she laid a small hand cautiously on his brow where a pulse was beating.

"Where is it worse, milord? Here? Or here?"

Forgetting he was her enemy, she rubbed his forehead, fingers gentle against his scarred face, replacing the small bags as they cooled. At last, he raised his hand to touch hers.

"I think you *are* a witch," he said. "The pain is gone."

Was he mocking her? "You cannot be serious," she said in a cold voice. "You do not believe in such things."

"Nay, I do not. I believe in *nothing*." As she gasped, he went on. "I shock you? 'Tis true. And spare me your sermons! God? Love? The milk of human kindness? 'Tis sour, milady. These things do not exist."

"But —" Adria began.

"But what?" His tone was cool, amused, his face sardonic. "You were going to remind me that you have been kind this day, in tending me. Am I correct?"

"Nay!"

"Oh, but you were! And since you obviously cannot, now that I have mentioned the subject, I will say it for you. You have been most kind to me, milady. What do you wish in return? More jewels, perhaps? A new gown? Surely, you have some reward in mind."

Adria stood, shaking with anger. "Only my freedom," she said stiffly. "Freedom to leave this dreadful house, if you insist upon regarding my actions in such light!"

Anthony did not answer. She turned away, resentment blazing inside her, making her fingers tremble as she gathered up the supplies she'd brought into the room. Lifting the tray, she walked stiff-backed, toward the door.

"Adria?"

"Yes, milord."

"You know I will not let you go. Why *were* you kind enough to aid me in my illness?"

Was there a new note in his voice? Or was he simply baiting her further? She placed her hand on the knob, wrenching the door open before she turned.

"As I told you," she said, her voice taut with repressed fury, "'Tis a wife's duty. Though I have never been able to stand idly by, and watch any ailing animal suffer!" She went out, slamming the door behind her.

For a long time, she leaned against the balcony railing, attempting to pull herself together before she descended the stairs. The man was a devil! Seeming so helpless one moment, almost boyish as his face relaxed, then his expression twisting, shifting as he lashed out at her with his hurting statements, shredding her control.

She straightened herself and swept down the steps. She would find Mistress Murchison, insist upon checking the linens and then the food supplies. In work, she would find release from her frustration.

Mark was at the foot of the stairs, looking up at her in admiration. He was so handsome, far handsomer than Anthony, with his brooding gloom. Mark was like sunlight itself, in his buff breeches, blue coat that matched his eyes, a ribbon of the same color tying back his unpowdered hair.

"I have been searching for you," he said, "But you are as elusive as a butterfly, lass. When you are upstairs, I am downstairs. Then we manage to pass somewhere. At least," he said ruefully, "until you decided to alight in Anthony's chambers. Do you prefer his company to mine?" He cocked his head to one side with a comical expression.

"I do not, you may believe me," Adria said, making a little face. "But he — is ill."

"So Mistress Murchison tells me. But he is improving? I'm certain I would be, with such a lovely lady to attend me."

"In all but disposition," she said, reaching the foot of the steps. Then she blushed. That had been an unwifely remark, and not at all in character with the personality she intended to maintain. Though it was true, it would not do to share her inner thoughts with a member of the household.

"If you will excuse me, Master Welles," she said, with a polite smile, "I have duties to attend —"

"Not Master Welles," he said, "but Mark. Say it. I want to hear you say my name."

"I think we must remain on a more formal basis." Adria shrank from the arm that went out to encircle her waist. "We — forgot ourselves yesterday, sir. If I am masquerading as Sir Anthony's wife, I must play the role. You are his friend."

He studied her. "So you've succumbed to the great man's fatal charm? You think you can compete with the Lady Jane? I cannot blame you. A man with his wealth —" He sounded stiff, hurt.

"Nay," she said, passionately, "Nay, Mark!" She stopped, seeing him smile at the use of his name, her face reddening. "'Tis only that under the circumstances there is no other honorable course. Until I am free —" She twisted her hands in an agonized effort to make him understand.

"You are quite right, madam." He bowed, his face impassive. "I but wished to tell you something to set your mind at ease. Perhaps you haven't noticed the wind has ceased and the sea is calmer. The — the lady's burial was accomplished early this morning. At dawn."

Adria stood silent, visualizing the scene as it must have been. The fog shrouding the waters, muffling the paddles as the boat moved into its depths; a body tipped over the side, drifting down to its silent grave. She shuddered.

"Thank you," she said, her face white. "Now — I must go."

Adria hurried across the great hall and entered the parlor. There, as might have been expected, stood Mistress Murchison. It was clear that she had been watching Adria and Mark, and that she was making something of their meeting in her mind. Adria suppressed the words of explanation that sprang to her lips and held her head high. There was no need for denial. She was mistress of Wyndspelle, was she not? She did not have to account for her actions. Not to a servant!

"We will check the linens this morning," she said.

"I see no reason for it," the woman said, sourly.

Adria looked at her, levelly. "As mistress of Wyndspelle, the running of the household is my responsibility. All must be in order when my husband's guests arrive. Come."

She turned, left the parlor and crossed the hall to ascend the stairs, grateful that Mark was no longer in sight, but conscious of the bristling animosity of the woman who followed her. As she passed Anthony's door, the resentment she felt toward him stiffened her determination. If she were mistress of this house, then mistress she would be. She would show him!

The generosity of the materials in the supply cupboards amazed her. She counted the linens, using the only method she knew. One knot in a length of wool for each item. From the cupboards, she went to the larder below, awed by the fruits and vegetables preserved between layers of straw; the strings of dried peppers hanging from the storeroom rafters; hare sausage, fried in patties and put down in crocks of fat. There were pumpkins and warty squash, haunches of smoked venison. Enough to feed the Puritan settlement for a year!

At last, tired and dusty, she returned to her room to ready herself for the evening meal. She had selected a dress and spread it across the bed when she realized she might be spared the ordeal of sitting at table with Anthony. Ill as he was, he would probably remain in his room.

Washing up in the now-cold water, she slipped into her gown, with a sudden feeling that all was not as it should be. Her hand went automatically to the locket at her throat, and she gasped in surprise.

It was gone.

Her locket, the only keepsake she had to remind her of her life with her parents, was gone!

Mother Moseby! Adria had passed through her kitchens a dozen times this day. What had Mark called the woman – the most proficient thief to escape the London gaol. But why would she take her locket? In this house filled with treasures, it would not count for much.

Adria's eyes were wet with tears of grief and anger. She would go down and face the woman — accuse her!

But what if she were wrong? Supposing the catch on the chain had come loose and the locket had slipped from her throat? Though it had never loosed itself before...

She would wait until she looked for it. Tomorrow, she would search. When it was light. Though her body felt cold now, and naked without the chain's familiar touch.

Clasping the ruby necklace around her neck, she paced the room nervously, waiting for the summoning bell. At last she decided to go down. Perhaps her locket was lying on the stairs.

When she stepped out on the balcony, she saw she had misjudged the time. The shadows had settled in, but the candles in the chandelier were still unlit. The stair was a tunnel of darkness.

Re-entering her room, Adria took up a candle. She went down slowly, praying she would find her keepsake. When she reached the last step and turned toward the hearth, she raised her eyes.

For an instant, she stopped stock still, her heart in her throat, for between her and the fireplace that was the core of Wyndspelle stood an elongated shadow.

The witch! Dear God, the witch of Wyndspelle! Dorrie said she'd seen her here. Adria closed her eyes, making a small whimpering sound.

"Did you call?" The voice came from above. Adria lifted her eyes to see Anthony Mordelle at the balcony railing. Then she looked back at the spot where she'd seen the apparition.

It was his shadow. A trick of light, perhaps, as he was silhouetted against the open door of his room. Yet there was something in the very fact that terrified Adria. It was as if the shadow was a part of the man; an extension of his dark nature.

"Did you call?" the man repeated, an angry edge to his voice. "I heard something!"

The cat rubbed against Adria's ankles, giving her a reason for the sound her husband had heard. For the mistress of Wyndspelle would certainly not cry out at shadows.

"Nay," she called up to him. "'Twas only the cat." Then, seeing he was fully dressed, "Should you be out of bed? Are you feeling well?"

"Much better," he said, coming down the stairs toward her. "Usually these spells last for some time, but —" He stopped, peering at her. There was something different about his eyes. Normally, they held an awful emptiness, but tonight a tiny light seemed to dance in each of them, as if an ember remained. "Why, you are wearing the rubies!" he said.

"You — you *see* them?"

"Why, yes." His voice was puzzled as he passed his hand across his eyes. "For an instant there, I could have sworn —! You *are* wearing them, aren't you?"

"Yes," she faltered. "Do you think your sight might be returning?"

"I don't know," he groaned. "Oh, God, if it only would!"

"Do you see now?"

"Only a blur," he said, turning his haunted face away. "As it has always been."

Then Adria saw Mark. He had followed Anthony down and stood several steps behind him. By the light of the flickering candle she held, he wore an expression that seemed, strangely, one of fear. Adria decided she was mistaken when he spoke in his usual lighthearted way.

"God's teeth! Are we saving on candles? Or is the fare so poor tonight we must eat it in the dark? 'Tis lighter than this in the cavern below!"

Anthony's call brought Mistress Murchison and Dorrie. He scolded them roundly for their tardiness in lighting the candles and ringing the bell for dinner.

"It was not my fault," said the housekeeper, tight-lipped. "What can you expect, with someone disrupting the household, changing the schedule all around?"

"That will be enough," Anthony thundered. He raised his cane, pointing it at the woman. "Do you dare to criticize your mistress?"

"Nay, sir," she said humbly, though she darted a venom-filled glance at Adria. "'Tis only —"

"No more excuses," Anthony growled. "Forget the overhead candles for this night. We will manage without them."

"I, for one, prefer it this way," Mark put in hastily. Turning to Adria, he said, "May I escort you to your chair, milady?"

Anthony scowled. "Are you not forgetting *your* place also, Mark? The Lady Adria is my wife, and it is my duty to seat her, not yours. I am not entirely helpless, you know."

Mark reddened, his eyes glinting with repressed anger, but he murmured an apology. The blind man extended his arm to Adria and, feeling his way with his cane, led her to the table where he insisted upon seating her himself.

Mistrusting his gallantry, Adria simmered with resentment. It had only been a method of showing he owned her. But it had shown her one thing. She was not the only victim of his subtle cruelty. Mark, too, writhed under its sting. She looked at the face of the blond man, subdued now as he stared down at his plate, and then at the ruined face of the master of Wyndspelle.

In the flickering light, it changed constantly, his dark countenance at once handsome and evil, strong and frightening. Yet there was something compelling about him that drew her gaze...

Tearing her eyes away, she looked down at her hands and uttered a brief and silent prayer. At least, he could not deprive her of that!

It was quiet, too quiet as dinner was served, then Mark said, "I heard you were ill, Anthony. I didn't expect to see you at table tonight."

Anthony inclined his head toward Adria. "I would not have been, except for my wife's excellent nursing. I do believe she has magic in her hands."

"Why not?" Mark said. "Is she not said to be a witch? Perhaps she has cast a spell on you."

It was not a jest. In fact, there was something insolent in his tone. So he *was* angry! Angry at her formal treatment earlier in the day, and at Anthony's high-handedness tonight. But there was no reason to punish her. She did not intend to become a bone of contention between the two men!

She glared at Mark, but he had ducked his head again. Her gaze met that of Dorrie, bending to pour Mark's wine. The girl's eyes widened. She began to tremble, then with a despairing shriek, she dropped the bottle. Its contents spattered across the floor beneath Adria's chair as it shattered. Then, hand over her mouth, the girl fled from the room.

"God's teeth," swore Mark, starting up. "Of all the clumsy —!"

"It's all right," Adria said, hastily. "I'll clear it up."

She was already on her knees, picking up pieces of the broken bottle, putting them into her napkin as Mark went for Mistress Murchison. She reached for a shard on the hearth that had almost gone into the flames, and then she saw it —

A gold chain, looping from between the logs where the fire blazed the highest.

A gold chain —

Careless of her fingers, she snatched at it, pulling it from the fire. The locket that was attached to it was now only a charred and broken lump of metal.

She was still kneeling there, staring at the remains of her keepsake, when Mark returned, the housekeeper and a weeping Dorrie in tow. And seeing the girl's start of guilty surprise when she saw what she held, watching Dorrie's eyes flicker and slide away, Adria guessed what had happened.

Dorrie, who was once her friend, had conspired with the thieving old woman in the kitchens below. They could not burn the witch, but they could destroy her talisman.

Adria returned to the table and finished the meal, sitting proud and erect, handling the silver utensils deftly in spite of her burned and blistered hand.

CHAPTER 9

The locket was surely beyond repair, the sections of it fused until it would not open. Though the chain was burned through in places, charred and blackened, Adria couldn't bring herself to discard it. She wept over it that night in her room, then stitched the remains into a lacy handkerchief, pinning it inside her bodice where she could keep it always with her.

The action gave her pause to think. She supposed that she *had* regarded the locket as a talisman. A sign that her parents were still near enough to protect her. Was this witchcraft?

Witchcraft or not, it was the one thing left that was her own. She would guard it carefully.

As though the locket had been a catalyst for the fearful happenings of the last days, life at Wyndspelle settled into boredom. Time stood still. It seemed as if the house waited, shadows collecting in the central hall, plotting some new horror...

The ship was late. Perhaps it had not survived the trip. She may have been sunk by pirates, or a storm at sea. And along with her, Anthony's stepmother, Lady Elizabeth, and the Lady Jane. It would serve them right, Adria thought with grim satisfaction. Then she uttered a silent prayer for forgiveness. It was not for her to pass judgment upon those women. Besides, it was only when they came that she could be free.

After nearly a week of gloom and what appeared to be rejection by the entire household, Adria rebelled. It had become unseasonably warm. She rose one morning to find the sleet had melted from the windows, little rivers of moisture glittering in the sunlight marking where it had been. Again, her heart leaped at the view, the combers, lazy now, rolling in toward the crag.

It was beautiful until she thought of the dead Emma, who had received a burial at sea. What had happened to her body? Had it been weighted, to glide straight down? Or might it someday wash ashore, perhaps even at the foot of the promontory? The notion cast a dark shadow on the sunny day.

Adria had had enough of water; the things that came from it and the things that were returned to it. She felt a desire for land, for trees about her, remembering that last idyllic trip to the spring before her life fell apart. The walls of Wyndspelle were like a prison around her. If only she could walk out into the sunlight…

Catching up a cloak, she hastened downstairs, hurrying through the great hall to the kitchens. There, she surprised Mistress Murchison in conversation with Mother Moseby. The housekeeper's eyes flicked over her, noting that she was dressed for the outdoors.

"Were you going someplace, milady?" The voice was a fine line between servility and insolence.

"Just out for a walk," Adria said, putting her hand to the door, pausing at Mother Moseby's outburst.

"Eee, 'er 'adn't oughter!"

"Let her go," Mistress Murchison said, a gleam of laughter in her eyes. "She won't get far!"

Adria turned away, pushing the door open, closing it behind her. Outside, she took a deep breath of the sea air, then stopped dead still, shocked at the sight before her. To one side was a long low building — housing for the guards, no doubt — but it was the land itself that gave her pause. It swept before her in a triangle with the crag as its apex, desolate, blighted, the skeletal remains of dead trees clawing at the sky.

She had heard this was cursed land. Now, she could believe nothing else. Even on a winter's day, it was plain that this was not a place of living things. But strangely enough, a fine wide pathway led downward from the kitchen door, crossing the property, branching at intervals. Here and there were lattices supporting no growth, benches placed where one might sit and gaze out upon utter desolation. A horrid travesty of a garden.

At least the air was fresh and clean, smelling of salt and seaweed. And she was rid of the brooding, waiting atmosphere of the house. She stepped out upon the walkway, only to be confronted by a dark foreign-looking man who blocked her path, moving in front of her as she tried to pass him.

Drawing herself up to hide her terror, she introduced herself as the mistress of the house, demanding that he step aside. "I only want to walk a little," she said, lamely, as he stared at her, his face impassive. What if she ducked around him? Would he dare *touch* her?

At last, she re-entered the house, humiliated at the expression on Mistress Murchison's face. "There's a gentleman outside who refuses to allow me to pass," she said, crisply. "Will you be kind enough to explain that this is my property, and that, as Sir Anthony's wife, he is expected to obey my orders?"

The woman shook with ill-disguised laughter. "Can't," she said. "He don't speak English. That's Petro. He's a Portygee. So's Rico. They take their orders from Vincente, who gets his from the master."

"Then I'll need to talk to Vincente," Adria said. "Where is he?"

The housekeeper shrugged and shook her head. Adria turned back to the inner house, climbing the stairs that led to the parlor, burning with the knowledge that behind her, Mistress Murchison and old Mother Moseby were laughing at her.

It did not help her disposition any when she entered the parlor to discover Dorrie, dusting the furniture. The girl mumbled something, the whites of her eyes showing like a frightened horse, and hurried from the room.

"Dorrie!" Adria called after her. There was no answer. The girl either hadn't heard, or had chosen to ignore her voice.

Disconsolately, Adria wandered to the windows, pulling the heavy drapes back. The windows were shuttered from the outside. Would they be the same in the study? She crossed the hall to the other door behind the great fireplace, entering the study to find Mark Welles at Anthony's desk, writing on a scroll of paper with a quill pen.

As she entered, he sprang to his feet, hastily turning the paper over to conceal what he'd written there, his face reddening a little. Adria suppressed a smile. Whatever he had been writing, he was in no danger from her. Did the man think she could read? How she wished she could! She glanced at the books around the walls, books filled with knowledge, knowledge that she hungered for.

"Were — were you looking for something, milady?" Mark asked, politely.

"I only wished to see if these windows opened on the grounds." She considered telling him how she'd been excluded from the grounds, then decided against it. She'd had enough of patronizing people! Her cheeks flushed with anger and she caught Mark's look of admiration. Did he think her blushes were for him?

"The shutters are kept closed," he said, coming toward her. "As you know, Anthony values his privacy. But I can have them opened for you." The expression in his blue eyes gave her an odd shaky feeling. She backed away from him, straight into Vincente standing in the doorway.

"The master wishes to speak to you, *senhora,*" he said over her awkward apologies. "He is in the upper room."

Bowing, he turned away. Adria hurried toward the stairs, hating herself for her clumsy exit. She would never acquire a lady's graces, that was certain!

She climbed the stairs, pausing a moment at the foot of the ship's ladder to catch her breath. Her heart was pumping too fast. Because of what she'd seen in Mark's eyes? Or because she would be in Anthony's presence soon? Forcing her nerves to calm, she lifted her hampering skirts and climbed the ladder. So Anthony Mordelle was waiting to speak with her! She might have a word or two to say to him! She would tell him she was not his wife, but his prisoner.

The memory of the man stopping her on the grounds; her humiliation before the cook and the housekeeper, was still with her as she made her way through the aperture that led to the upper room.

As usual, the very power of the man's presence overwhelmed her, stifling the words she'd been rehearsing on her way. He was standing as he had before, his back to her, looking from the window that faced the sea. But he had heard her approach. Her heart thudded as he turned his haunted face in her direction, reaching out a hand to her.

Fighting his compelling magnetism, she stopped stock still, stubbornly resisting his invitation to approach. Whatever the reason for his seeming friendliness, she did not trust him.

"You wished to speak to me, sir?" she asked coolly, noting even in her dislike of her situation that, here in the light, he was a very handsome man. He looked much as he did on that first night, his white silk shirt partially unbuttoned, showing the brown chest that tapered to a slim waist. Except that now his somber countenance was somewhat lightened by his smile. A smile that did not reach his eyes. They were still dark, fixed, brooding...

"Yes," he said, "I sent for you. Come here, milady."

His tone commanded her, and she took several steps before she remembered her resolution. Then it was too late. He had grasped her hand and was drawing her toward the window. A strange sensation shivered through her at his touch. A thrill of fear — and something else she did not recognize.

"I thought you might wish to come here for a while," he said. "It must be rather dull for you in this house at present. This is my own favorite haunt. From here, one can look out over all of Wyndspelle. The sea, of course," he gestured in that direction, "and the gardens in spring —"

Gardens! Adria shuddered. From this elevation, the grounds looked even more bleak and devastated. From this height, she could see the contour of the earth. Wyndspelle stood on a promontory that sloped suddenly downward behind the house; the grounds bordered in the far distance by a continuous cliff, horseshoe-shaped. Only beyond the cliff could she see a trace of color or vegetation.

"Of course, the gardens will be at their worst now," he said, "after the sleet storm. But the sea is always exciting. Ever-changing. Have you ever used a glass?" He indicated the telescope, his grip tightening as he led her toward the open window.

It would be so easy, she thought, for him to push her from here! One shove and she would be over the low sill to fall upon the jagged rocks below. Perhaps he had already decided his marriage was a mistake, that he needed no wife…

She was certain of it when his hand touched her head, closing firmly against the nape of her neck, the other clasping her shoulder. She was paralyzed with terror for a moment until she realized his intent. He was merely trying to maneuver her into position to look through the telescope.

"Close one eye," he said, "and look through here. There is a small island out there. I cannot see it, but I know that it is there." Still with his hand at the back of her head, he adjusted the scope.

Nervous at his touch, weak with the aftermath of fear, she watched as something came into focus, blurred, and reappeared.

"I can see it now."

The island seemed to be composed mostly of granite boulders piled one on the other, though there must have been soil to account for the scrubby bushes that appeared at the southern side.

"They tell me there are birds there in the spring," Anthony said. "It is their breeding ground. Herring gulls. Great black-backed gulls. Night herons and cormorants. And would you believe they have the island divided fairly among them? Each type of bird has his own particular area. The black-backed, or parson gulls, have a small section on the western end. The night herons' nests are built in the bushes. Look at the northeastern point. Here, let me move the glass a little. Do you see the remains of the cormorants' nests? They are about a foot high, woven of small sticks, just out of reach of the waves—"

"Yes," said Adria, faintly, more conscious of his nearness than she was of what she was seeing.

"The herring gulls occupy the remainder of the island," he said. "In the spring you can hear them from here. You won't see their nesting places. Those are rather crude affairs. The herring gulls choose hollow spots and place a few twigs around the edges. The interesting thing is that the birds are so like people, each group keeping to itself —"

"But that is not true," Adria said, hotly, recalling the philosophy he'd revealed when he was ill. "People are friendly. They help one another."

"Do they?" His face was sardonic as she looked up at him. "Tell me, milady, do the Puritan folk intermingle with the godless at Wyndspelle? Or with the Catholic Portuguese fisherfolk down the coast? Surely you've been told that the devil resides at Wyndspelle. Only the reputation of the place prevents them from driving me from my own home, and for that I am grateful!"

Adria searched for words to refute his statement and found none. Anthony slid his hand beneath her chin and tipped her face upward as though he would look into her eyes. She trembled beneath the inspection of his blind gaze.

"I have heard you wish to walk on the grounds," he said, gently. "Vincente told me of your attempt this morning. I wanted you to understand why I feel it necessary to keep a guard posted at the rear of the house, and why I do not feel it safe for you to walk there alone. I have issued orders that you be allowed to pass. But I will ask you not to stray too far without a companion. Perhaps Mark —"

She moved her head back, escaping the touch of Anthony's hand. "Nay," she said, "I do not deem it proper. I have been brought up most strictly. A wife — even a wife such as I — does not seek the company of a single man."

To her surprise, he threw back his head and laughed. "So be it," he said, teasingly. "Then my good and faithful wife must promenade with her husband. I will be your escort and you must be my eyes."

All that mattered was the thought of getting out of this dismal house! Out into the sunlight. When she spoke, her voice held more warmth than she intended.

"I would like it very much, sir."

At her tone, his smile faded, his hand going up to touch the scar that marred his dark face. He looked angry, as though he had forgotten himself, revealed that he was a human being.

"Very well, then," he said coldly. "I will make arrangements with Vincente. We will walk together shortly after the noon hour." He turned his back to her, resuming his blind study of the sea. It was a summary dismissal.

Adria stood for a moment, perplexed at first, then a slow anger began to simmer. "I prefer to walk alone, sir. There is no need for you to accompany me."

He turned, brows lowered, his face harsh and forbidding once more; the impact of his impenetrable eyes making her reel as if she'd been struck.

"We will not have any further discussion, milady. As I told you, we will walk shortly after noon."

Adria whirled, blind with fury, and descended the ship's ladder. Opening the door to the stair room, she hurried down the steps, stopping before she entered the door that led out to the balcony. Tears burned behind her lids, and she was certain her quandary showed upon her features.

She was equally certain Mistress Murchison was waiting out there to guess at what had taken place in the upper room. She would wait until she had pulled herself together.

Turning, she walked the length of the small room that held the stairway, then back toward the door. As she did, she caught sight of something she hadn't taken notice of before.

There was a small door, evidently leading to a storage space beneath the steps. What would be kept here? More linens, perhaps? The housekeeper had not mentioned this space during Adria's check of supplies. Perhaps she was taking a delight in knowing there was a wrong accounting. It would be something she could report to the master!

With a wave of hatred for Anthony and his minions, she fumbled among the keys at her waist, at last finding one that would open the door. Then she gave a small cry of surprise, forgetting her hurt and anger at the sight of what lay before her.

A treasure trove!

The small room was crammed with bundles of cloth, with chests; the one nearest her open, spilling out jewels that seemed to glow even in the semi-darkness of the narrow space. And looping from a corner of the chest, was a plain gold chain.

Adria fell to her knees, separating the chain from its companion pieces, expecting to find a locket at its end. Instead, it proved to be a ruby, surrounded by gold filigree like fine lace.

She slipped it on. It lay warming against her, feeling like the keepsake that was burned. She was reluctant to return it to the chest. And why should she? Was she not the mistress of the house? Surely Anthony would not begrudge her one small jewel!

Then she remembered his words in the sickroom. *"You have been most kind to me. What do you want in return? More jewels, perhaps?"* She wanted nothing from him! Nothing but her freedom! Her hand went to the chain. She would remove it and put it back where it belonged.

"God's teeth!"

Mark's expletive brought Adria to her feet so swiftly that she caught her heel in the folds of her gown and pitched forward. His hands closed on her arms in a tight and bruising grip, his face white as he jerked her to her feet, almost throwing her into the stair room where she stumbled and fell against the opposite wall. Shutting the small door, he turned to her.

"What were you doing in there?" he demanded through gritted teeth. When she stared at him, her eyes enormous with shock, he grasped her arms again, shaking her. "I asked you, what were you doing in there? Answer me!"

"I noticed the door and was checking to see if there were additional supplies," she said, finding her voice. "I do not understand your concern, sir! Now, if you will release me…"

He obeyed, stepping back and breathing heavily. "These things are not for your eyes," he said more gently. "Those are choice pieces, put aside for the Lady Jane upon her arrival. I'm sure you understand."

"I — I suppose I do," Adria said in a small voice, rubbing her arms where the print of Mark's fingers was already beginning to show.

Mark's expression had changed. No longer white with fear or anger, he had regained his normal, boyish charm. "I'm sorry I handled you roughly," he said. "The truth is, I was concerned for your safety, lass."

"Safety?" She did not understand, unless Anthony would be so furious at her intrusion into these things he'd set aside for someone else…

"Many of these things, the bales of cloth and some of the chests come from the Orient or the Indies," he explained. "'Tis not uncommon to find poisonous creatures among them. Spiders that have hatched out upon being kept in a warm, dark place. Small snakes. We are careful to sort among these objects with gloved hands."

Adria looked at the door with a shudder of revulsion, brushing at her skirts.

"I'm certain that you are all right," Mark laughed. "'Tis only rarely that such things occur, but 'tis best to remain at a distance from such goods. Or to enlist the aid of someone more experienced. I would be happy to offer my services."

Embarrassed at being caught rummaging through Anthony's private property — jewels that were destined for another woman, at that — Adria suddenly realized she was closeted in the small stair room with a man to whom she was attracted, and who seemed to reciprocate her feelings.

Murmuring something to the effect that she wouldn't open the door again, she fumbled at the door to the balcony.

Instantly, Mark was at her side. "No harm done," he said softly, slipping a hand beneath her elbow, turning the knob for her. "'Tis just that we want nothing untoward happening to such a lovely lass —"

As Adria had expected, Mistress Murchison was waiting just outside. Tossing her head, the housekeeper marched away, her black skirts rustling. Another item to add to the tale the woman would take to Sir Anthony one day, Adria thought forlornly. Unless the tale-bearing had already begun!

Excusing herself at the door of her room, Adria entered, closing it against Mark with a sense of relief. Troubled, she wandered to the window that looked out over the sea. It had been a most dreadful morning. A morning in which she had felt hatred, fear and humiliation. The sun, winking off the waters below her seemed to mock her, showing the extent of her imprisonment.

Leaning from the window, she looked down at the tiny half-moon of beach below, at the precipice she had negotiated that first awful night. Perhaps if she tore linens into strips, knotted them together and used them to aid in lowering herself down the cliff's sheer side — But then where would she go?

As always, when she was troubled, her hand went to the locket at her bosom. She ran her thumb and forefinger along the chain. Then with a sense of horror, she remembered her locket was gone. Its remains were wrapped in a kerchief, pinned inside the bosom of her gown.

The thing about her neck was the ruby pendant.

She removed the thing, entangling it in her hair in her haste. How could she have forgotten it was there! Now she desired it no longer. The thought that it was intended for Anthony's Jane made it repulsive to her. She must return it to the place where she had found it. Perhaps Mark would do it for her. She could give it to him, explaining how she'd taken it by accident.

Nay, it would be too degrading. He might believe her covetous of something destined for another woman. She wanted nothing that belonged to Jane. Nothing! Though the thought of snakes and spiders made her skin crawl, Adria intended to return the jewel herself.

But as she turned to leave her room, a rap sounded at the door. Adria stood for an instant, panic-stricken, then shoved the thing she held in her hand beneath her pillow.

CHAPTER 10

The door opened to reveal Mark Welles. "I must talk to you," he said, entering and closing the door behind him. "I've just come from Anthony," he said. "He tells me you are walking with him in the gardens this afternoon."

"Yes," she began, "but —"

"But there are no gardens. The land here is blighted. It will not bear. Anthony does not know it. He believes we've planted the shrubs and flowers he's requested, and that the place will be a bower in summer."

"You wish me to lie about what I see there? 'Tis dishonest!"

"Why, if it makes him satisfied to remain here? Where else is he to go? A blind man, an expatriate from his own country! We've tried to follow his instructions, but nothing can live."

"The curse," Adria breathed, her eyes wide. "The curse upon the land —"

"It has nothing to do with a curse, lass. The land is dead because of its salt content, that is all. Nothing would grow here after the great wave that swept over it. Is it wrong to keep up our little charade to make Anthony happy?"

She stared at Mark, wondering how Anthony could command such devotion. The two men were as different as light and shadow; the one of such a sunny nature, the other dark, sinister — a mystery.

Anthony was not worthy of Mark's friendship, but she would do as the blond man asked. Not for Anthony, she told herself. But for Mark.

"I will watch my words," she said. "You are a good friend to Anthony."

"He was wounded saving my life," Mark said. "The blow that was struck was meant for me. Thank you, milady." He bowed and left the room.

Before Adria could move to return the pendant, Mistress Murchison appeared with her luncheon tray.

"I noticed Master Welles leaving as I came up the stairs," the woman said, her expression curious.

"He came to give me a word of warning," Adria said, coolly. "The master and I are walking in the gardens this afternoon. He asked me not to mention the condition of the grounds."

"A pity," the woman nodded, removing the covers from the dishes on the tray, "but the land is barren. It is cursed land."

"Not a curse, but the salt left by the waters. Master Welles explained it to me."

Mistress Murchison's eyes narrowed. "Little he knows! This is a doomed place. Can you not feel it? A place where nothing lives or grows. And that woman walks here. I have seen her myself, in the great hall."

"Who?" Adria asked, the hair prickling at the nape of her neck.

"Why, Elizabeth Miller, of course. The witch."

Then she was gone, leaving Adria with little appetite for the contents of her tray.

Less than an hour later, Adria stood with Anthony outside the door that led from the kitchen into the so-called gardens behind the house. She had intended to send word that she had changed her mind. But the thought of fresh air and sunshine won out.

Now the men, Petro and Rico, waited before them, Vincente serving as spokesman as Anthony introduced his wife.

"*Senhora,*" each said, bowing. Then the formalities were over and she and Anthony were free to begin their promenade.

Adria tried to ignore the arm Anthony extended toward her, then took it, remembering his sightlessness. He managed quite well in the house with his cane, but here he might need her support. Though it would serve him right if she allowed him to stumble and fall!

She slipped her fingers through his crooked elbow, trembling at little at the feel of his warm arm burning through the silken sleeve, searching for a topic to cover the strange sensation that had shaken her.

"The men," she said. "Only Vincente speaks English. Why do you employ Portuguese?"

"They've attached themselves to my service," he said. "In fact, 'twould be difficult to rid myself of them. We picked them from the waters as we sailed here. Their boat had foundered in a storm. They have remained with me since."

Perhaps that was the secret of all Anthony's faithful servants, she mused. He had risked his life for Mark, rescued these men from the sea, had even taken Dorrie and Mother Moseby from prison. And in return, he owned them — as he was attempting to own Adria. Well, he would not! She resisted an urge to break free of him and run. In the distance she could see a tiny, twisting path that climbed the horseshoe cliff at one point. So there was a way out, if she could but reach it —

No, Anthony had only to call and his men would be on her heels. She wondered how far their loyalty to the man would take them. What would they do to her if they caught her?

"Are you chilled?" Anthony had felt a tremor in the hand that rested on his arm.

"Nay, 'tis quite warm."

"If only it were spring. I would like you to see the flowers in bloom. There," he pointed with his stick, "will be my English garden. And over there I'm hoping to grow some of the more exotic plants from the Indies. Though I fear it will be impossible in this climate."

Or in this land, Adria added silently. Then, to cover her thoughts, she asked, "You have been to the Indies?"

"I have been many places. I suppose I've seen enough to last the remainder of my lifetime."

His words evoked a pity that she did not want to feel. Here, in the sunlight, it was easy to forget he was a murderer; that his hands were stained with his own brother's blood; that he was her jailor.

"And you, milady. Have you seen other than these shores?"

"I have been nowhere. My parents came to this country from Ireland before I was born. Their lands were taken from them in the Rebellion so they settled here, far to the north along the coast. This is all I have ever known. Though I suppose all countries are much alike —"

He laughed, a sudden spontaneous burst that made her stiffen. He was laughing at her ignorance!

Then he said, "You cannot know if you have not seen these places." He began to tell her of warm islands teeming with jungle growth, bright birds, and small brown people. Of islands where no white man had set foot before, where food might be plucked from trees, and babies run naked in the sun. Where every day there was dancing and singing…

She listened, so enthralled that she forgot her animosity for a moment. "These are godly people?" she asked.

"In their way."

From his answer, she knew that Reverend Potts would regard them as sinners. Yet, why was happiness and joy in living so wrong? She had a strong desire to see these places, know these people…

As Anthony talked of palm trees and flower-scented winds, Adria looked at the bleak land about her, stark and ugly beneath a sun that gave no warmth. "I should like to see those islands," she said.

Anthony dropped his arm, releasing her hand, and turned to face her, his hands on her shoulders. "Someday, I will take you to see these things."

On the last word, his eyes widened. He had a strange expression, almost of shock as his eyes stared down into hers. In them, she could see a difference, as if a small flame danced in each of them. His hands clenched convulsively upon her flesh.

"Adria!" he said hoarsely. "Adria —!"

Then, giving his head a shake as though to clear it, those eyes looked beyond her. Turning a little away, he seemed to grow rigid, his face turning as harsh and bleak as the landscape about him.

"Go back to the house, lass." His voice was flat, expressionless. "Quickly."

"Are you ill?"

"Do as I say. Leave me! Send one of the men to me. Mark Welles, or Vincente."

Adria stood, irresolute. If he were ill, she surely could not leave him here alone! He took a step away from her, staggering a little, and she grasped his arm.

"Please," she said, "Let me —"

The face he turned toward her was black, glowering, the very face of a demon: a mask of murderous hatred. "Damn you," he snarled. "Damn you! Do as I tell you! Leave me to my own private hell!"

As she still stood, too terrified to move, his hand lashed out, striking her across the cheek. "Go!" he said in an awful empty voice. "Go, damn you!"

Hand to her face, Adria drew in a shuddering breath, then she turned and ran. At a safe distance, she turned to look back, still not able to believe he had struck her.

Anthony stood, face turned to the heavens, his clenched fists upraised. "Oh, God!" he cried out in a terrible agonized sound.

It is not a prayer, Adria thought. *Not a prayer, but hatred! Blasphemy!*

She ran as if the devil were back there behind her.

Perhaps he was.

She stumbled toward Vincente and Mark who were already coming along the path in answer to the sounds from the garden. Mark grasped her arm as she reached them.

"What is it?" he asked, his voice showing fear.

"Anthony," she panted. "There is something wrong with him. He is either ill or — mad —"

Mark looked at her welted cheek, touching it gently with a finger tip, then turned to Vincente.

"You go to him," he said. "I'll see the mistress to the house."

As Mark led her away, Adria looked back once more. In the distance, she could see Anthony standing, his arms at his sides now, shoulders squared as he stared with blind eyes toward the horizon.

"What happened?" Mark asked. "Did he hurt you? What brought it on?"

"I don't know," Adria said, numbly. "We were talking and suddenly he looked — different. Then it was as if he could — could stand me near him no longer."

"What were your last words? Can you remember?" Mark guided her toward the door that led into the kitchens. She

113

searched her mind, frantically trying to recall the conversation of that last moment.

"Islands. We were talking about islands, where it is always warm and there are flowers. I think I — I expressed a wish to go there. Then Anthony said — he said —"

"Go on," Mark encouraged, "What did he say?"

"He said, 'Someday I will take you to see these things.'"

"Perhaps he forgot who you were," Mark said softly. "Just for a moment. Then he realized he'd made a promise he could not keep."

It was possible, Adria thought dully. Once Anthony might have promenaded in another garden with his Lady Jane, talking of faraway places. Today, in what he'd visualized as a romantic setting, he'd forgotten himself. But that did not explain the violence of his reaction, nor did it excuse it. The man was surely possessed by the devil, she thought, as she touched her stinging cheek. And the devil was welcome to him.

"No gentleman would strike a lady," she said, crisply. "And if _you_ were a gentleman, sir, you'd call him out!"

Mark laughed, putting up his hands before him in a mock gesture of self-defense. "Is this the little Puritan I hear speaking? The lass who believes murder is an ugly deed? And from the look of you, you are ready to perform it yourself! You frighten me!"

She was aghast. It was true what Mark had said. How she had changed from the girl who came here... Anthony had done this to her! Anthony, and the great house with its curse and its ghosts...

"I'm sorry," she said, listlessly, pushing back her hair. "I did not mean it."

"I am sure of that," Mark soothed her. "And I am sorry, too — sorry that he frightened you. The man is mad, but he is still my friend and I owe him much. But when the ship comes and he no longer needs you, I will take you from this place."

They had reached the door of her room, and as Mark opened it for her, he turned, taking her in his arms for a long moment. Then he placed a gentle kiss on her mouth.

"To seal a bargain," he whispered. "Now try to forget what happened on the grounds."

Then he was gone.

Down the hallway, Adria heard a door close. The sound came from the direction of the stair room. Mistress Murchison, no doubt, she thought tiredly. At her eternal spying. She raised her chin. What did it matter? Let the housekeeper spy to her heart's content! Let her go to Anthony with her tales! She hated him!

And hatred was a sin upon her soul.

Better to have been burned as a witch, she thought. At least she would have been innocent, except for small things...

She closed the door behind her, and crossed the room to the window. The sun had gone, and there was a dark, greenish cast to the sky. How soon the atmosphere changed here, she thought. Like Anthony Mordelle himself! Below her, the waves crashed against the rocks as the wind began to rise. And with it, that pervasive, whispering sound as the house breathed again...

Closing her eyes against the view of the sea, she thought of blue waters, warm islands where naked brown babies played in the sun. Where there were exotic birds with brilliant plumage and flowers with dragon faces. Places she would never see.

Places that were reserved in Anthony Mordelle's mind for Jane.

Trying to clear her mind of ugly thoughts, she set to work laying out a gown for the evening. That done, she brushed her hair, thoroughly, attacking it with a brush as though her actions might also erase the memory of the day.

It was futile. Even the face that looked back at her from the mirror was tainted. There was a new look to the eyes. The expression of a girl who might hate enough to destroy a man. And her mouth was no longer soft and young, but tight, hard. She forced it to relax.

She could not remain in this house! It was changing her.

Yet there was Mark. Mark with his warm arms, his tender kiss, his promise. She must pin all her faith on him, have patience as he suggested — go on as if nothing had happened on that walk. It was difficult to do, with Anthony's fingers still imprinted on her cheek.

When the bell rang for the evening meal, she remained in her room. When Mistress Murchison tapped at her door in a second summons, Adria told her she was ill, and needed nothing.

Then, as an afterthought, she called out before the woman could leave her door. "Mistress Murchison!"

"Yes, mum?"

"Is — Sir Anthony recovered? Is he at table?"

"Yes, mum."

"Thank you," Adria said, dully. She hated herself for having asked the question. After all, she need have no concern for him. She hoped the housekeeper would not mention that she had inquired about his well-being.

The hymn of hate began singing in her brain again, and she rose and prepared herself for bed. As she removed the packet that held her burned locket, pinning it inside her sleeping shift, she looked about for the cat which had taken to occupying her room. Even the cat had deserted her this night, she thought, disconsolately.

Kneeling beside her bed, she tried to pray. But she could see only the Reverend Potts' face before her, hearing his voice in her head.

"There is evil in you, girl," it said. *"Evil!"*

Finally, she crept between the silken sheets, feeling small, lost and alone as she tossed and turned until sleep came at last.

She dreamed. In that dream, she was standing before the Puritan congregation in her shift. Everyone was looking at her. And the Reverend Potts was preaching his favorite sermon.

"And then she cried out, the smoke rising round her. She called to the spirits of the wind and the sea."

"Nay," she moaned, twisting her head on her pillow. But the voice went on, inexorably.

"Those who watched from the promontory above saw a gull rise against the black sky as the fires of hell crackled around them, and they smelled the fumes of the netherworld, of fire and brimstone, of evil —"

He paused, and there was only the sound of his breathing. In and out, in and out. Then it was not his breathing she heard, but that of the house —

Adria's eyes flew open as a jagged bolt of lightning crackled across the sky, illuminating her room. *Fire and brimstone!* She could smell it, here in this room! There was a glow between the bed and the doorway, shining through the filmy draperies she had drawn about the bed before she slept.

Paralyzed with fear, she turned her eyes toward that glow. And then she saw it —

A black figure, silhouetted against the draperies! An angular shadow in Puritan garb. The witch! Dear God, the witch! *And the fumes of the netherworld, of fire and brimstone, of evil —!*

Adria drew in her breath, choking on a scream as flames licked upward from the hem of the draperies, turning the canopied bed into a flaming shroud.

Leaping from the other side, Adria ran around the bed, screaming, tearing at the blazing material with her bare hands, calling for help.

It came in the person of Mark Welles, still booted and dressed. Ripping the remaining material from the bedframe, he stamped out the flames. The fire was out by the time a robed and gowned Mistress Murchison appeared in the doorway, Dorrie lurking, white-faced, behind her.

The flames extinguished, Mark brushed at his face with a sooty hand. "God's teeth!" he gasped. "What happened here, lass?"

"The witch," Adria whispered. "I saw her! She came while I was sleeping —"

Dorrie made a peculiar whimpering sound and fled. Mark turned to the housekeeper. "I blame you for this," he said in an icy voice. "I blame you!"

"For what? 'Tis true I mentioned the witch to the girl, but I cannot be blamed for her wild imagination. See, here is how the fire began!" She picked up a candle that lay on the floor beside the bed. "Carelessness," she said, sternly. "A burning candle, knocked from its stand —"

"But I did not leave a candle burning," Adria said. Her voice sounded childish in her own ears. The last words were drowned out by a roll of thunder and another flash of lightning that deepened the crevices in the illuminated faces before her, making them suddenly frightening. "And I saw," she went on, "I saw —!" She was unable to finish the sentence.

"We'll have to move you to another room," Mistress Murchison said.

"Nay, I — I prefer to stay here."

The woman shrugged. "Then you'll need more sheets. We'll try to repair the damage you've done in the morning."

She left the room as Adria, angry now, said, "But —!"

"No matter what she thinks," Mark soothed Adria. "Tell me what you — thought you saw. From the beginning."

Shuddering, Adria described the scene the best she could, the figure that had appeared, the smell of burning. Mark inhaled, deeply. "Gunpowder, I think," he said. "Your visitor was no witch, lass, but a human. Someone who intended to do you hurt or frighten you away."

"Mistress Murchison? Dorrie? It was a woman's figure that I saw."

"Was it? Could it not have been a man?"

Adria thought of the angular shadow that appeared so briefly in silhouette. "I — I don't know," she faltered. Vincente? Petro or Rico? Or — *Dear God, no!* Anthony's room was nearest, only a door between them, and he had not even appeared.

"Who — who would want to harm me? And why?" She could not control her trembling.

Mark moved toward her, his blond head haloed in the candlelight. Putting forth a hand to touch her bare arm, he had a disturbing expression in his eyes. "I do not know. But I will protect you, lass."

For the first time, it dawned on her that she was not properly dressed. She was appearing before a man in her night wear, her hair down around her shoulders like a wanton. She retreated from him as the housekeeper appeared with fresh linens.

Snatching the bundle from Mistress Murchison's arms, Adria held the things before her. "I — I will make up the bed," she said. "I thank you both for coming to my aid."

Mark left, reluctantly. At the door, he turned to say, "I would lock my doors at night if I were you." Then he was gone.

Adria stood pondering on his words. *Doors,* he had said. Not door. So he knew the secret of the tapestry on the wall. Did Mark think she might be in danger from her husband? She thought of the walk in the bleak gardens, Anthony's face in that last moment of their camaraderie, his eyes suggesting some inward horror. And then he had sworn at her and struck her!

Perhaps it was then that he made his decision. When he finally concluded he would be happier without a wife to hamper him, regretting his decision to wed her. And it was then that the devil in him spoke out, telling him to destroy her...

Shuddering, she made up the bed, unable to keep her eyes from the tapestry that covered Anthony's door. It seemed to move, undulating in the shadows of the candle's light, hiding a door for which there was no key. She flinched as the lightning arced across the sky again and the wind made a low, mournful crying. The rain hissed at the glass, timing itself to the breathing of the house, the labored, measured breathing...

Adria knew she could not sleep. If Anthony was plotting against her, it would be better to face danger when she was awake. She would not lie cringing in her bed! She would face him with her suspicions.

Taking up the candle, she moved, trembling, toward the door, walking softly on bare feet. Pushing the tapestry aside, she tapped gently. When there was no answer, she entered her husband's bedchamber, drawing near to his bed.

He was sleeping soundly, face dark against his pillows. Asleep, when the room adjoining had been afire!

"Milord," she whispered, her heart pounding in anticipation of the moment he would open his eyes and direct that blind gaze at her.

He did not answer, but stirred restlessly, the covering sheet falling away from his upper body, his brown chest gleaming in the firelight.

Adria backed away, her cheeks reddening, a memory of Reverend Potts' voluminous nightshirt in her mind. It was indecent! Her nervousness made her voice a little sharper as she spoke again. "Milord! Sir Anthony!"

He did not wake.

Disturbed at the depth of his slumber, Adria had no choice but to step forward and study him. He was breathing deeply, but this was no natural sleep.

Her eyes went to the low table beside the bed. There was a goblet upon it. She took it up. Wine. But wasn't there a hint of an odor about it? Reminiscent of the drug she'd been given on her wedding night?

Did someone drug him so that he could not come to her aid? Or had he set the fire himself, then downed the drink in order to disclaim knowledge of the deed?

She shivered as thunder rolled across the skies and a gust from somewhere set the candle flame a-tremble. There was danger in this house. She could feel it. Had felt it from the moment she entered the huge front door. Danger and hatred. And it was directed at her. But for what reason?

Numbly, she went over the names of the people in the house. Of them all, only Anthony had a true reason to want her dead. But would he go to such lengths to rid himself of an unwanted wife?

There was Dorrie, who feared her for a witch. And burning was the prescribed treatment for witches, was it not? Mistress Murchison was jealous of her authority, but that seemed small cause for what had happened to Adria tonight. Mother Moseby? Vincente? Petro? Rico? They had little to do with her.

Which left only Mark. And Mark was her friend, her protector. She thought of the way he had rescued her this night, of his promise to stand by her. He was her friend and if it were not for her relationship to Anthony, Mark's expression had told her that he would be much more…

Which brought her back to Anthony again. Adria studied his sleeping face. Even in sleep, there was strength there, perhaps a bit of cruelty. And a lack of sadness about the mouth. He was a strange man, a mysterious man. She recalled his diabolic anger as he struck her, the way he had shaken his fists at the heavens in blasphemy —

"Leave me to my own private hell!" he had said.

Her enemy had to be Anthony, or it was nothing human. She shivered again as she thought of Elizabeth Miller, witch of Wyndspelle, said to return on dark nights when storms raged at sea.

She walked toward the door that led to her room, then paused. The wind was screaming at the windows, and there was a frightful draught in the room. When the fire died down, it would be bitterly cold.

Turning, she marched back to Anthony's bed, pulled the sheet and coverlet up over his bare brown chest and tucked it in. Then, her face flaming, she hastened to her own room, carefully pulling the tapestry straight over the door. There had been a reason for her impulsive act, she told herself. She had been returning good for evil, as any Christian should.

But all night long, she tossed and turned in her smoke-scented bed, the house breathing around her until at last she slept.

CHAPTER 11

Adria came awake to the sound of the knocking at her door. For a moment, she was not in her bed at Wyndspelle, but a small child standing before the charred ruins of the cabin in which her parents had died, smothered with grief and the scent of smoke. Then she remembered.

"Yes?" she called.

"Your breakfast, milady," the housekeeper's voice said from beyond the door. "And your door is locked against me."

Adria winced as her bare foot came down hard on something sharp. Investigating, she found the pendant she had taken from the storage room beneath the stairs.

It was no longer intact. Hidden under her pillow, it must have been pulled to the floor during the melee in the night. It had been stepped upon, probably by Mark's booted feet. Now the jewel was broken into several pieces, the delicate filigree that surrounded it crushed and ruined.

Adria stared down at the broken pendant, sick at heart. She should have returned the object instead of moping the evening away as she did. Now it seemed to be a symbol of her misery.

"Milady!" The housekeeper's voice was impatient. "Are you awake? This tray is heavy!"

"A moment," Adria called. She scooped up the remnants of the damaged pendant and looked about for a place to hide them. Spying the jewel box, she dumped them into it, closing the lid. Then she hurried to the door, apologizing for her tardiness.

"I was still asleep," she said. "I didn't rest too well after the fire."

The housekeeper entered with the tray, banging it down upon a table as her eyes darted over the room. "A proper mess, this is," she grumbled, sniffing at the odor of charred material. "'Twill take Dorrie and me most of the morning to clear this out."

"I will help with the cleaning," Adria offered.

"No, we will manage. Get your breakfast over so we can get started in here."

Adria's ire rose. The woman's attitude was more that of mistress than servant. Biting back a sharp retort, the girl turned to her breakfast, hoping the housekeeper would leave. Instead, Mistress Murchison remained in the room, her arms folded.

"We've decided to say nothing to Sir Anthony about the way you set your bed afire —"

"But I did not," Adria said, spilling her tea in her fury. "I told you! There was someone in my room!"

"Be that as it may, Master Welles thinks there's no point in getting Sir Anthony stirred up. Says it's better to be still about it, with him blind as he is. But if you don't agree —"

"I suppose you're right," Adria said wearily. "I will not mention it. But how do you expect to explain away the smell of smoke?"

"I already have. I told him you burned some torn gowns in your fireplace. That you didn't know any better —"

Adria managed to hold her temper until the housekeeper had left the room though she trembled with the effort to restrain it. For one dreadful moment, she'd felt the urge to fling the tray, hot tea and all, into the woman's smiling face.

Mistress Murchison knew she would not go to Anthony — *could* not go to Anthony — with any complaints. And she was taking full advantage of the situation.

Adria's chin tipped up. She would find a way to handle her herself!

She would not let Mistress Murchison or the terrors she'd endured in the night disturb her this morning. She must brace herself to meet the day, and first she must have a hearty breakfast. If she found her situation difficult to face when well and healthy, it would be doubly so should she allow herself to become ill.

For some reason, she found it hard to swallow. All her nerves seemed to have concentrated in her throat. A result of having inhaled so much smoke, no doubt. Burning gowns in the fireplace indeed!

She pushed the tray away.

Rising, she made an attempt to wash off the soot that streaked her face, then ruefully surveyed the results of her efforts. She looked dreadful in the gray light of this rainy day. Her eyes were swollen from lack of sleep and her hair refused to go up in any order. She struggled to pin it into place with blistered hands, finally giving in and leaving it down.

After all, what difference did it make? Her crisp morning gown was one any fine lady would wear, thus filling Anthony's requirements. As for Mark — Mark had seen her at her worst. Adria's cheeks turned crimson as she recalled her *déshabillé* of the night before. There was no point in dwelling upon what was over and done. It could not be helped.

She removed the burned locket from the bosom of her shift, transferring it to the bodice of the new gown. Her action brought the pendant to mind, and she opened the jewel chest, praying that by some lucky accident it wasn't as badly damaged as she thought.

Tis worse, she mourned, fingering the shattered stone. How odd! She had always believed that real jewels were of sturdier stuff. And the ruby of the pendant seemed duller than that of the necklace. One would think they would look the same...

"Milady!" It was Mistress Murchison's voice. Adria opened the door to admit the woman, laden with rags and a pail. "If you're ready to leave the room," the woman said, sourly, "I'll get onto it now."

"I suppose I could go down to the parlor —"

"I wouldn't do that," the housekeeper said. "Dorrie's dusting in there. You seem to have an upsetting effect on the poor child."

"Where is Sir Anthony?" Adria asked, holding back her irritation at the woman's insolence.

"In the upper room, mum."

As Adria turned to leave, she heard the housekeeper gasp.

"Why, what is this?" the woman asked. She was down on her knees, inspecting the charred carpet. And she had something in her hand, something bright —

Adria looked at the shard of ruby the woman displayed. "I have not the slightest idea," she said. Then, despising herself for letting the woman force her into a falsehood, she hurried toward the stairs. Her first thought had been to take the pieces to Anthony and confess, but that was impossible, now. Would it be so dreadfully wrong if she hid it away, or returned it to the place she found it, saying nothing?

The study was empty. She sank into a deep chair, but with the horrors of the night still in her mind she was too nervous to sit still. And this room seemed filled with Anthony's presence. Some time today, she would have to face him. The thought bothered her.

Rising, she turned toward the windows, but the shutters were still closed. She was obscurely grateful for that. The dreary landscape had been frightening enough yesterday in the sunlight. She could imagine how it would appear in the rain.

Moving to the desk, she looked down at the hieroglyphics that would be Mark's writing. It was a listing of some sort, one word below another. Again, she felt a yearning to be able to read. Looking at the book-lined shelves, she thought of the wonder those books might hold. The very scent of paper and leather bindings seemed to have a kind of magic.

She went to a shelf and took down a book, delighted at the feel of it in her hand. Pages of small, indecipherable print danced before her eyes. Trading it for another, she was pleased to see that this one was illustrated, filled with engravings. She recognized a map, knowing it by the galleon drawn upon an area representing the sea, where an improbable fish rose from the waters.

She took the book to a chair and sat with it open in her lap as she wondered what country was pictured here. Was this the land of mosques and minarets? It might even be the country from which her parents came! And here — these could be the islands where it was summer all the year...

She dreamed away, coloring the pages with her imagination before she turned the page.

"Mark?" It was Anthony's voice.

Adria shrank in her chair, making herself very small and still.

"Mark?" His voice held an edge of anger. "I know there is someone here! I hear you!"

"It is only I." Her tone was higher than she would have liked.

"Adria? But I thought I heard the sound of pages turning. You are reading?" He came toward her as he spoke, his face its usual dark mask. It was as if yesterday had not occurred.

"Yes," she said, looking up at him with dislike. She could still feel the bruise from his hard hand across her cheekbone.

"Indeed! The Puritan folk are rising in my estimation. Imagine, teaching a young lass her letters!" Without giving her a chance to refute his notion, he went on. "I trust you slept well?"

"Well, indeed," she whispered. As he gazed down upon her, she wondered what his expression would be if she told the truth. If she said, instead, *^I did not sleep well. I was occupied with hatred for a man who struck me. And then someone — or something — came into my room in the darkness and tried to burn me alive!"*

"I slept like the dead myself," he said. "I suppose 'twas due to getting a breath of fresh air yesterday. I have you to thank for that, milady. Though I suppose I should apologize for my evil temper. There — was reason for it. A reason I do not care to discuss at present." His words were halting, grudging, as if it were an effort to say them.

"I — I'm glad you had a restful night," she said, formally.

"Enough of small talk," he said, abruptly. "Tell me, milady, what book do you have there?"

She looked at the volume in her lap, not wanting to admit her ignorance. It was very likely the Lady Jane would know its title. Adria's mind raced as she searched for release from her predicament. She could not bear to be humiliated again!

"'Tis only a tale," she said, her voice defensive.

"Indeed?" Reaching out with his stick, Anthony felt for a chair. Finding it, he pulled it into a position to face her, his blind eyes intent as he fixed them upon her face.

"I should like to hear this tale," he said. "Pray, what is it about?"

"It would be of no interest to you." Red flags of color flew in Adria's cheeks. "'Tis not a thing a grown man would enjoy, milord."

"Let me be the judge of that. Will you read to me, lass?"

"But — 'tis only a fairy tale," she said, drawing on her memories of the stories her mother told her when she was small. "A story such as children read."

His brows shot skyward. "I have such a book in my possession? Then I must hear it! Come, Mistress!"

She shrank in her chair, staring at him wide-eyed. She was trapped by her own words! Reverend Potts had said one falsehood led to another — and then another. Now she had only two choices. She could confess that the printed page meant nothing to her, or she could try to improvise. Her mind whirled as she touched the tip of her tongue to her lips.

"'Tis a tale — about leprechauns," she said finally. "They are little creatures, tiny and green, who have pots of gold. And if you catch one, he must give you his riches. Well, once upon a time…"

She began to weave a story about a young lass in love with a woodcutter's son. Unwittingly, she described herself and the man who sat listening to her, his dark features alive with interest.

"The two of them wished to wed," she said, "but their wicked stepparents would not let them. Their only hope was to catch a leprechaun. So the girl went to her friends, the animals in the forest, to whom she had been kind. All the animals in Ireland helped her, because they loved her so! And then —"

"Animals?" Anthony's voice sounded strange. "And what kind of animals were these, pray? It does say, does it not?"

Adria faltered. Should she mention the ones with which she was familiar? Deer, squirrels, bears, perhaps? Nay, Anthony had said all countries were different!

"All kinds," she stammered. There was a pause as she studied the page before her as if searching for the information he requested. The words swam before her eyes as she thought, frantically. Surely there were different creatures in the Bible — Daniel! Daniel in the lions' den!

"Lions," she told him. "Lions and other ferocious animals. They all came out of the caves and the forests, and they helped her trap a leprechaun, who gave her all his gold. Then the girl married the woodcutter's son, and they lived happily forever after —"

She stopped as Anthony made an odd, choking sound. His shoulders were shaking. He was *laughing* at her! Adria leaped to her feet, her face flushed with anger and shame as he reached out to her.

"Oh, lass, lass," he chuckled, "I do not know when I have enjoyed anything so much in my life!"

She jerked her hand away from the larger one that enveloped it. "You do not need to —!" she began.

Then her fury faded at the sound of running feet. Anthony's blind eyes turned toward the doorway as Vincente burst into the room.

"Senhor!" the man gasped. Remembering his manners in time, he made a stiff bow in Adria's direction. *"Sen-hora."* After that, his words disintegrated into a garble of English and Portuguese until Anthony lifted a restraining hand.

"Stop it, man!" Anthony said, his own face glowing darkly. "Speak a little slower! I cannot understand you at that rate. Do you say what I think you say?"

"A sail, *senhor! Senhor* Welles says he believes it to be your vessel! He is watching from the upper room."

Anthony stood up, bumping the chair he had pulled into a different location, and reached his hand to take Vincente's proffered arm. "Take me to Mark. And alert Mistress Murchison. All must be in order when they arrive!"

And they were gone. Adria stood alone in the study. Her long wait was ended, now. Today the Lady Jane would arrive; the girl Anthony Mordelle loved so much that he had killed his own brother for her. That love would be revived and Adria would be free to go with Mark, as he had promised.

Why did she not feel happier?

Now that the ship had come, she could admit it to herself. Though she hated Anthony for what he had done to her; though she simmered with resentment at the humiliations he had heaped upon her, she had felt strangely attracted to the man. A feeling that surely came from the devil.

"You are a fool," she told herself. "A fool!"

Head high, she crossed the hall and climbed the stair to her room. Around her, the house of Wyndspelle came alive with preparations for the coming of Lady Jane.

CHAPTER 12

Several hours later, Adria stood with Anthony at the trapdoor that opened into the chasm. At Anthony's left was Mark, resplendent in peacock blue, his fair hair shining in the darkness of the wine cellar. Drawn up behind them the servants stood: Mistress Murchison, a twittering Dorrie, and the old crone, Mother Moseby, looking rather respectable for once. Petro and Rico had taken the small boat to ferry the passengers from the vessel, and Vincente waited below to assist the ladies upon the boat's arrival.

Adria fingered the material of the mulberry velvet she had donned, disobedient to her husband's demands that she wear bright colors. At least, it had the effect of making her appear a little older. She had managed to put her hair up, too, despite her burned hands. There was no way of knowing if she presented a proper appearance. Even Mark's eyes were fixed upon the boat that bobbed in the swelling sea, gray rain obscuring it from time to time.

I hope they get wet, Adria thought mutinously. *I pray they're soaked through when they arrive.* Then she sighed. Perhaps she was being uncharitable, though the story Mark told her had little to recommend the ladies' characters. Perhaps Jane and Anthony deserved each other!

"I seem to smell smoke," Anthony said suddenly, sniffing the air like a hunting hound.

Adria's heart sank. All her gowns had smelled of smoke, absorbing it from the blaze the night before.

Mark Welles came to her rescue. "The torch below, I imagine," he said, "Or perhaps the kitchen fires."

Anthony wasn't listening. He'd already forgotten his observation as he stared down the chasm, watching for a boat he could not see.

At last the small dory bumped against the stony landing below. Vincente seemed to be assisting the boatmen in lifting three oilskin-wrapped bundles ashore, carrying them up the rough-hewn steps to a spot that was protected from the rain and flying spume. There, the coverings were peeled back, first revealing a majestic, dowager-like woman, then the slender figure of a girl. The Lady Jane.

Adria stared at her. Dressed in a gown of the palest blue, the girl had blonde hair, swept high, with a long curl falling along her white throat to her shoulder. Adria had never seen a woman so fair! She raised one blistered palm to her own brown cheek as she looked down at the lady who was Anthony's love.

So bemused was she that it was fully a moment before she noted the contents of the third oilskin-wrapped bundle. A small rotund man, busying himself with flipping his limp wrists in order to get the ruffles that surrounded them in proper order.

"Damme!" His high voice carried to them. "They should return this land to the savages!"

Then Vincente and the boatmen were assisting the guests up the stairs. The older woman, Anthony's stepmother, deigned only to rest her hand on Vincente's arm. Behind her came the Lady Jane, leaning heavily on Petro in languorous exhaustion. Rico came up last with the foppish little man, who slipped and swore until he reached the point where the treasure room was visible. There he made much of withdrawing a scanning glass and placing it to his eye.

"Damme," he said in an awed tone, "the fellow has a fortune!"

The dowager did not turn her head. "Come along, Edwin," she said.

When the small party reached the door to the wine cellars, Anthony helped the older woman through, lifting her to one side as he assisted Lady Jane. The women safely deposited, there was an awkward silence as he smiled down at them, a grave smile that did nothing to light his brooding face.

Adria's heart caught in her throat as she surveyed him as he would appear to the newcomers' eyes. Anthony was dressed in a coat of the darkest crimson, with cream-colored trousers and high soft boots, his dark presence seeming to dwarf even Mark who stood beside him. *He looks like a king,* Adria thought, feeling an irrational pride in his appearance.

Then, turning toward the women who stood studying his blind face, Adria knew with a flash of intuition that they did not share her opinion. They were repelled by his infirmity! But even as the thought struck her, Anthony's stepmother came forward.

"Anthony, dear boy," she said, kissing him coolly on the cheek. "How well you look."

Lady Jane followed suit, clinging to him. "Oh, Anthony," she said in a soft voice, pressing her face to his shoulder, "I've so longed to see you. It has been too dreadful at home, then this journey has been quite frightening. I cannot believe I am here, safe at last! With you!"

'Tis a lie! Adria thought, watching the interchange. *A lie!* She felt as if an iron band had tightened around her heart. Anthony was blind. He would not see that these people were acting. She

could feel her eyes narrowing, her mouth growing tight, and was certain her dislike for the ladies was showing in her face. Hastily, she readjusted her expression. After all, it was none of her business.

"'Tis good to have you here, Jane," Anthony said, removing the girl's clinging arms, "I hope you will be happy here. But now you must be introduced to the mistress of the house. Adria, my love?"

She moved toward him, touching her hand to his arm to indicate her presence. To her surprise, that arm went around her. Of course! It was a wife's place to stand so at her husband's side. She would play her part well. Adria held her head high.

"Adria, this is my stepmother, Lady Elizabeth Mordelle, and Jane — my dear sister-in-law. Jane, I am certain you and Adria will be great friends."

The girl stared at Adria, smiling, though her blue eyes were flat and expressionless. "La," she said prettily. "What you must think of me? I believed you to be the housekeeper!"

Adria, who had prevented herself just in time from making a servant's bobbing curtsy, moved forward regally. "You are very welcome here," she said stiffly, her face scarlet.

"My faith," the girl said with a charming *moue*, "how *formal* we are! You need not stand on formality with me, Adria, dear. Not when I know your husband so well!" Taking Adria's blistered hands in her slim white ones, she showed an instant's surprise at their roughness. Then she said, "Oh, but she is a sweet little thing, Anthony!"

Adria was rescued by a testy voice from the chasm steps. "Well, damme," it said. "Have you forgotten me, Lady Elizabeth? You might get me out of this hole and introduce me to the gentleman and the lady!"

"Sir Edwin Osmund," Lady Elizabeth murmured as Anthony extended a hand to the fussy little man. "He is an old friend. Kind enough to offer his protection on the voyage. 'Tis hard for women alone, Anthony, impoverished as we are — with no one —"

It seemed a barb at Anthony, and Adria felt the muscles tighten in his arm beneath her fingers.

"Sir Edwin," Anthony bowed, "'twas most kind of you —"

The gentleman waved a limp hand in negation, "Nay," he said, "'Twas a pleasant duty. In addition, I had a curiosity to see this barbaric country, and being in bad odor at Court, the journey could not have taken place at a better time."

"Sir Edwin is a painter, Anthony," Jane said with a tinkle of laughter. "He did a portrait of a duchess which was far too lifelike to suit the lady. She took offense."

"Sir Anthony!" Edwin bowed. "And your Ladyship!" He bowed again and snatched the startled Adria's hand, planting a damp kiss upon it.

She shivered, wanting to snatch it away, then wiped her hand surreptitiously upon her skirt as the attention turned to Mark, whom the ladies appeared to know quite well. And as Jane greeted Mark, too, with an effusive kiss, Adria decided she had been right in her estimation of the lady. She did not like her at all!

Turning away, she found herself face to face with the ludicrous little artist. "Have you ever been told you have a *most* expressive face?" he asked, his china-blue eyes filled with malicious amusement. "One can almost read your thoughts!"

Adria reddened. "I was only thinking," she said stiffly, "that we should repair to the upper rooms where the ladies would be more comfortable."

As Adria spoke, Jane swayed like a wilting flower, catching at Anthony's arm. "I feel quite faint," she apologized. "The excitement of seeing you again —"

"I've been thoughtless," Anthony said. "We must get you upstairs. I have forgotten my manners."

Mark assisted Lady Elizabeth up the steps into the kitchen. Jane followed, leaning on Anthony, while Adria came up alone, the other men having been sent to retrieve the guests' baggage.

The girl even smells like a flower, she thought, almost suffocated by the scent of smoke that hung to her own heavy velvet gown. It suddenly seemed a most unsuitable dress.

When they entered the kitchen, Adria caught a look of dismay on Lady Elizabeth's face as she looked at the soot-blackened room, the sweating stone walls. The expression changed, however, when they climbed to enter the ladies' parlor with its luxurious furnishings. She and Jane were fairly beaming when they stepped out into the great hall.

"You've been far too modest, my boy," the older woman said, tapping Anthony's wrist playfully. "To tell you the truth, I had not expected such luxury."

There was a look of eagerness on Anthony's face as he turned his sightless eyes from the old woman's face to that of the younger. "I'm pleased that you like it," he said in a low voice. "All that is in it is yours. I want you to consider Wyndspelle your home."

"If Adria is willing," Jane cooed, though her eyes sparkled with malice as she looked at her.

I am the mistress of the house, Adria thought, *in spite of the circumstances.*

"You are welcome," she said, simply. "And now, I'm sure you'd like to rest and refresh yourself after your long journey. Mistress Murchison," she turned to the housekeeper, "Will you see Lady Elizabeth Mordelle to the gold room? And Dorrie will see that Lady Jane is made comfortable in the blue room." Having dispatched them, she turned to the gentlemen with a slight curtsy. "And now, if you will excuse me, good sirs," she said.

It would have been a dignified, ladylike exit, but for the fact that at that precise moment, Edwin Osmund drew a small silver box from somewhere in his clothing. He took a pinch of some sort of powder from it and put it to his nostrils, inhaling.

Adria sneezed. And sneezed again.

Gathering her skirts, she hurried up the stairs, cheeks crimson. *I can't do anything right,* she thought, savagely flinging back the door to her room. Then she stopped short. It was almost as she had left it. Tatters of charred draperies still fluttered from the canopy top, the walls were soot-blackened, and the smell of smoke still lingered. At one side sat scrubbing rags and a pail. All efforts to clean this room had been dropped when the sail was sighted, so that accommodations would be perfect for Lady Elizabeth and Jane.

She would clean it, herself, she thought. But not now. Now she had to ready herself for dinner with Anthony's guests. The long evening ahead hung over her like a shadow.

Well, she would have to make the best of it. She would try to dress richly enough to suit the occasion. And surely her position at her husband's table would establish her as the mistress of the house in the eyes of their guests. She went to the wardrobe, shoving gowns aside as she searched for the most appropriate one to wear.

She finally settled on a gown of scarlet. It was daringly cut, exposing her throat and shoulders, but it complemented her dark coloring. Donning it, she looked into the glass, suppressing an urge to change to something more modest. The bell ringing for dinner, sounding from below, decided the issue. She would not have the time. And the ruby necklace would take some of the attention from bare flesh.

She lifted it from the chest and fastened it around her throat, then stopped, her pulse racing as she stared into the box. The pendant was gone. Every bit and piece of it! Who could have taken it? And why?

Her reverie was broken by the shrill sound of a woman's scream.

CHAPTER 13

Adria rushed to the balcony to discover the cry had not emanated from a woman's throat, but from that of a man. The artist, Edwin Osmund, was flattened against the railing, peering into the shadows, his eyes popping with fright.

"Keep it away from me," he babbled. "Keep the thing away from me!"

Adria went weak, her skin prickling as she thought of the apparition that had entered her room the night before. She willed her eyes to follow the man's pointing, trembling finger. And then she saw it.

The cat! It was only the cat!

She picked up the animal and carried it into her room. Thinking of the reaction of the absurd little man who had destroyed her dignity with his snuff box, she suppressed a giggle. *"Thank you,"* she said, placing the cat on her bed, stroking its silken head. Then she went out, closing the door behind her. To her surprise, the artist was waiting for her.

"I owe you a debt of gratitude, milady," he said, adjusting the ruffles at his wrist. "Can't abide the blasted creatures. And there's something about this house — that infernal *breathing* sound!" He shivered, delicately, to indicate he didn't like the atmosphere.

"It's because of the way the house is built," Adria explained. "Something to do with the waves, and pressures in the chasm below. It is worse when it storms, but it is a natural thing."

He rolled his eyes in a parody of relief at her words. "Glad there's a reason for it. At any rate, I was coming along to dinner, and the beastly creature attacked me!"

He still looked unnerved, and she could sympathize with him in a way. A strange house, smothered with shadows, a brooding note about it, the cat's sudden appearance. How well she remembered her own welcome here!

"'Tis a nice cat, really," she said, taking the man's proffered arm. "I think it was only trying to be friendly."

Edwin Osmund shuddered. "All the same, I can't stand the things. Makes me think of a witch's familiar. I shall be forever in your debt!"

Adria couldn't resist smiling. In all the time she'd been in this house, she'd done nothing that was right. Now, she was appreciated, and for something so ridiculous. Still, despite his absurdities and affectations, the man seemed to be sincere. Actually, he had done *her* a kindness. Now she would not have to walk down those stairs and face a barrage of waiting eyes alone.

Descending to the great hall, they found Mark at the foot of the steps, coming to seek the origin of the cry they'd heard from below. As they went toward the table where the others were waiting, Edwin gave a gory account of his narrow escape from a ferocious animal, his voice still high and excited as he helped Adria into her chair.

She was glad for the cover of his conversation, for the seating arrangement was not as she had foreseen. The Lady Jane was in Adria's place on Anthony's right, Lady Elizabeth at his other side between Anthony and Mark. Adria was seated between Jane and the voluble artist.

It had not been Anthony's doing. Adria realized it at his change of expression when Jane spoke up beside him. "I do hope you don't mind my usurping your place, Adria," the girl said sweetly. "'Tis just that we haven't seen Anthony in such a long time."

"'Tis most understandable," Adria murmured, though she had felt a peculiar wrench at her heart. The two of them seemed to complement each other so well. The somber dark man in his throne-like chair, and the fragile blonde girl.

"They look well together, do they not?" the painter said into Adria's ear.

"Yes," she said, honestly, "They do. My — my husband is a very handsome man."

"With a lovely wife." Edwin Osmund said generously, helping himself to a liberal swallow from his wine goblet, patting his pouting lips with a napkin. "Do you know your husband begins to sit for me on the morrow?"

Adria didn't understand his meaning. She sat quietly, hoping further conversation would supply an explanation. It did.

"I have never painted such a face before," the man said, musing. "'Twill be a challenge." His blue eyes were fixed on Anthony's ruined features. "'Tis a tragic face, tortured, some anger in it — a certain nobility. The face of a man at war within himself…"

As he talked, Adria marveled at his perception. For such a silly little man, he had the understanding to depict Anthony quite well. And her opinion seemed justified when he added, "I feel it would be difficult to know this man, completely, even for a wife. There is a strange mixture there, of saint and Satan—"

Adria turned from the artist as she heard her name on Lady Elizabeth's lips. But the woman was talking about her, not to her.

"Adria," the woman said, as if she were tasting the word and finding it unpleasant. "'Tis a heathen-sounding name. I thought the girl's name was Emma."

Before Anthony could speak, Mark answered for him. "The Lady Emma is deceased," he said smoothly. "This is the *second* Lady Mordelle." He smiled at Adria as Lady Elizabeth inspected her as if she were some strange insect.

"Where did he find this one?" she inquired.

Adria raged inside. It was dreadful being discussed this way, like a — a *thing*! An animal without sense enough to answer for itself!

"She comes from the Puritan settlement below," Mark grinned. "I believe it all began with a meeting on a path to a spring. It was a brief courtship."

"I'm sure of that," the Lady Jane giggled. "After all, as I recall, Anthony is a hot-blooded man, romantic, impatient —"

Anthony's stepmother frowned. "As I was saying, earlier," she said, "Jane and I do not intend to be charity cases. We shall make every attempt to be of use in the household here."

"That will not be necessary, Mama," Anthony murmured. "As I explained in the packet I sent you, our home is yours. There is no need for you to concern yourself."

"But I insist! As you know, I'm experienced in the niceties of managing a great house such as this. I'm planning to take the burden from your little wife's shoulders. 'Tis obvious that she was not reared to such responsibility."

Adria flinched and sat up straighter, trying to still the angry response that sprang to her lips. Luckily, before she lashed out at the woman, the Lady Jane preempted her.

"I, too, would like to do my bit," she said in a sad little voice. "But I've always been such a helpless creature, Anthony. However," her voice took on a lilt, "there *is* something I can do! I do understand styles, and I know all the latest fashions at Court. And I'm surprised at you, allowing your little bride to wear things that are so out of mode! I can teach her to dress in a manner that befits her position. To use colors more suited to a — a sallow complexion."

Adria sat still for a moment, seething with rage. Then slowly, deliberately, she stretched her hand toward her wine goblet, tipping it. It spilled its contents into the Lady Jane's ice-blue lap.

With an unladylike screech, the drenched girl jumped to her feet, scrubbing at the spreading stain with her napkin. Adria pretended shock at the thing she had done until she met Mark's eye.

He was looking at her with an expression of amused admiration. He gave her a congratulatory nod. She blushed as she realized he had seen and approved her action. But Anthony—?

Anthony's blind face was impassive as he waited for the commotion to cease. Then he asked, "What is it? What has happened?"

Adria stiffened her shoulders. "A small accident, milord." Turning to the furious Jane, she said, "I beg your forgiveness. It was clumsy of me. I am certain we will be able to remove the stain, but if not," she shrugged, "you are most welcome to something of mine."

Mark nodded again in approval. It gave her courage to go on.

She spoke to Lady Elizabeth. "We will have no more mention of charity, milady. Though our staff is small and I am inexperienced, we manage quite well. And after all, you are our guests."

"Well said, milady." It was Anthony who spoke, his sightless face turned toward her with an expression of — almost affection. "There will be no more argument on the subject," he said to Lady Elizabeth. "I am certain your offer of assistance will be accepted should it be required, but my wife is a most capable woman. I defer to her in all household matters since, after all, she is the mistress of Wyndspelle."

His unexpected championship was almost too much for Adria's shattered nerves. She felt hot tears spring to her eyes and looked down at her plate to hide them.

"At least," Jane said, but less surely, "I may help plan entertainments. You do entertain?"

Adria saw Anthony's face harden. He would have to explain that he was an outcast, even on foreign shores. Before he could speak, she interrupted, answering for him.

"Entertain? As much as you wish! Though I fear there is scant material for a guest list. There is the Reverend Potts, of course, though he would not approve of your gowns or wine-bibbing. Then there is Granny Goodhue who has enlivened many a table with her tales of midwifery. Joseph Shanks, a widower with good lands and many children —" She looked meaningfully at Jane. "He is looking for a young wife."

Jane looked horrified. "This is your social set? There are no others?"

"Oh, many! There are the folk from the Portuguese fishing village two days distant. And, of course, the native Americans."

Edwin broke into the conversation, twittering with excitement. "We must have the natives, by all means! Oh, what tales to take back to Court! Tell me, milady, are there any lovely princesses among them? And are they considered dangerous?"

"They murdered my mother and father," Adria said, a lump in her throat. "Burned them in their cabin — alive."

"Damme," the little man said, his round face showing a flustered sympathy. "Well, damme!"

Adria's comment put a damper on the conversation. Those about the table were quiet for a time, then Anthony and Mark began to discuss the ship now standing off at anchor, worried about its safety, should the storm increase in intensity. The ladies picked desultorily at their food.

Adria was grateful for the gregarious Edwin Osmund at her side, filling her ears with tales of intrigue at Court, though some of his tales shocked her. She did not know men and women pursued such wicked ways.

Then something Jane said at her other side attracted the artist's attention.

"What are you discussing up there?" he asked, leaning across Adria. "A curse! What curse! On *this* place? Surely you are jesting!" He looked enchanted.

"The servant told me about it while I was dressing," Jane said. "A witch's curse!" She looked over her shoulder in mock horror. "I know I shan't be able to sleep a wink tonight!"

"You will be protected," Anthony said. "There is no such thing as witchcraft. 'Tis only an illusion held by the ignorant and untutored to be true. We will watch over you and keep you safe."

Will you? Adria thought grimly, memories of her own terrifying night returning. *Will you watch over the lady as you did over me last night?*

At Edwin's insistence, Jane repeated the story. It tallied much with that of Reverend Potts, though his had been more dramatic. The little painter was entranced, insisting that he knew the place was haunted, had felt it all along.

"You must remember," Anthony interposed. "Elizabeth Miller is dead."

146

"But could she not come back in another form? A cat — or a *woman?*" Jane's question was artless, but Adria caught its inference. Evidently Dorrie had filled her in well as to the peculiarities of Anthony's bride.

"Forget this gloomy subject," Anthony said. "I suggest we retire to the parlor. I recall how you used to play and sing, my dear Jane. Will you honor us?"

The group moved into the parlor where Adria sat uncomfortably, listening as the girl performed. Looking at her, candlelight gleaming on her fair head, Adria envied her the voice that, though a trifle shrill, was clear and true.

It isn't fair, Adria thought, listening to the haunting melody of "Greensleeves." *It just is not fair!*

"But I have played enough!" Jane turned to her audience. "'Tis Adria's turn. You *do* play?"

"Nay. I had a Puritan upbringing. We had no music."

"Oh?" The girl cocked her head to one side, putting a world of sympathy into her voice. "What a pity!"

"Anthony," Lady Elizabeth broke in, "you do marry the most *different* wives. Charming, of course, but *different!*"

Anthony looked thunderous, but before he could speak, Mark had pulled Adria to her feet. "She *is* different," he said. "I know of few ladies who would remain to entertain guests when they were ill and should be abed. I am breaking a confidence in mentioning it, Anthony, but Mistress Adria caught a chill yesterday, walking in the gardens —"

"She did not tell me —"

"She did not wish to worry you. May I have your permission to escort her to her door?"

"'Tis unnecessary," Adria said, flashing him a smile of gratitude. "Though I appreciate your concern for my health."

Excusing herself, she stepped out into the great hall, a feeling of relief welling inside her. She could not have stood much more. But now, crossing the cavernous room, she began to wish she had accepted Mark's offer. The overhead candles had been extinguished and those on the table were burning low. The fire was only a red glow, since the log had charred through.

There was no reason for her nervousness. The house was filled with people. As proof, she heard the tinkling of the spinet through the closed parlor door. Jane had wasted no time!

Timorously, Adria crossed the great hall, heading toward the stairs. And then she saw it, a black shadow reaching across the floor, reminiscent of the monstrous horror that loomed above her the night before as her draperies went up in flame —

Stiffening, she raised her eyes to the balcony above, to see a white, triangular face.

Vincente!

For a long time, their gazes held. Then he backed into the shadows. As she mounted the stairs, she heard the door to the stair room close. Why was he here? Had he been watching throughout the meal? Whatever he did, it was in Anthony's interests, she was certain of that.

Still pondering on his presence, she entered her room, wrinkling her nose at the stale smell of burning that still lingered. She would have to sleep with that odor again; the scent that proved someone — or something — tried to burn her as she slept.

Again she ran over the list of people who might have had reason to set fire to her bed. Now it seemed plausible to add Vincente to their number. But Vincente could have no possible motive — unless he acted on Anthony's behalf.

It came back to Anthony again. Anthony, who had tricked her, humiliated her, sworn at her — and laughed at her. Yet, tonight, he had treated her with kindness, behaved as a husband.

Sighing, she loosed the ruby necklace, replacing it in the chest, wondering again at who could have removed the pendant and why. The incident had been completely erased from her mind, what with Edwin Osmund's altercation with the cat, along with the rest of a miserable evening.

The cat! She turned toward the bed, puzzled. She had left him here, shut in. He had not passed her when she entered. Surely, he was somewhere in the room. She searched its nooks and crannies, calling softly, finally giving up. There was no other opening by which the animal might have escaped. Someone had been in this room! But who?

Dorrie and Mistress Murchison had been serving and assisting Mother Moseby. The rest of them had been at table, or in the parlor. Only one person could have invaded her sleeping quarters.

Vincente!

But why? Was it possible that Anthony's trusted henchman was a thief? Surely she had nothing worth stealing. Not in comparison with the riches in this house. She had worn her only thing of real value, the ruby necklace, down to dinner. And it would not compare to the jewels in the chasm, or in the storage under the stair — except that he would need a key.

Her eyes went to the ring of keys lying on the chest. She hadn't left it there. She remembered dropping it on the bed when she changed to her formal gown. And a key was missing! The one that fit the small door in the stair room. It had been smaller than the rest, and of a different shape. If Vincente had been on a legitimate errand, acting upon Anthony's orders, he could easily have obtained a key from the housekeeper.

She would have to talk to Anthony about it. And tonight. But she could not bring herself to face the women in the parlor. She would wait until she heard him come upstairs.

Opening the door a crack, she seated herself in a chair and waited for the sound of his steps, the tapping of his cane. Exhausted by the fire of the previous night and the emotions of this day, she fought the drowsiness that threatened to envelop her.

She woke up with a start. How long she had been asleep, she did not know. But the candle before the mirror was now only a feeble flicker of flame in a puddle of melted wax. Rising, she went to her door and looked out. There was no sound from below. Except for its occasional sighing, the great hall seemed dead and still. Evidently the master and his guests were all abed. Should she disturb Anthony now? After all, she had nothing concrete to tell him. Only her suspicions.

As she waited, in a state of indecision, a door across the way opened, the light from within illuminating Mark's fair head as he emerged.

Mark Welles! In the Lady Jane's sleeping quarters at this hour of the night? Instinctively, she stepped back into her room, closing the door softly.

Adria turned to her bed, hating herself for letting the thought of Jane and Mark Welles together matter so much. It had given her the same dull ache she felt when she saw Anthony with Jane.

Then, after a while, she turned her hatred toward someone else: the Lady Jane. Jane was pale, alluring, seductive, and gracious. All the things that Adria herself could never be.

CHAPTER 14

Despite her exhaustion, Adria slept fitfully, her night a crazy patchwork of waking and dreaming. The door clicked. Someone entered her room and towered over her.

Fire!

Her eyes would not open and her throat was too dry to scream. She lay rigid until she realized it was only a nightmare brought on, perhaps, by memories of the night before and the scent of smoke that lingered in the room. Turning over, she willed herself to sleep again.

In the morning she came awake with a sense of something wrong. Something was different about this day, this waking. Then she remembered that there were guests in the house. That Anthony's stepmother and Lady Jane had arrived to stay.

She sat up, hollow-eyed and pale, brushing back hair that felt damp and tangled after her restless night. Drawing her knees beneath her chin, she sat, arms clasped around them, and moodily surveyed the room. In the morning light, it was even more of a shambles. Indicative of her position in this household, she thought rebelliously.

When Mistress Murchison tapped at her door, Adria bade her enter. As the woman set down her breakfast tray, the girl studied her. There was a certain attractiveness about the housekeeper, she saw with surprise. The whiteness of her face was accentuated by her black dress, and with her dark hair parted in the middle and drawn smoothly back, she had a sort of fascination. If she would only smile —!

"I'm sure the guests are causing much extra work," Adria said, impulsively. "If things become too difficult, perhaps we might find additional help. Someone from the fishing village, perhaps —"

"It is not necessary, mum." The woman eyed her, a dour amusement in her face. "'Tis a pleasure to be ordered by someone so efficient as Lady Elizabeth. 'Tis always easier to work for an experienced mistress."

It was a deliberate snub and Adria reddened. When she could speak, she asked, "My husband — I must speak to him this morning. Has he breakfasted?"

Mistress Murchison's eyes shifted. "He has already eaten and gone to the upper room, mum."

"Then I will go to him, as soon as I have eaten." Adria noted the look of fear in the woman's eyes. It was obvious that she would go as far as she dared. She was still uncertain of the relationship between Adria and the master of Wyndspelle. Now she was wondering if Adria would inform on her. Let her think it! She would keep an upper hand at least.

"Can you spare a few moments to clean here today?" Adria asked.

"I will try," the housekeeper said, sullenly, "but 'tis difficult, what with the guests.'Twould be best to take another room for a while."

Another room, away from that tapestry-covered door. Adria's face brightened, then fell as the woman added that the only rooms available were those usually allotted to servants — if Adria did not mind.

She did mind. She would remain where she was. She could not give Lady Jane the satisfaction of knowing that she could be so easily deposed.

"I will stay," she said.

As she ate her breakfast, sickened at the odor of stale smoke, she wondered if she had done the right thing. She really held no place here, after all. Wife in name only, mistress in name only. And it was wrong to be prideful. Vainly, she sought for feelings of meekness and humility and could not find them. Perhaps it was the devil in her, but she would not humble herself before Jane!

Finishing her meal, she hurried toward the upper room, formulating in her mind the things she would tell Anthony. But no sooner had she emerged from the opening than she was summarily dismissed. Evidently Anthony and Edwin Osmund had come to an agreement the night before. The talked-of portrait was already in progress.

"I do not like an audience when I paint," the little man said, fussily.

"But it will only take a moment. I must speak to my husband." She looked at Anthony, but he did not speak.

"Every moment counts," the artist said. "We will be working here each morning, so I can catch the light. So if you will keep that in mind, milady, so there will be no intrusions?"

"But since you are just beginning —"

"Another time, Adria," Anthony interrupted. "I like this no more than you. But if it must be done, I say let us get on with it!"

Chastened, Adria descended the steps. She felt like a child, scolded and sent to her room. Still, she was almost relieved at having her confession postponed. The story of the pendant could wait. And as far as Vincente was concerned, there was probably some logical reason for his actions.

Hurrying back to her room, Adria set to work cleaning. In the course of her scrubbing, she found the key. The small object was lying at the foot of her bed, where it might have fallen from the ring.

The key could not have loosened, she discovered as she tried to return it to the proper place. Then how had it fallen there? Unless someone took the thing and returned later to drop it so she would believe she had handled it carelessly?

She recalled her dream. The dream that someone entered her room in the night. Was there a possibility there was an intruder?

Her head ached. She tried to put her confusing thoughts from her mind as she set to work again, her labors seeming to make her feel a bit better. It was something she had missed. For a moment, she thought of her years in Reverend Potts' home with nostalgia. The simple life, rising early. Washing clothes in the black boiling pot in the yard, the scent of ashes-and-lye soap bleaching the air. Candle-making, spinning —

The devil finds work for idle hands, Reverend Potts had said. Perhaps he was right.

Within a short time, she had the charred draperies stripped from their supports and lying bundled in a corner. The carved wood of the massive bed showed little damage, she found, once the soot was wiped away. Only the floor covering, the priceless carpet the housekeeper mourned, was ruined. Perhaps it might be covered with a small rug, Adria thought. Or she could cut a length of fur to place beside the bed.

The smell of brimstone was strongest here, she found. She recalled Mark's mention of gunpowder. It appeared that someone might have laid a trail of it, igniting it to be certain the draperies would catch. She smoothed the scorched nap thoughtfully, wondering who the intruder had been.

She was so lost in thought that she jumped, startled at a lilting laugh behind her. "My stars," a voice trilled, "it is *you,* Adria! I thought it was a charwoman."

Rising from her kneeling position, Adria faced Jane. The other girl was becomingly gowned in yet another costume of blue, her hair perfectly groomed. At the sight of Adria's smudged face, she broke into fresh laughter.

"I'm sorry," she giggled, "but you do look a fright!" Then, looking curiously about the room, "What happened here? This place is a ruin!"

"A fire. I was careless with a candle. I — I trust you are happy with your quarters?"

The girl wrinkled her nose. "They will do. Though they are somewhat provincial, don't you think? To tell the truth, I had thoughts of having a look at *your* room with an eye to trading. But I see you have some of the same crude furnishings. I'm surprised at Anthony!"

Adria swallowed her anger at the girl's contemptuous remark. "'Tis very hard to lay hands on fine things here," she said, her mouth dry, "and though I am not accustomed to luxury, I am sure some of the furnishings are of great value."

"No doubt." Jane shrugged. "But 'tis such a hodgepodge. I suppose we shall have to become used to it. Well, now that I have seen *this* room, I believe I'll remain in the one I have. I will go now, so that you can get back to your work."

Jane walked toward the door, then stopped, staring at the ruby necklace in its open box. She went to it, picked it up, and admired it in the light.

"Such a pity," she said, "that rubies are so wrong for you! Surely you have other things."

Without waiting for an answer, she snapped it about her white throat, turning to see its effect in the mirror. "'Tis most becoming to me, is it not?"

"Yes." Adria almost choked as she answered, truthfully.

"Then I'll just take it along with me! You don't mind, do you? 'Twould only point up your dark skin. However, I do have some powders that would improve *that*, you know, and I will gladly give you some. Though they are poisonous, except in small doses —" She looked at Adria, a question in her eyes.

"Thank you, but — nay. I fear they would not help me."

Jane studied her. "I suppose not. I do hope my taking the necklace does not upset you. Anthony said I was to have anything I wanted." She danced toward the door, then looked back, surveying Adria critically. "You really mustn't work so hard," she said, "and at such menial labors. That sort of thing tells on one's looks. Of course, you're lucky Anthony cannot *see*. But somehow men sense these things." Then she was gone, leaving Adria flaming with rage.

When the girl was out of earshot, that rage exploded. Stamping her bare foot, she said, "Curse you! And may the devil take you!" Then she clamped her hand over her mouth. What on earth was she doing? To curse somebody as if she were indeed a witch!

She thought uneasily of Jane's comment at table last night. "Could Elizabeth Miller have not come back in another form? A cat — or a woman?"

Would this account for all the vices Adria was discovering within herself? The ability to tell tales? Vanity, stealing, hating? And even worse, jealousy? An attraction toward two men at the same time?

Again she turned to her work, seeking peace of mind. Now her labors no longer proved to be healing. Her hurt and anger at Jane still rankled in her breast. Dark skin, indeed! And that parting remark — *"You're lucky Anthony cannot see, but somehow men sense these things."*

Looking at her small soot-stained hands, roughened from the scrubbing she'd done, the blisters broken, Adria, ruefully, had to concede that Jane had made her point.

CHAPTER 15

At last, back aching, palms raw and almost bleeding, Adria stood back to view what she had accomplished. Though the room before her was not up to Lady Jane's standards, it would do. It was clean and shining, though a hint of smoke still pervaded its atmosphere. The draperies about the bed had not been replaced. She thought of asking Mistress Murchison for materials, but decided against it. For however many nights she was allowed to keep this room, it would be best to have a clear view from where she slept. To be on guard for any danger.

Now, there were other things to do. She must get dressed in something clean and fresh and go down to her guests. Dreading the ordeal, she went first to the window and stood a while, hands pressed to her aching back, gazing out at the rain-swept sea. It looked sad and cold, just as she felt. She turned away.

Descending the stairs, she found only the artist. Edwin Osmund had taken possession of Anthony's throne-like chair and presided with comic dignity over the table in the great hall, empty except for the tray of cheese and fruit set before him. So his work on the portrait was finished for this day. But where were the others? Had the ladies not come down?

"Where is Sir Anthony?" Adria asked.

"Still above," the little man said, peevishly. "I daresay he was glad to dispense with my company. Your husband is a surly man, madam! I paint him only at Lady Elizabeth's insistence!"

"I am certain he will be happy with your work," Adria said, placatingly. "'Tis only his way. But where is the Lady Elizabeth — and Jane? Have they not come down?"

"Come down?" He sipped deeply at his goblet of wine and coughed. "Indeed they have. They are in the cavern below with Master Welles. Some nonsense about sorting and listing the valuables there, I believe. A way of repaying dear Anthony for his hospitality!" He mimicked Jane's babyish voice with droll malice. "They will only earn themselves an ague, down there in the damp and the chill, if you ask me! I want no part of it!"

"Then Anthony is alone?" Adria was surprised at the wave of relief that washed over her. She had been so certain he and Jane were together. Before Edwin Osmund could answer, she was hurrying toward the stairs.

Anthony stood at a window in his customary moody pose. This time he was not gazing seaward, but at a rear window, toward the land.

"Jane?" he asked.

"Nay, 'tis Adria." Her heart turned over. Was he expecting the girl?

"Adria." His voice was oddly gentle. "Come here, lass." She went toward him, a little fearfully, and he slipped his arm about her waist. She fought to control the little shiver that ran through her at his touch, setting her blood to humming as he drew her toward the window.

"Look out there, lass, and tell me what you see."

"'Tis raining," she began, uncertainly.

He jerked his head impatiently. "I know that. 'Tis the garden itself I want to hear about. I know 'tis winter, but tell me how it will look in spring. Are the plantings well-spaced? Will there be blooms, d'you think?"

159

Adria looked out at the barren land, now a sea of mud and stones. The wind lashed at dead and twisted trees, breaking rotten limbs, strewing the ground with twigs and debris.

"It will be very beautiful," she said, tears stinging her eyes.

The arm that had been tender at her waist tightened. "Thank you, my dear," he said. Then, looking at her with an expression that was haunted, lost, bewildered, he said, "You don't know what it is like to be punished for your sins. To be doomed to hell. To blight everything you touch." He pulled away from her as though her fingers had burned him. "My God, girl! You should never have come to this house! And I should tell you to run, now. Run for your life. But I need you."

Adria had cringed before the bitter onslaught of words, but now she spoke up impulsively. "If you need me, milord, I will be here."

"I should not have said that." He spoke coldly. "I need no one. No one. And for now, you'd best leave me."

"I have something to discuss with you," she said.

"Not now, lass. I have too much on my mind. Just go."

The man thought of no one but himself!

She, Adria, had been forced to run away from the only home she knew, then pressed against her will into this situation that was more servitude than marriage! With inimical forces around her — without protection.

She left him and went downstairs, remaining in her room until dinner.

The atmosphere was not so stiff and stilted this night. Those who had been searching through Anthony's treasures were filled with excitement over the rare and lovely objects they had found in the chasm below. The talk was all of coronets and collars of gold until Jane said, "Anthony, there is a length of material I simply must have. A peacock blue, so like the one I had when we first met."

Anthony was a little slow in answering. Perhaps, Adria thought with an ache, he was remembering how the girl looked in those days.

The Lady Elizabeth spoke up. "Surely you would not begrudge Jane a small thing like this, Anthony! After all, you owe her much."

Anthony, his face set, did not reply. Adria frantically searched for something to say to change the subject.

She did not need to, for it was changed for her. As she opened her mouth to speak, Edwin sprang to the seat of his chair with a squalling sound. Thence, he jumped up to the middle of the table to land squarely beside the steaming joint of beef.

"Take the beast away," he babbled. "Get rid of the monstrous creature!"

Adria looked down. The black cat stared up at her with unwinking eyes, then rubbed against her ankles, purring. Unable to stop herself, she committed her final social crime. She burst into laughter.

Blessedly, Mark followed suit. Then, as Adria rose, clutching the animal, he said, "Nay, put him down. 'Tis all right," he chuckled, assisting the red-faced little man from his perch, "He will not harm you."

"He scratched me with his beastly claws," Edwin said, crossly. "Is that evidence of his intentions?"

"Possibly after your snuff box," Mark said. "This happens to be a very sinful cat. He was our ship's cat, and our bully boys taught him all the vices. Tobacco. Strong drink. See?" He poured some wine into a saucer, and the cat lapped at it, avidly.

"Well, damme!" the artist said, admiringly. "But keep the dratted thing away from me!"

"I will," Adria promised. "I shall keep him in my room hereafter."

"Damme," the little man said, again. He turned to Anthony. "I must admit to having had romantic designs upon your wife, sir! And now she has made it impossible for me!"

The others laughed, and Adria's face flushed. Her cheeks were still pink when Mistress Murchison carried in the dessert.

"Why, what is this?" she asked. "I believe I requested a steamed pudding —?"

"A trifle," the housekeeper said. "Lady Mordelle prefers it." She looked toward Anthony's stepmother as she spoke, bobbing a curtsy.

"I hope you don't mind," Lady Elizabeth smiled at Adria. "And she said you had suggested jugged hare for the morrow? I took the liberty of changing it to fish."

As if he sensed a tension in the air, Anthony's hand went to his head. Adria forgot her irritation in her concern. "Are you ill, sir?" she asked, forgetting the others at table. "I can —"

"Quite well," he interrupted. "Just in haste to finish this meal, since I am looking forward to another concert such as the one we had last night." He smiled at Jane.

Adria bent to her dessert, trying to mumble polite responses to the gossip Edwin Osmund was pouring into her ears.

It seemed hours later when Adria finally trudged up to the silence of her room. Her muscles ached from the scrubbing she had done in the morning, and it had been a long, tiring day. Anthony felt it, too, she could tell. Throughout the evening, his face had grown weary and drawn.

As she prepared for bed, she vowed to herself that she would be cool and calm at all costs, no matter what was said or done.

For Lady Elizabeth had seemed especially vindictive, tonight, in her veiled proddings at Anthony's guilt-ridden mind. And Jane had been equally adept in her contemptuous remarks to Adria. Adria felt the two of them had been besieged, saved only by the comic pomposity of the little artist and the tact of Mark — blessed Mark!

Cuddling the cat — the *sinful* cat, she thought, with a smile — into the crook of her arm, she fell asleep.

How late it was when the sound intruded into her dreams, she did not know. One moment she was sleeping, the next awake, the hair prickling at the nape of her neck as she listened. And the sound came again. A moan. A man's voice, groaning in pain.

Anthony!

Springing from her bed, spilling the indignant cat to the floor, she ran to the tapestry-covered door, placing her ear against it. It was he. Turning back, she lit a candle from the fire's embers, slipped a cloak over her shoulders, and entered the man's room.

"Can I help you, sir?" she whispered. He raised a fever-flushed face, looking at her with his sightless eyes.

"Adria?"

"Yes, milord."

"I'm sorry to have disturbed you, lass. My head — my head!" He groaned again and she hastened to his side, putting a cool hand to his hot forehead. The eye on the marred side of his face looked inflamed, the scar red and pulsating. She would try the remedy she had used before, but she must go down to the kitchens…

Assuring Anthony that she would return as quickly as possible, she stepped out into the darkened house, candle in hand, to go down the shadowed stairs.

Entering the great hall, she heard the wind screaming at the door. And as she moved toward the fireplace, the house creaked and groaned around her with the fury of the storm — breathing.

Adria jumped as a log shifted on the hearth, sending sparks flying. She ran for the safety of the parlor. For a moment she remembered dead Emma as she had lain there in state, and her heart was in her throat.

'Tis only the memory of that first night, she told herself. Still, she was reluctant to make her way down the steps that led to the kitchens. Below the kitchens was the wine cellar. Below the cellar, the chasm. And she could remember what she'd last seen *there*!

Only the thought that Anthony needed her goaded her on.

The kitchens were empty. Mother Moseby slept down here, she knew. Somewhere in the warren of small rooms used for storage and drying. She did not want to come upon the woman in the darkness. Her appearance was fearsome enough in the light.

Adria was relieved to find the kettle on the hob, the fires banked, but water being kept hot for the morning. She would fill a small pot and take a spill of tea with her, fashioning the bags when she returned to Anthony's side.

First, the tea. Entering the larder, she held her candle high, searching until she found what she had come for. Lifting it down, she began to measure a small amount into a spill. A strangled sound came from behind her.

She whirled, searching the darkness, then took up her candle in a trembling hand. There was something in that far corner! A bag of grain, perhaps, or rice? Nay, it *moved*!

Dear God! A human! It was Dorrie! Crouching on the cold stone in a sodden mass, crying her heart out.

"Dorrie, what is it?" Adria touched her, and the girl shuddered away, babbling in grief and fear. "I won't hurt you, Dorrie! Believe me! I only want to help you. Don't be afraid."

"I b'ain't afeared," the girl sobbed. "'Tis nothin can 'urt me now! Wisht I was dead, that's wot! 'E went to 'er again. 'E dunno I be alive! 'E don't care!"

"Who, Dorrie?"

"Vincente, that's 'oo! Eeee, I wisht I was dead!"

"No, Dorrie! Don't! Don't!" Kneeling beside the girl, Adria smoothed back the wet wisps of hair that clung to Dorrie's feverish face. "Tell me about it," she whispered, trying to calm her. And at last the story poured forth.

It was a simple one. The girl was hopelessly in love with Vincente. He, however, loved someone else. A girl from the Puritan settlement, whom he met when they could arrange a rendezvous. He had been meeting her for nearly a year, and now Dorrie had given up hope.

Adria was shaken. She had made no friends among the girls in the colony. They had all seemed too sanctimonious and holier-than-thou to her. Out of reach of an orphaned, wilderness child. Yet, one among them had been meeting Vincente, secretly, all the time. It was dangerous, she knew. If the girl were caught out, she would be put down in Meeting, beaten — or worse!

"Do you know the name of the girl?"

Dorrie shook her head.

"See if you can learn it." It seemed very important that Adria know who it was. Names ran through her mind. Mercy Parrish, Hope Timmons, Elspeth Grey —? She must try to stop these meetings, warn the girl, Vincente! It was sinful.

Was it? Supposing she had remained in the village. Would she have slipped out to meet Mark, if she were asked, or — Anthony?

"'E's with 'er now," Dorrie snuffled. Then she went into a rambling dissertation on how she might have attracted him, if Adria had only given her a potion or charm.

"That's nonsense, Dorrie!"

"'Elp me," the girl sobbed. "'Elp me!" Then she went on to state that after seeing Vincente go from the house this night, she had planned to throw herself into the sea.

Adria was horrified. "'Tis sinful to take your own life, Dorrie! 'Tis the same as murder!"

"Then 'elp me!"

The servant clung to Adria tightly, as a drowning person would clutch, tears wetting Adria's cloak, her lumpy body shivering in Adria's arms. Adria was torn between the two of them: Anthony upstairs, in pain, and Dorrie who sounded desperate enough to do anything. If she could only quiet the girl now, talk to her in the sanity of daylight!

Her hand went to her throat, seeking the locket as she had in other troubled moments, and she remembered the small bundle pinned inside her sleeping shift.

"Dorrie, if I give you something — a charm — will you come and talk to me in the morning?"

"Oh, yes, mum!" The girl's weeping was noisier in relief. "Yes, mum!"

Reluctantly, Adria unpinned the handkerchief in which her locket was knotted, giving it to Dorrie. Then, looking down at the girl's swollen face, the straw-like hair matted and tangled, she knew that Dorrie's love for Vincente was hopeless. Despite the fact that Vincente was only a Portuguese fisherman and a servant in this house, he had a neatness, an elegance about him.

"Dorrie," Adria said, "This charm won't work without your help. You must keep saying, 'I must help myself!' Do you know what I am telling you?"

"Oh, yes, mum!" The girl grasped at Adria's hand, covering it with damp kisses. "Bless you, mum!"

Tearing herself free at last, convinced that Dorrie would do nothing desperate this night, Adria completed her preparations and hurried to Anthony's side.

This attack was worse than the one he had suffered before. She sat with him most of the night, caring for him, placing the warm healing poultices on his eyes, bathing his hot forehead, listening to his feverish mutterings.

It is as if I were a wife, she thought. *A true wife.* A warm wave of tenderness flooded through her as she closed her eyes, shutting out the sight of his haunted dark face, feeling only the touch of his hand beneath hers. For a moment she dared to weave a dream of a small house, with a hearth and kettle, its wooden floor covered with the hooked rag rugs she would make, curtains at the glassless windows, a loft above with pallets of straw for the children…

She opened her eyes and shivered, hating herself for her moment's lapse. What strange power did this man have over her? To attract her and repel her at the same time. To leave her feeling so torn and confused.

"Adria?"

"Yes, Anthony." Her voice trembled.

"You are a good lass," he said.

"Nay, Anthony." Her eyes brimmed. Since she had come to this house, she had been guilty of many a sin.

"You will never know," he said, bitterly, "what it is to have something eating away at your conscience. To know that your hands are stained with blood, and whatever you do, you can never make up for it! You cannot repay those whom you have hurt most."

He's thinking of Lady Jane, Adria thought. *And his stepmother.*

"You must ask God's forgiveness," she whispered. "'Tis all that is required of you."

"No, I must pay for what I have done. I'm only sorry that I have involved you in my life. Everything that I touch dies. Everything! Can you not see it?"

Was he trying to tell her she could expect to die, too? Like Emma? Trying to justify himself for whatever might come? That now Lady Jane had arrived, seemingly still in love with him, he saw marriage as part of his payment? And first, Adria must be removed from the scene —

She took a deep breath. "Nonsense," she said, as she had to Dorrie. "Now, you must sleep."

She stayed by him through the night, the house breathing around them, wind shrilling with demon fury at the windows. From time to time, she ministered to him. In the gray light of morning, she retired to her room, shaken and exhausted.

It had been a night of harrowing emotions.

Slipping the cloak from her shoulders, she returned to her bed, but she could not sleep. For one thing, she missed the comforting presence of her locket. For another, the cat, made restless by the storm, was prowling and wailing, his eyes green and shining, his fur raised and stiff.

At last, Adria was forced to get out of bed and pick him up. Holding him close, she smoothed his fur and talked softly, but to no avail. She could not stop his mournful crying.

"Nay," she said, hopelessly, "Not you! Not you, too!" So much unhappiness in one house! So little she could do! She could not even help herself. For, in spite of her situation in this house, the indignities she had suffered at Anthony Mordelle's hands, she had begun to acknowledge the feelings that raged, tempestuous, in her breast. There was something in the man that drew her, as helpless as a moth to a flame. And it was wrong! It was wrong!

At last, dropping to her knees beside the bed, she prayed. A small, raven-haired Puritan girl, in a harlot's silken gown.

CHAPTER 16

Adria woke to a tapping on the door. It was Dorrie, with her tray. A new Dorrie. Her hair was combed and she looked less slatternly than usual, but there was something different about her face. A look of calm resolve in her blue eyes.

"I been thinkin' on wot you said," the girl smiled, "and I'm goin' to do it!" Nodding mysteriously, she set the tray down and left the room.

What, exactly, was it I did say? Adria wondered, struggling to focus on the day. Surely she had not closed her eyes until dawn. The night before seemed to have been a hodgepodge of nightmares.

Anthony! Jumping from her bed, Adria pulled her cloak about her, and went to the tapestried door. He was still sleeping, and the lines of pain had been erased from his features. She stood looking down at him for a long time, recalling her fantasy of being his wife, having a little house of their own. But this man, a dark pride in his face, would never be content with such a simple life. No more than she with this! Sighing, she tiptoed away, thus beginning a long and dreary day.

It would have been a lonely one without the presence of Edwin Osmund. Dorrie and Mistress Murchison had been set to work repairing ravages to Jane's and Lady Elizabeth's wardrobes, while those good ladies returned to their labors in the jewel-packed chasm below. Anthony remained in bed most of the morning, Adria running up occasionally to check on his well-being.

He was strangely quiet at these times, answering in monosyllables, turning his face away from her. It was as if he were ashamed of his confidences in the night.

It was from one of these excursions to his bedside, descending the stairs, lost in thought, that Adria ran into Sir Edwin.

"Damme," he said, "'Tis good to see a pretty face in this mausoleum. May I inquire as to your good husband's health? He did not sit for his portrait, today, you know." His pink lips pouted, as if he had taken Anthony's failure to appear as a personal slight.

"Anthony is much better," Adria hastened to assure him. "He will be down later this afternoon, I'm sure."

"Too late for the light," the little man fussed. "I like to work a bit each day, to keep my hand in. And there's nothing to do in this barbaric place, except to go down into that hole!" He pointed downward, then searched for his snuff box and inhaled a pinch of dust. "Well, I shall wander about, find something to sketch —" He stopped, looking at Adria in such a way that she brought her hand to her face to cover her confusion. "Damme," he said, excitedly. "Why did I not think of this before! You will sit for me, milady! Fresh, unspoiled colonial beauty!"

"Nay," she said, backing away. "I am no fit subject —"

"But you are! Does your mirror not tell you, girl?" He put his hand beneath her chin, tilted her face, bringing his own close. "Interesting. It has character! None of your pink-and-white beauty like Jane, but you have something —! Shall we go to your bedchamber? I like privacy for my work."

"The parlor, I think," Adria said.

There she sat for him, acutely self-conscious at first, then forgetting herself in the sparkle of his conversation as he talked

171

about life at Court, the glittering life to which Anthony and Mark really belonged. After a while, he moved on to more personal matters. From what country had Adria's people come? Was there perhaps a hint of Gypsy in her blood? She had a look of the Romany to her. What were the Puritan people like?

Questions. So many questions. Even so, she did not expect the one that slipped into the conversation smoothly, darting out at her like a snake.

"And Anthony. Do you mind about him and the Lady Jane? Having the woman he loves beneath your roof?"

Adria gasped, unable to speak.

After a silence in which her thoughts whirled, he spoke again. "I suppose it does not matter. The servant, Dorrie, says you do not share his bed."

Anger began to rise inside her, both at his presumptions and Dorrie's gossiping. "I fear Dorrie would not know," she said, her head high.

"Damme," Edwin swore petulantly. "I cannot get this right! The Puritan maiden —" He tossed a paper to the floor — "or the mistress of Wyndspelle!" Another paper followed after he had crumpled it in his hand. "There is something in your face I cannot catch. Here —"

Rising, he came to her, turning her face to the light, running a finger along her cheekbones. "Damme," he said, thickly. "You have something these milk-and-water ladies do not have! There is a fire here —!"

"Sir!" Adria struggled in his attempted embrace, finally freeing one hand to rap him smartly across the cheek. "Sir," she said, her face scarlet, "I must ask you to remember you are a guest in my husband's home!"

For an instant, Edwin Osmund was not a silly little man. The eyes that stared into hers were those of a man of pride; he had offered her the gift of his attentions and that gift had been rejected. He looked at her for a moment and turned away, obviously piqued.

"I was in error," he said. "My apologies, milady. I thought perhaps you were lonely, and sought to honor you with my advances. Though if I were Mark Welles, it would be a different story, eh? I've seen the way you look at him. Perhaps the little bride is not so lonely, after all."

Adria was speechless. Had it been so obvious? She thought she had relegated Mark into the category of friend. "You misjudge me, sir," she whispered, finally.

But Edwin had already returned to his sketching. "Don't move," he said, crossly. "I'm getting it now!"

Adria sat stiff and silent as the man worked on. At last they were interrupted as Mark appeared at the parlor door.

"There you are," he said to Edwin. "I wondered where you'd got to. Could I enlist your aid? Or will you be able to tear yourself from such charming company?"

Adria ducked her head, pleating a fold of her gown with her fingers, certain that Edwin Osmund was looking on with knowing eyes.

"The truth is," Mark said, turning back to Edwin, "We need your professional opinion down below. We've found a painting, a royal hunt, that appears to be of value. Would you care to estimate its worth?"

The artist rose with alacrity, dropping his sketches into his chair, and followed Mark from the room. As the door closed and she heard their feet on the stairs, Adria rose, snatching up the crumpled papers from the floor.

The first was of a plain girl in Puritan garb, but there was a hint of rebellion in the huge dark eyes. The second, that of mistress of the house, was more flattering, but he had made fun of her here. The girl in the drawing looked awkward, uncomfortable, as though she did not belong and knew it. She wore her fine gown like a gauche country lass. And the third—

Adria's breath caught on a sob as she studied the sketch that was still unfinished. Edwin's chalks had portrayed her unkindly. It was an evil face, sensual and seductive. A cat's face. *A witch's face.*

"The devil is in you, lass," the Reverend Potts had thundered. Adria wondered, dazedly, if Edwin Osmund's artistic eye had seen the truth.

Dropping the sketches, she wandered across the room to the windows. The shutters had been opened, but she still felt imprisoned as she gazed out into the wind and rain. Suddenly, she ached with nostalgia. If she were in Reverend Potts' house, now, she would be kneeling, baking cakes on the hearth, filling the small cabin with the smell of good, plain food. They would dine early, and there would be prayers at table. Afterward, the Bible reading. There would be nothing to worry over. Her life would be planned for her. In the hands of Reverend Potts — and God.

She felt so lost, so cut off from everything that was familiar. If she could only go back, stand up in Meeting and confess to her sins, repent of them! Would they not forgive her?

Turning from the window, she ran her fingers lightly along the spinet keys until they touched a familiar note. "Greensleeves," the tune the Lady Jane had sung so sweetly. Pursing her lips, she whistled the melody. It faltered at first, then the notes rang clear and true. Experimentally, she added the note of a lark, an oriole, the image of green fields and trees unfolding before her. She put spring into the song, then summer with its warm, night sounds. And finally, fall, with a lone leaf spiraling down —

"God's teeth!"

She jumped, to find Mark Welles in the door that opened on the stairs to the kitchens. Behind him was the artist, his mouth agape, and beyond them, the ladies, Jane and Elizabeth.

"Damme," Edwin Osmund said, "I thought we'd been invaded by a covey of birds!"

"Excuse me," Adria gasped. "I must see to Sir Anthony." Gathering her skirts, she fled from the room.

She did not return to their company until the bell rang for the evening meal. There, she sat small and quiet, grateful that no one had mentioned the whistling incident. Anthony, the harsh lines of last night's pain about his lips, guided the conversation toward the weather. He had been aching to board his ship since it arrived, but due to the tempest, it had been forced to stand off to sea to avoid being dashed against the rocky shoreline. He and Mark were intent upon a discussion as to when the storm might end.

"I do not think the weather will ever clear," Jane pouted. "It is no wonder we were told this was a strange and savage place. The wind! The waves! The sounds of this house! Does it not tell on your nerves?"

"I suppose not," Anthony answered. "But then, 'tis like a ship, the creaking of the hull, the sound of the wind in the sails."

His voice was flat, but Adria could hear its sadness. How he must miss the sea! Then, after a pause, he went on, explaining that the warm Gulf Stream, sweeping north, and the frigid Labrador Current flowing south, met just off the New England Coast, creating fog and breeding weather. Neither ocean current was irrevocably committed to a fixed course, and they whipped back and forth to a certain degree, causing the air and water temperatures alongshore to deviate.

"So the climate can change in moments," he went on. "Tomorrow, we might rise to a balmy day. Is that not so, Mark?"

"True," Mark said. "And I can tell you, no one longs for clearing weather more than I!"

The conversation was interrupted as Mistress Murchison brought in the main course. Adria looked at the great planked fish that was a substitute for her own menu. She felt nauseated. It had been baked whole and it seemed its goggled eyes were staring at her. At least, she thought, swallowing, with a joint or a hare, one might be able to forget it was once a living creature.

She picked at her plate until the interminable meal was over and Anthony suggested they retire to the parlor where Jane went at once to the piano. Adria found herself a shadowed corner to wait out the evening. Then a new horror began.

"Your wife is more talented than you know," Edwin informed Anthony. He explained his statement, and nothing would do but that Adria perform.

Forced to the center of attention despite her denials, she found she was trembling. "You're frightening the poor thing to death," Lady Elizabeth interposed. "'Tis obvious she has not performed socially. I'm sure Jane will be happy to sing in her stead."

Adria looked at Jane, at her self-assured smile, and straightened her shoulders. "I shall be glad to entertain you," she said quietly. "If it will please you."

Going to the window, she looked out into the night. "It is spring," she told herself, "and I am alone. Alone at the watering place on a spring morning." She could see herself against the forest with its greening trees, a small plain figure in Puritan dress, and above her, on a branch, a bird —

The notes came to her, true and clear, the air around her trembling with birdsong, warbling, twittering, dying in a wintry farewell.

The room was silent as Adria came back to herself. Anthony's face was rapt with attention. "Beautiful, lass," he said, unsteadily. "'Twas beautiful!"

"Indeed it was!" Jane cried on the heels of his words. "How I envy your little wife, Anthony! But I had been taught such things are not natural to a female. I am certain it is not to me. All I have is my small voice —"

"Which we would like to hear now," Anthony interrupted, gallantly. "Will you honor us with a ballad?"

Jane moved to the spinet, seating herself, spreading her skirts gracefully. *She looks like a painting,* Adria thought, reddening at her own presumptuousness. What a great loon *she* must have looked, standing before them all, whistling like a — a man.

She moved back against the draperies at the window, wishing she could hide herself behind them. And from where she stood, she could see a bobbing lantern moving off across the grounds toward the horseshoe cliff. Vincente, gone to keep another lover's tryst? Poor Dorrie.

Maybe, she thought miserably, nobody in the world was ever really happy. Anthony, Dorrie, herself. Nobody in all the world.

She was glad when the evening came to a close, and she could flee to the privacy of her room at last. For the first time in her life, she felt beaten, old beyond her years. And as she changed into her silken shift, she realized how much she missed the locket. It was something of herself, that helped her retain her own identity.

And from the locket, her thoughts moved to Dorrie. She would know Vincente had gone to meet the girl again, tonight. How was she taking it? She remembered Dorrie's desolation of the night before, her wild statements about dying for her love. It came to Adria in a chill premonition that all was not as it should be with the servant girl.

Sighing, she pulled on her cloak over her nightdress. She could not sleep unless she had gone to see.

She entered the stair room with a tense feeling as she thought of the storage under the stair; the treasure trove that might also harbor a spider or a snake. Then, mounting the steps, she paused at Mistress Murchison's door. It was closed and she thought she could hear the woman's even breathing as she slept. Then she tapped, timidly, at Dorrie's. When she received no answer, she pushed it open a little way, holding her candle high.

The narrow cot the servant's room held was still made up. The room was empty.

Her mind whirling with a dreadful surmise, she ran down the steps, along the balcony, and into the great hall. As she turned toward the parlor, she stopped short at the sight before her.

Edwin Osmund sat in Anthony's place at table, his chubby legs thrust forward, too short for the seat of the throne-like chair. His eyes were closed, and he snored gently, the empty wine bottle before him offering sufficient reason for his slumbrous condition.

Adria looked at him, her anger at his presumptuousness mitigated by the humor of the situation. Obviously, the artist had slipped down here in the darkness to play at being the master of Wyndspelle. He would be most undone if he knew what a comical sight he presented! Still, just knowing he was here made her journey to the cellars less frightening.

Almost smiling, she hurried through the parlor and down into the kitchens. There she stopped, drawing in her breath in a retching sob. The huge room was empty, but directly across from her, there was a yawning hole in the surrounding shadows.

The door to the cellars was standing open!

It did not necessarily mean that Dorrie had gone down there. Perhaps Edwin Osmund had opened the door, in search of wine. Still, Adria felt cold as she descended into the lower regions. In the far corner of the wine cellar, a lighter square intruded into its blackness.

So the trapdoor, too, was open! The entrance to the chasm. The room echoed with the sound of booming surf.

"Dorrie!" Adria whispered. Then, heart in mouth, she hurried toward the opening, only to halt at the sound of voices below. A woman's voice? Dorrie's?

A man's!

Kneeling, she peered down into the chasm. She could see them down there in the flickering torchlight. Mark. Lady Elizabeth. Jane, whose voice she now heard raised in petulant complaint.

"God's teeth!" Mark swore in reply. "I promise you 'twill be calm in a day or two! I know this coast, and you do not. We've got to finish this job. There's no time to waste! Now, look at this. What value do you put on it?"

Adria withdrew, quietly. She had had enough of Jane and Lady Elizabeth for one evening. And Dorrie, no matter how heartbroken, would not fling herself into the sea with such an audience. Indeed, she was probably down there with the trio, aiding them in their work.

But Adria had thought the guests to be safely abed. What was so urgent about sorting and listing valuables that they must

179

work in the chasm by night? The ladies were greedy, it was true. Perhaps they were making certain they obtained the best of Anthony's treasure for their own use.

But were not the things he had set aside for them in the space beneath the stairs above?

Was there reason to wake Anthony? Of course not! He would only be angered at her suspicious nature. After all, Mark was in charge of household matters. Since he was there, it was certain that whatever they did was with Anthony's permission. In addition, it was none of her business!

Tiptoeing past the table where the artist still snored in Anthony's chair, she returned to her room.

There, she stood at the window for a long time, dismissing Dorrie from her mind, returning to the humiliation of the evening. She clung to the notion that Anthony had enjoyed her whistling. At least, his face had shown signs of pleasure. Was he only being kind?

There was a clawing sound at the door and she caught her breath, only to relax as a faint mewing followed. The cat. Only the cat.

Opening the door a crack, she watched him slide around it, silent as a shadow. Then, with a graceful leap, he was in the center of her bed where he yawned pinkly and preened himself. And she recalled Edwin Osmund's words.

"A witch's familiar," he had said.

Dear God! She began to tremble. Dear God! No!

Jumping from her bed, the black cat twined himself around her ankles and began to purr.

CHAPTER 17

Morning brought a harried Mistress Murchison. Both ladies were ill, she told Adria as she slammed down her tray, and Dorrie was no earthly use, having just gone into a state of hysterics in the kitchen.

"Did she say what was wrong?" Adria asked. She thought she knew the answer, but there was a chance the girl might be ill, also.

"She did not. But if you'll just tell me how I'm going to manage, with those women wanting me to wait on them hand and foot?" Mistress Murchison pushed back her hair, and again Adria noticed how attractive the woman was once she dropped her hard, professional look. "Up the stairs, down the stairs ... you'd think they were dying! And it's just a case of the sniffles, if you ask me!"

"You tend to your other duties," Adria sighed. "I'll see to them." Dressing hastily, she ignored her breakfast, settling for a sip of tea before she hurried to Lady Elizabeth's room.

"Come in." The answering voice was weak and filled with self-pity. Adria pushed the door open. The older woman was not so overpowering, with her eyes watering and her hair askew.

"'Tis this house!" the woman grumbled. "Cold, damp! This barbaric coast!"

And spending half the night rummaging through the wealth in the chasm, Adria thought, though she said nothing. The woman went on with her diatribe. It was all Anthony's fault for bringing them to this heathen place.

"Is it not cold and damp in England?" Adria asked.

Lady Elizabeth glared at her. "At times, but at least 'tis civilized. There is someone to care for you when you're ill."

"I have some knowledge of herbs —" Adria began.

"With which to poison me!" The woman sat upright, forgetting her ailments for the moment. "You cannot be happy to see us here! To know that your husband loves Jane! Loved her enough to kill my only son."

"But Anthony is your son, milady."

"Not my true son!"

"He only wishes to care for you," Adria said, in a low voice.

"And so he shall," the woman said, triumphantly. "I will have my due — you may depend on that!"

Adria was quivering with anger as she stared at the old woman in the bed. Without makeup and wig, her features were haggard and unpleasant. "You shouldn't talk to me of these things," Adria said, finally.

"And why not? You will not tell Anthony. You wouldn't dare! Don't you think I recognize this as a marriage of convenience? There is nothing between you, I have been told!"

By whom, Adria wondered. Dorrie, again, with her gossip? Mistress Murchison? Mark? Or — Anthony himself?

"I only came to help you," she said, finally. It would do no good to deny the things the woman had said, since they were true. "I would like to make you comfortable, if I may."

Grudgingly, the woman consented to Adria's ministrations. At last, dressed in a clean shift, her pillows plumped, she ran through a litany of her ailments. Her cold had settled in her back, she said. She was certain that she would worsen and die here in this dreadful land. Temper soothed by her comfort, she consented to Adria's offer of medication.

"I'll check on Lady Jane, first," Adria told her, "and see what she needs. I'll be back in a short while." Closing the door on the woman's complaints, Adria hastened to Jane's room, her face still flushed with anger.

Jane, too, was not so impressive this morning. In fact, with her pink nose and red-rimmed eyes, she quite resembled a rabbit. Sprawled rather ungracefully in her rumpled bed, she made no effort to change her position when she saw that it was only Adria.

"Oh," she said, rudely, "'Tis you."

"I was told you were ill. I came to see if I could help in any way."

"About time someone came!" The girl's voice was a nasal whine. "I'm miserable! Bored to death! And this room is a shambles!" Then, when Adria started to open the drapes at the window, she screamed, "No! Leave them closed. I cannot stand the view! It's too depressing."

In the brief moment they were open, Adria had to agree with her. This window looked out over the blasted land that was the garden of Wyndspelle. She closed the drapes quickly and set herself to picking up the rubble of gowns and slippers entangled on the floor. Apparently Jane had tried on and discarded many costumes before appearing at dinner the night before.

"Where is Dorrie?" the girl asked, pouting. "I thought she was to be my personal maid."

"Dorrie is ill." The mention of the servant brought a new worry to Adria's mind. She would see to the girl as soon as she had finished here. "I will do what I can," she said to Jane. "I see Mistress Murchison has brought hot water. Would you like a fresh shift?" She took one from the wardrobe.

"Not that one," the girl said, imperiously. "The blue silk, and the bed-sacque to match. The one with the white fur trim."

Doggedly, Adria set about making the girl comfortable, conscious that Jane was watching her all the while. The intensity of her gaze made Adria feel awkward and self-conscious. Picking up the girl's hairbrush, Adria dropped it, hating herself for her clumsiness.

"Why did Anthony marry you?"

The question was so sudden and unexpected that Adria was at a loss. "Why — for the reasons most people are wed, I suppose."

"It cannot be your looks," the girl said, speculatively. "For you certainly do not have the appearance of a lady, with that brown skin. Still, my poor Anthony cannot see —"

"There — there are other things than appearance, I am sure."

The girl hooted. "Are you trying to tell me he wed you for your soul? That is an old wives' tale! Men are not made in that fashion!"

"I know of no other reason," Adria whispered.

"Perhaps you bewitched him," the girl said, mockingly. "Dorrie swears you're a witch."

"If I were," Adria muttered to herself, later, as she went down the stairs to the kitchens, "I would put a curse on the guests in this house! Instead, I am trying to heal them!"

Heal them? They weren't really ill. They had both caught slight chills and were feeling sorry for themselves, yet she would be expected to provide some sort of medication. Lady Elizabeth had complained of her back, which might indicate a need for pumpkin-seed tea. And for Jane's faked cough, she would prepare honey-and-onion syrup, though she was certain that the women's colds had not settled in their lungs.

Or had they? Perhaps on the assumption that the ladies suffered from near-pneumonia, she should prepare mustard poultices. Reverend Potts swore by them; perhaps he believed in giving the sick a taste of hell's fire here on earth. Adria's brown skin had been blistered once. What would it do to the aging skin of Lady Elizabeth? The tender white flesh of Jane?

She shouldn't! But she would. Perhaps she could not destroy them with a witch's curse, but she could do the next best thing — and in the spirit of mercy.

She caught herself smiling as she entered the kitchens. In the stone room that was Mother Moseby's realm, Mark stood, coattails to the fire, his face drawn and a little grim. His gloomy expression lightened at seeing Adria. "How are our patients?" he wanted to know. "Are the ladies ill, or having an attack of the vapors?"

"They both have caught slight chills, I think."

"God's teeth!" He turned away from her, looking toward the door that led to the wine cellars and thence to the chasm. "I didn't think they could bear a little honest work! I need their aid, and the weather shows signs of clearing —" He stopped, then said, "And what of Sir Edwin? At work on the portrait, I suppose?"

Adria nodded, wondering at the desperation in the man's eyes. Why was it so important that the work in the chasm be done so hurriedly? Unless — her heart plunged sickeningly — Mark was using it as an excuse to enjoy the company of Lady Jane.

"Perhaps Vincente could help you," she offered, timidly.

"I cannot trust Vincente. At any rate, I would not ask him for any favor today. He seems as sour as a spinster at someone else's wedding."

Adria couldn't help laughing at his analogy. Then she sobered as she considered what he had said. *"I cannot trust Vincente."*

She thought of the missing pendant with its broken stone, the key —

"You must excuse me," she said. "I have promised to prepare some medications."

A little nervous under his amused gaze, Adria set to her preparations. She sliced red onions into a shallow pan and dribbled honey over them, placing the pan in the hot ashes to one side of the hearth. Here it would simmer into a syrup that would ease coughing. Then she put pumpkin seeds on to boil and set about preparing the poultices.

"And what is that?" Mark asked as she folded the steaming mixture into flannel cloths. "God's teeth! Is it what I think it to be?"

Noticing the guilty look on her face, he began to laugh, laughing until the tears came. He was still chuckling when she placed the poultices on a tray, covering them with a heated towel, and started toward the stair.

"I wish I could watch this," he said, wiping his eyes. "Would that I were a mouse, a very small one, to hide in a corner of the room as those are applied!"

"That would not be seemly, sir," she said, demurely.

"Tell the ladies those applications must be made repeatedly until they are completely recovered," he called after her, "and see how speedily they return to health!" And as she reached the door that led into the parlor, he called her name. "Adria?"

She turned to look down. He stood below her, his fair hair shining, all the light in the dark kitchens seeming to concentrate in his being, his merry eyes as blue as the coat he wore.

"Lass," his voice was a teasing caress. "Lass, I love you!"

Her knees weak with a new and unfamiliar feeling, she turned to her duties, carrying his words with her through the remainder of the day.

True to his prediction, the ladies made speedy recoveries. They both came down for the evening meal, with pale, long-suffering faces. "Yes," Lady Elizabeth told Anthony, "We both feel quite well. Though your little wife," she added, "insisted upon using some barbaric medication far too strong for a *lady's* tender flesh."

Adria was certain that her poultices had been no more blistering than the hateful glances of the two women. Only the twinkle in Mark's eye kept her upright in her chair, head high, a fixed smile on her face throughout the evening.

Thankfully, it ended early. Dorrie was still confined to her room, and Mistress Murchison accepted her extra duties sullenly. Anthony was somber, gloomy. He seemed unnaturally quiet. Even the little artist appeared daunted by the atmosphere. Only Mark Welles was his gay, charming self as they parted for the night, relinquishing the parlor session for the sake of the convalescents.

The others went to their rooms and Adria remained behind to give Mistress Murchison her instructions for the morrow, and to inquire about Dorrie.

"Do you think I should look in on her?" she asked.

"I wouldn't," the woman said, bluntly. "Fact is, she don't want you near her. Said so, in plain words, if you want to know."

Probably, Adria thought wearily, Dorrie believed that she had failed her. But it wasn't Adria's fault. It was Dorrie who had insisted she had supernatural powers.

"No point in getting her stirred up again," the housekeeper pointed out.

She was right. Adria was exhausted; the day of running up and down the stairs, tending two demanding patients had begun to tell on her. She would go to her bed.

Dragging herself up the stairs, she found Mark waiting outside her door. "I've got to talk to you," he said, urgently, taking her two hands in his. Adria drew back, the traitorous weakening of her knees betraying her reaction to him.

"Not tonight," she begged. "Please." To her surprise and shame, her eyes brimmed. "I'm tired," she said. "So tired —"

"Tomorrow, then." His handsome face was serious. "But I want you to think on something. Remember my promise? I told you I would take you away when it was time. That time is drawing near. Anthony and Jane have reached an understanding, lass. 'Tis as I said it would be. And now you stand in their way. I have work to finish here, as a matter of honor; then when the seas are calm, we will go. But a decision must be made now. *You will go with me!*"

Adria pushed her hair back with a trembling hand, her eyes dazed with fatigue as she looked up at him, seeing the eagerness in his face; the way he flinched at a sound, his eyes sliding furtively to right and left to see if their conversation was being observed. He did believe there was danger here. He feared for her.

"Yes," she said, "I will go."

But after he had left her and she had retired to her room, her mind was racked with an agony of indecision. She wanted to leave Wyndspelle more than anything in the world, but something seemed to hold her back. What if Mark were mistaken, and Anthony and Jane had *not* renewed their romance? Would she not be leaving a blind man helpless in the hands of two unscrupulous females who had undone him before? Adria had made a pact with her own conscience — to act as mistress of Wyndspelle as long as she was needed, to owe no debt to its sightless master.

She could not, she told herself stubbornly, walk out on that bargain until she was certain! It would not be right.

Or was it true what Mark had said? That Adria, herself, was attracted to Anthony — setting herself in competition with Lady Jane?

Whatever it was, her blood was singing through her veins, and her face felt hot.

Going to the window, clad only in her thin shift, she pulled the velvet drapery aside and stood looking out into the night. Leaning out, the wind wet against her face, she could see Anthony's ship silhouetted against the horizon. The rain had stopped, and a pale moon shone sporadically between the scudding clouds that swept the night sky, their shadows racing along the sand below Wyndspelle. In a little while, with this change in temperature, the fog would come, shrouding the Druid stones on the strip of beach below.

Looking downward toward the shore from which she had climbed on that first night, her heart caught in her throat. The place looked different, somehow. That tall stone. Had it been there before? It seemed as though it moved. She peered into the darkness as a cloud blotted out the moon, so intent that she did not hear an opening door.

"Adria." It was Anthony's voice that jerked her to attention. Anthony's voice, with a new note in it. Pleading, unsteady, unsure.

Wheeling, she looked first toward the door that opened on the balcony, then toward that which connected their two rooms. Her husband stepped from behind the tapestry, his face unreadable, masked in shadow.

Saint's face — or Satan's? She thought of Edwin Osmund's words as she stood poised, heart thudding in her ears until he spoke her name again, this time like a command.

"I am here, milord," she whispered.

He came toward her, looking much as he had that first night, shirt open, his bronzed body gleaming in the firelight, blind eyes intent upon hers, but with that small flickering flame.

He stopped before her, his hand touching her shoulder, sliding onward to circle her bare throat, tightening until he could feel the pulse that beat within her body and shook her with its violence.

"You are afraid?"

"Nay," she whispered. "Nay —"

"I had to come. I could not help myself. I need you." His words held all the anguish of loneliness and love.

"I am here, milord." Then, with a sob as his arms tightened about her. "I am here."

I cannot help myself, she thought as he lifted her, carrying her to her marriage bed. *I love him! Man or demon — I love him!*

And then the world rocked and spun and exploded in a kind of glory...

CHAPTER 18

The dim light of morning sifted into the room and Adria came awake with a feeling that something was different in the atmosphere. A sound? Nay, it was the absence of sound. The house was still around her, neither creaking nor breathing.

Then she remembered she, too, was different. Last night, she, Adria Anne Turner — nay, *Mordelle!* — had lain in the arms of a man.

Or had it been a dream? Anthony had gone from her as she slept, but the pillow beside her still held the imprint of his head.

Sitting up in the big bed, hugging her knees, she thought back over the events of the night. She had not known love could be like this. So warm. So close.

Anthony loved her! It had been a time of wonder, of tenderness. And she had reciprocated his love, not as a wifely duty, but wantonly, shamelessly.

Now, in the gray dawn, her face flushed as she recalled the way she had responded to his caresses. "I love you!" she had cried. "Oh, Anthony, I love you!"

"Don't speak," he had said. "Just let me hold you —"

He had not spoken of love! She realized it now. But surely he would not use her to fill a need, and then when that need was gratified —

Nay! He loved her. His actions had not been those of a man who cared for another. Still, there had been that tortured cry: *"I had to come! I could not help myself!"*

And now he was gone from her bed.

Longingly, she looked toward the tapestry door, wanting to open it and go to him. But she was unsure of what was expected of her. She must let him dictate the rules that governed their relationship. After all, she was only a simple country lass.

One thing she knew, she need not fear their guest now. She could even feel pity for Jane, now that Anthony was truly her husband. Husband! The thought was exultant in her breast. She would bring happiness to his haunted face. Devote her life to his well-being.

She thought of Mark, and dismissed a flicker of concern for the blond man. He would be happy when he learned it was Adria Anthony loved, not Jane. Sitting up, she swung her bare feet to the floor. Though the fire had burned low in the fireplace, the room was warm. *Tis an omen,* she thought. The predicted weather change had come. It seemed almost balmy, with a feel of spring.

A false promise, she discovered when she reached the open window. For while the sky directly overhead was shading into grayness with the dawn, thunderheads were building up out at sea. It was an awesome sight: the storm static on the horizon, the cotton-wool fog blanketing the sea immediately below, the angry waves reduced to a fretting murmur.

Yet, as she watched, the first winds came, shredding the fog with nervous fingers. Like that first night, she thought as she looked down toward the beach, seeing the mists scatter like ragged wraiths, swirling across sand and stone —

And then she saw it.

For a moment, she could not move or breathe. Then fear began to beat inside her, her throat closing, suffocating her as she stared into the fog below with terror-blinded eyes. Praying that she would not see it again —

But the mist swirled, and it was there! *It was there!*

Screaming, she ran from the room, straight into the arms of Mark Welles, still fully dressed. Behind him stood Mistress Murchison.

"What is it, lass?" he asked. "What is it?"

She could only stare at him, her face horror-stricken. Then she heard Anthony's voice, stern, commanding.

"Adria! Calm yourself! What has frightened you?"

Turning toward him, seeing his fear for her in his haggard face, his reaching hands, she sensed his feeling of helplessness. Blind, not knowing what had happened, unable to protect his wife as a husband should.

Backing away from Mark, she sobbed, "The window! Down on the beach! I saw it! Oh, dear God! I saw it!" She threw herself into Anthony's arms, shivering, on the verge of hysteria.

"There's nothing there," he comforted her. "Only your imagination. Mark —?"

But Mark hadn't waited for Anthony's request. He had already gone. Adria could see him through her open door as he leaned to look out from her window. When he turned, his face was the color of chalk.

"There *is* something down there, Anthony. The girl is right. I'd better get help. Vincente, Petro." His voice sounded queer, jerky. And when his eyes met hers, she knew he saw what she had seen. Her last conscious thoughts were of horror that the vision existed — and relief that she was not mad.

For the thing she had seen as she looked from her window, rising from the mists that swirled about the cairn of stones below, had been the figure of a girl. A maiden in Puritan dress, tied to a timber, facing the sullen sea. She had seen the ghost of Elizabeth Miller — come home to Wyndspelle.

193

CHAPTER 19

Adria came awake in a room filled with night shadows. *'Tis not morning, yet,* she thought, drowsily. Then she remembered that Anthony had been here. Turning her head toward the pillow beside her, she saw that it was empty. A bewildered frown creased her brows as memory came back to her, slowly. There was a bitter taste in her mouth. She remembered, now. She had fainted, then they had given her something to drink. She had fainted because —

Dear God!

She sat up with a little whimper, her eyes going toward the window, where the drapes were now drawn, the picture of the obscene thing below imprinted in her mind.

"Adria? You are awake?"

It was Anthony's voice. Relief flooded through her as she saw him in a high-backed velvet chair before her fire. She was not alone. "Anthony!" She said his name with a sob, holding out her arms toward him. "Oh, milord!"

He did not move, his face still wearing a tired, reserved expression. It seemed closed against her. Puzzled, she dropped her arms.

"I waited to be certain all was well with you before I retired," he said, almost formally.

"The witch?" she whispered. "There was something there? Mark saw it —"

"There was something there, but 'twas not a witch. 'Twas a Puritan maid from the settlement below. Wyndspelle seems to collect them." His laugh was bitter.

"She was tied to a stake?" His face answered her question. "She is — dead?"

"Nay. She is in poor case, however. She has been whipped, soundly, and exposed to the night mists. God knows how long she hung there."

God knew — and Adria knew. With a sick feeling, she recalled those moments at the window, just before Anthony came to her bed. She thought she had seen something then, but his coming had taken her mind from it. While she had lain in her husband's arms, the poor girl had been out there suffering. Tears filled her eyes.

"Do you know her name? And how she came here?"

"According to Vincente, her name is Prudence Shanks. He has been meeting her for some time, I understand. I gather the girl is still too crazed with fear to make sense."

Prudence! Joseph's daughter, who would have been Adria's stepdaughter, had they been wed! Pale, quiet Prudence — and Vincente. It could not be!

"I must go to her," Adria said. She sat up, the room wheeling around her in her dizziness from the drug.

"You will not," Anthony commanded. "She is terrified of seeing you. In her mind, you have some part in the thing that has happened to her."

"I?" The girl's voice was filled with disbelief.

"You — and I. It would seem Wyndspelle has been singled out as the reason for the girl's fall from grace."

"She told you this?"

"It was not necessary. A note was pinned to the girl's bosom. It said, *Devils, Begone.*"

"Oh, Anthony!"

"I have no intention of being driven from my own home," he said, rising, his face grim. "Now, I would suggest you try to sleep. We will probably know the rest of the story later in the morning."

Going to the tapestry-covered door, he turned once more, his voice harsh, as if the words he uttered were being torn from him.

"My apologies for last night, lass. I had no intention of coming in to you as I did. Loneliness, perhaps — or madness — drove me. Whatever the reason, it was inexcusable, and it will not happen again."

"Milord —"

What she would have said, she didn't know, because his own words interrupted her.

"The girl would not allow herself to be brought into the house," he said. "She is lodged in the building behind the house. Vincente and Mother Moseby are caring for her. I intend to get my cloak and join them, so you may count yourself safe tonight. Tomorrow, I shall have a bolt fitted to your door."

Then he was gone.

"Just put it on the table," Adria said in a muffled voice, as the housekeeper brought her breakfast tray. Adria tried to make herself eat, but she was only able to swallow the scalding tea. All the while, her mind was whirling with indecision.

She could not face Anthony today. She could not face Mark. And, dear God, she could not face the ladies, especially Lady Jane. There was no help for her, she thought, numbly. Not unless she remained in her room, pretended she was ill. Still, she could not hide in this space all the rest of her days. There would come a time when she must leave it, so it might as well be now.

At last, dressed in the drabbest gown she could find, her hair put up as severely as possible, she surveyed herself in the glass. It was not a wanton who looked back at her. Just a slip of a girl, with a trembling mouth, and heartbreak in her eyes.

Stiffening her spine, head high, she stepped out onto the balcony.

To her relief, no one was in sight, save Edwin Osmund. As she descended the steps into the great hall, the little man minced toward her in his red heeled shoes. Shaking the ruffles at his wrists into place, he produced his snuff box and inhaled a pinch of the gray powder before he spoke.

"Well, milady," he said, "You find me alone again. Damme, I've begun to wonder if there is a stink about me. He peered at Adria, anxiously, as though the thought had just occurred to him and he might find affirmation written on her face. "The ladies have not come down," he said, petulantly. "They plan to keep to their rooms until the witch has gone from the premises."

Witch?

"Prudence Shanks is no witch," Adria said, trying to keep the irritation from her voice. "No more than I!"

"Indeed?"

"I thought you would be working on the portrait," she said, evenly.

"Would be," the man sighed, "Except that my subject seems to be closeted in the study with all his minions. Seems to be a council of war, or the like. Well," he swept Adria a dramatic bow, "I suppose I shall go on up and get things in readiness, should he decide he has *time* for me."

With a flip of his lace-covered wrist, Edwin Osmund turned and marched up the stairs, ludicrous in his offended dignity.

Adria waited until he was out of sight, then headed for the steps that led to the balcony. She did not intend to be caught here, standing outside the study door as if waiting to be included. Her first impulse to stay in her room had been quite correct. Like Edwin Osmund, she did not belong.

But as she set her foot upon the first step, the study door opened. Dorrie rushed from it, her mouth square and ugly, emitting little whimpering sounds. She passed Adria, nearly knocking her down as she shoved her to one side.

Adria looked after Dorrie in wonderment, then turned to see Vincente leaving the study. His face was white and set as he passed her. He turned into the parlor where the steps led down to the kitchens and then to the outside.

On Vincente's heels came Mistress Murchison, her face alight with a kind of morbid glee as she saw Adria.

"There you are, mum! The master was just sending me to fetch you." She beckoned Adria toward the study door, putting a hand on the girl's arm as if to prevent her from escaping, barring the door once Adria had entered the room.

Trying to conceal her trembling, Adria looked at the men before her. Anthony's face was bleak. Mark looked sheepish and apologetic, spreading his hands in a gesture designed to absolve himself from whatever was to be said.

"You may leave us, Mistress Murchison," Anthony said, his voice like ice. Then, "Adria?"

"Yes, milord."

A muscle twitched along his jaw as he stared at her with his blind eyes. At last, he said, "You tell her, Mark." He turned away, his hands behind his back, his shoulders stiff with anger.

"I don't quite know where to begin," Mark said, hesitantly. "It — it's Dorrie's doing, Adria. It seems Dorrie followed

Vincente when he went to a — a tryst with this girl we found here. You know about this?"

"I knew about the girl, but not that Dorrie —" She paused and he continued.

"Dorrie followed them to their meeting place, then trailed the girl to her own house. Her name is Prudence Shanks, and she lived with her father. You know the family?"

"Yes," Adria said in a stifled voice, "I do."

"Dorrie informed the father, and the next night the girl was caught out. Worse, she was wearing a Catholic cross, which Vincente had given her. The girl was beaten, and accused of heresy and consorting with witches. She was brought here — and you know the rest."

Adria's eyes brimmed with tears. But for the grace of God, she would have met the same fate. "How dreadful," she whispered. "How dreadful! I must go to her —"

"You will not see her, milady!" Anthony's voice cracked like a whip. "Have you not done enough with your meddling? This poor child! Dorrie! Vincente! Putting us all in danger?"

"I?" Adria stared at him, hurt and incredulous. "What are you saying? I have had nothing to do with this!"

"According to Dorrie, you have," Mark said, gently. "Vincente faced her with the girl's story a few minutes ago, right here in this room. And Dorrie said it was you who had instructed her to search out the girl's name, then move to 'help herself'. She said you — bewitched her with your magic."

"I can work no magic! I am no witch!"

"Are you not?" It was Anthony speaking, his words breaking through the haze of anger that burned in her. Dorrie had accused her falsely, to cover her own misdeeds! But Anthony had drawn something from his clothing, something terrifyingly familiar. He tossed it to a table. "And what is *that*?"

Adria looked at the small soiled bundle. It was her burned locket, done up in a kerchief. The packet Dorrie had believed to be a charm. And Adria had given it to the girl. She could not deny it.

"But I am no witch," she repeated.

"Of that, I am certain," Anthony said, coolly, "since I have never believed in witchcraft. Yet one small maid, playing a pretend game, has put all I own in jeopardy in a single night."

"I do not understand."

"In addition to informing on the girl, Prudence, Dorrie told the father that you are here. The Puritans know you are at Wyndspelle. There has been sickness in the village, and they lay it at your door. Also, it is believed that you led Miss Prudence into — imprudence. With the good Reverend at the helm, they plan to drive the devils of Wyndspelle into the sea."

"Nay," Adria whispered. "Nay!"

Anthony silenced her with an impatient gesture. "Now we must decide how best to set up our defenses. Vincente will be gone. He has asked leave to take the girl to his parents in the fishing village down the coast. So, Mark, if you will call Petro and Rico —"

"I will go back," Adria said with a sob. "Send me back to the settlement and they will have no further reason to disturb you."

"If we sent you to them," Anthony said with a kind of grim humor, "we would only have you back, tied to a stake on the beach below."

"Then let me go with Prudence and Vincente." Adria was crying in earnest now, tears streaking her cheeks faster than she could wipe them away.

"Do you think Vincente would take you?" Without waiting for an answer, Anthony turned away from her. "As I was saying, bring Petro and Rico to me. I will see them in the upper room, where we can study the layout of the land. When this new storm passes, we can bring in a few of our lads from the ship. For now, here's what I want you to do..."

Adria stood waiting until it was obvious she was no longer included in the conversation. Turning to leave, her tear-blurred eyes chanced upon the locket. Taking it, she moved toward the door, pausing once to look back. She was praying for a word. Just one soft, kind word. None came.

Blindly, she made her way back to the sanctuary of her room.

There, huddled in her bed, forlorn and miserable, Adria considered her life. The night she was born, her mother had told her, there was a dreadful storm that unroofed the hut at the hour of her birthing. Her mother and father had teased her, lovingly. They had ordered a nice, orderly child. Instead, they'd received a storm child. A changeling.

She shivered. Reverend Potts had said much the same, but he'd said it differently. She had been born with evil in her, he'd explained. The evil of original sin. And her parents' death had been part of God's plan to bring about her sanctification. His punishment, because she was not a tractable and humble soul. She had not believed him — then.

Too confused to think clearly, too numb to cry, she sat very still. It was as if by waiting long enough, she might receive an answer. Something would guide her, tell her what she must do.

Tiptoeing to the door, she opened it a crack and saw Petro, Rico, Mark, and Mistress Murchison. They were moving along the balcony toward the stair room. They were met by Edwin Osmund, who seemed to be in a huff. Making a remark to Mark concerning his inconsiderate host who had sent him from his work, the artist slammed into his own room, banging the door behind him.

The others went on their way, summoned by Anthony to hold their council of war. To plan for the safety of Wyndspelle.

With Vincente gone and the other men above, there would be no one guarding the rear of the house. It would be simple to slip away, to return to Reverend Potts and say, *"Here I am. Do what you will."*

Adria put on a cloak, then turned toward the gilt-framed mirror. The face that looked back at her was haggard, with huge haunted eyes. She looked like a witch in the dark cloak. It was surely appropriate for her return to the settlement.

Going to the door, she had an overpowering desire to turn once more — to look back. Back at the bed with its silken sheets; at the tapestry over the connecting door.

She had changed, but the room had not. It still seemed as cold and cavernous as it had on that first night, shadowed even in the day. And apparently the storm was pushing the waves toward the shore, for the house had begun its labored, measured breathing once more. An inimical room, a frightening room, cold even though the fire blazed on the hearth. It needed only the body of Emma to make it complete—

Adria jumped as something touched her ankles. The cat. She had forgotten him. Scooping him up, she held him for a moment, feeling the warmth of his purring body, then reluctantly put him down.

She must run.

Through the parlor, down the stairs, and into the kitchens. Blessedly, Mother Moseby was not in sight. Unseen, Adria slipped outside.

For a moment, she could not see. A gust of wind caught her hood, blowing it back, lashing her hair across her eyes. Fighting it back into place, she looked nervously at the sky above her. The rain had not yet begun, but seaward, the sky was black and boiling. Already a few ragged, dirty-looking clouds were skimming overhead. Thus Wyndspelle had greeted her, she thought sadly, and thus it was sending her away.

Stepping out onto the fine path that had been laid through the desolate land, she began to run, cloak flying in the wind, arm shielding her face from the gale-driven debris.

Where the path ended, she stopped to rest. And here, she turned to look back. Back across the blighted ground with its twisted tortured trees, at the house that loomed starkly against the coming storm. For just a space, the bleak sun was unshrouded. It cast a glint that reflected from the windows of the topmost room. Anthony was there.

The trail was now stony and broken, with puddles of water standing here and there. The curve ahead was marked by an enormous boulder. From there, it was a straight, uphill climb.

There was no longer any need to run. No one in the house could catch her now. For a moment, she was honest with herself, confessing that all along she had prayed someone would stop her and take her back.

She reached the boulder, lifting her eyes to gauge the steepness of the trail. And she saw them, on the rim of the cliff. Two dark-clad figures, one with a musket.

Staring at the men above her, she lost her footing and fell down. The world seemed to explode around her as the musket fired. She stood up, wavering, looking at her bleeding hand. It had been struck by a chip of flying granite.

"You missed her," a voice shouted. "Missed her! And 'tis her! The witch. Reload, man! Hurry!"

Such excitement she had heard from men returning from the hunt, gloating over their kill, carrying home the bleeding deer with something in their faces that was more than the reward of bringing meat for the larder. A bloodlust! And the innocents had suffered.

Fury blazed inside her, stiffening her knees as she lifted her hand, fingers clawed, toward the men on the cliff above. They froze there, staring down at her as if mesmerized. At the girl in the wind-blown cloak, dark hair whipping around her face, the blood-streaked hand extended toward them.

"Yes," Adria screamed, *"It is the witch! And I curse you! I curse you! May the devil take your souls to hell!"*

Her voice was drowned out in a roll of thunder as the sky blackened about her. Then, from the mass of clouds that blotted out the day, lightning jagged downward to strike the cliff with a spitting, crackling sound.

For an instant, all was silent. Then, with a strangled shriek of fear, the men fled. The musket came tumbling down the cliffside, bouncing from stone to stone as a dazed Adria watched its descent.

Had any of this been her doing? She swayed again, weak with fear and shock, now that the danger was past. Then, falling to her knees, her face white except for a streak of blood across one cheek, she lifted her eyes to the stormy heavens, thanking God.

CHAPTER 20

Adria looked back toward Wyndspelle. The storm had been a shallow one. Already the worst of it had passed over the house, leaving it limned in a golden light. Like an omen, telling her to return...

But then, what other choice did she have? She could not hope for justice now. And perhaps she had some value here at last. Fear had been Wyndspelle's defense for all these years. She had renewed that fear today.

Exhausted, chilled, she began to stumble back along the trail, thunder rolling ominously overhead. When she reached the path, she saw Mark running toward her. He, like the house, seemed ringed with light.

"God's teeth!" he swore, reaching her. "What do you think you are doing? You little fool! You little fool!" Snatching her to him, he held her close. She could feel his heart beating against hers. At last, he held her away, looking at her anxiously. "You're bleeding! You're hurt!"

"Just scratches." She tried to smile at him, but it was a dismal failure. Her lips began to quiver and he hugged her close again.

"I saw it," he said. "I saw it all from the window. The cowards — the beastly sniveling cowards!" He scanned the cliff. "Shoot at a lass, but when a man appears, they run!"

Adria realized he had not seen the final scene: the curse she had flung at her attackers, the lightning streaking from the heavens. She opened her mouth to speak, then thought better of it. She had been damned as a witch already. Only Mark believed in her now. She buried her face against his chest, shivering, unable to stop.

"She's all right," Mark said. "Only frightened. Someone had better go and tell Anthony."

Surprised, she raised her head to find that Petro and Rico had joined them. "God's teeth," Mark swore. "I forgot!" He rattled off a few words in a foreign language, and the men left. Adria flushed, wondering what the thoughts had been behind those expressionless faces. What had they made of finding her in Mark Welles' arms?

"Now to get you back to the house," Mark said practically. Adria leaned against him as he half-led, half-carried her along the path. Once inside the kitchen, he took both her arms in his hands and held her away from him looking down into her blood-stained face.

"Promise me you won't try anything like that again," he said.

"I only wanted to go away," she said in a forlorn voice.

"And you shall. I told you I had plans! Give me a few more days, and we'll both go! Just the two of us!" Pulling her to him, he kissed her. She was too tired and shaken to resist.

"Sir Anthony wishes to see you, Master Welles."

It was Mistress Murchison, who had come quietly down the stairs from the parlor. The ever-present Mistress Murchison. This time she did have a tale to carry to Anthony. Adria was too weary to care.

It was Mark who was abashed. "'Tis not what it seems," he spluttered. "How long have you been standing there?"

The woman didn't answer. Turning her back, she mounted the steps. She was gone by the time Mark and Adria climbed to the parlor and entered the great hall.

"I will go ahead to my room," Adria said. "And — thank you." She was beginning to shiver again.

Mark squeezed her hands. "Remember what I said."

Wrapping herself in blankets, she huddled close to the fire. Strange that her forehead was so hot, yet she couldn't stop shivering...

She woke up with a start, realizing she had fallen asleep. But she still felt feverish. Perhaps a cup of tea. It would be difficult to bring herself to go downstairs in the darkness. There was no reason to be afraid of the dark, she told herself. So many dreadful things had happened. Fate couldn't possibly have more in store!

She drew on a cloak and, candle trembling in her hand, made her way to the kitchens. The door to the wine cellars was ajar. Would Mark be down there? Mark and their guests? She went to the door and listened. There was no sound. She made her tea. Then, carrying the pot with her, she moved toward the stairs.

She met a white-faced Dorrie coming down. The girl clutched at her, and Adria backed away, feeling a sense of revulsion toward the one who had brought so much trouble to the house.

"What is it, Dorrie?" she asked, trying to quiet the girl's wild babbling.

Dorrie fell to her knees, clutching the hem of her cloak. "I didn't want to 'urt nobody," she whined. "Now I want to 'elp. I know summat, see? Summat bad, wot's goin' to 'appen. You 'ave to stop 'im. Mayhap another spell, like —!"

Adria shivered again, but whether with illness or with anger, she did not know. "Get out of my way," she said, through gritted teeth. "You've done enough harm. Get out of my way, or I'll put a spell on *you*!"

Eyes popping with fear, Dorrie released her grip on the cloak. Adria brushed by her, hurrying up the stairs.

The tea had its desired effect, easing her shuddering body, though it could not ease her mind. She went to the window and looked down at the beach below, thinking of the thing that had stood there the night before.

She saw a light bobbing in the waves.

The ship? No, it still stood far out to sea, the moonlight picking out its sails. This light was nearer to the shore, though it seemed to be moving away. A small boat, perhaps? Who from Wyndspelle would slip out to the vessel at night? The boat was heading for the ship, she knew. For someone was signaling, now, with a swinging lantern.

It must be someone from this house. The craft from the chasm, since Vincente had taken the small dinghy he kept beached somewhere along the sands. Surely it could not be the Puritan folk, seeking to destroy Anthony's vessel. They were not seafaring men.

Perhaps she would wake Anthony. That idea died aborning as she thought of his harsh words.

It was later, much later, when she heard the moaning sound that brought her upright. It was Anthony, she knew. He was having another night of pain.

She leaped to her feet, then stopped, mind torn with indecision. She could not go to him. He wanted nothing more to do with her. He had shown her that.

Still, if he were ill…

Another moan ended her hesitation. Hurrying across the room, she paused with her hand on the tapestry. Then, lifting it, she put her hand to the door. It did not move, and she saw the thing that held it. The bolt.

The bolt which, in spite of all the confusion, Anthony had remembered to have installed. The bolt that said, *I do not want you. I do not need you, for any reason.*

CHAPTER 21

The next morning, the customary tray did not arrive. Her fire had gone out, and though it wasn't cold, there was a feeling of dampness in the room. Washing up in cold water, Adria fumbled into her clothing, wondering if things had gone wrong in the kitchens, or if she were to be ostracized henceforth; no longer mistress of Wyndspelle, but an unwelcome boarder, forced to fend for herself.

She had finished dressing and was brushing her hair when there was a tap at the door.

"Come in," she called, with a sense of relief. But the door did not open.

"It is I, Anthony. May I speak to you for a moment?"

Her heart pounding, she dropped the brush and rushed to open the door. Anthony inclined his blind face toward her, his expression somber.

"Things are at odds below stairs, milady. I believe we may require your assistance."

"What seems to be wrong, milord?"

"Mistress Murchison has injured her ankle and can but hobble. And Dorrie," his lips thinned, "Dorrie has disappeared."

"Disappeared!" The memory of the girl's frightened face struck Adria like a blow. "When? Where can she have gone?"

He shrugged. "Perhaps to her new friends in the settlement below."

To the Puritans? Not Dorrie — blowsy, slatternly, her manners none too circumspect. The Puritans would have none of her!

"I cannot think that," Adria blurted. "We must rout out the men and have them search —"

"It is too late for that. She left early in the night. Her bed has not been slept in."

"We still must look for her," Adria persisted. "What if she is ill or in danger?"

"Then she deserves it, does she not? You forget, milady, that she is a spy, an informer, and has brought trouble upon us all!" The man was unmoved.

"I will go down to the kitchens," Adria said, icily, "and see what I can do." She would search this house, the grounds, every inch of Wyndspelle. She would enlist Mark's aid.

In the kitchens she discovered that all was chaos. Mistress Murchison, gray-faced, sat in a wooden chair, her foot propped on a cheese box as she issued orders to Mother Moseby, who grumbled at the fire.

Adria carried the trays to the rooms above. The ladies received theirs with chill disdain, waiting for her to remove the covers and pour their tea. *Like a servant*, she thought, returning with Anthony's breakfast.

He received it at the door, closing it quickly against her, as if to be certain she would not enter his domain. Edwin Osmund, upon getting his tray, only grumbled at its tardiness. It was an angry Adria who climbed the steps the last time with a tray for Mark.

Mark took her wrist and drew her into his room. "I've got to talk to you."

"There is no time," she said. "I must get back. There is much to do, and Mistress Murchison is a hard taskmaster."

"But I must see you."

"Later," she said, then she plunged ahead. "Mark, Dorrie's gone, and I'm frightened. She tried to talk to me last night. She seemed terribly upset. Would you look for her?"

"I already have, lass," he said. "From the minute I heard." He indicated his cloak, thrown over a chair, a pair of wet boots leaning against each other. "I have been up since dawn. Mistress Murchison alerted me as soon as she rose to go to the kitchens."

"And you've searched the house?" Adria persisted.

"She is not in the house, Adria. Take my word for it." Taking the tray from her, he placed it on a table, then came toward her, reaching out to her.

She backed away. "I must hurry," she gasped. She fled to the safety of the kitchens.

The day was a shambles. No sooner had the trays been delivered than it was time to pick them up. Lady Jane needed assistance in doing her hair, and Adria bit back angry words as she combed it for her and piled it on top of her head. Every instinct within her urged her to give it a good hard tug. She was somewhat mollified, however, to note that the coquettish curls were false as Jane added them herself, settling them to drape across her snowy shoulders.

Unconscious that she was staring, Adria caught the girl's eyes inspecting her in the mirror also.

"You have such an interesting face," Jane cooed. "Your coloring is most unusual! You were born on these shores?"

Adria nodded, flushing under the mocking eyes. "Up the coast from here, a great distance." She faltered as the other girl smiled knowingly.

"Your mother must have had a liking for the natives," she said.

Adria started to answer, to say that her mother loved all creatures, but she stopped, aghast, as she caught the inference in the girl's remark. She dropped the jeweled brush, then whirled and ran from the room.

The day was dreadful. Soon it was time for a light luncheon. After that was cleared away, Adria finally found time to administer to the housekeeper's injury. The woman's ankle was swollen, but a little tender probing revealed that nothing was broken.

"How did it happen?" Adria asked.

It developed that, finding Dorrie missing in the early hours, Mistress Murchison had gone looking for her through the darkened house, and had slipped on the stairs. After Adria had applied compresses to the ankle and bound it, the woman reluctantly consented to be helped to her room.

Then there was dinner to prepare. Aiding Mother Moseby, chopping vegetables, lifting the heavier kettles, Adria realized how exhausted she was. Alternately hot and cold by turns, she was beginning to feel a little giddy with fever. She could not become ill! How would the household manage?

Or perhaps that wouldn't be such a bad idea! She could imagine Jane in the kitchen, smelling of onions; Lady Elizabeth fetching her own tea; Edwin Osmund scrubbing smoke-charred pots with that lace at his wrists, his artist's hands. She smiled at the pictures her imagination presented.

"Eeee?" Mother Moseby asked, shooting her a suspicious look, one eye settling on Adria's face, the other veering toward the wall. "Wot you thinkin'?"

"Nothing," Adria answered. "Nothing at all."

As she worked, however, she came to a decision. Dinner would not be served tonight. It would all be placed on the table, colonial style. Those who wished could help themselves.

She would not be placed in the position of a slavey before the guests.

Afterward, it seemed a mistake. She had forgotten Anthony's blindness and was forced to watch as the ladies, Elizabeth and Jane, made much of seeing that his plate was filled with items of his choice. She wasn't certain as to whom she hated most. Jane, Anthony — or herself for even caring.

Anthony reached for his goblet and it was empty. "The wine?" he asked, his dark brows raised.

Adria leaped to her feet. "I'll get it," she said, "Right away."

But Mark had already risen. "The lady has worked much too hard, Anthony," he said. "And she doesn't look well. I will go."

Adria felt a warm wave of gratitude at his words, but she refused. Only as she went down through the kitchens to the wine cellar did she realize how much she welcomed the respite from the table.

Candle in hand, she searched through the dusty bottles until she found the type Anthony preferred. It seemed different here, this night, she thought. She missed the booming sound. The waves washed in gently, with little wind, producing a sort of sigh — almost a sobbing. Her eyes went toward the trapdoor in the floor, the door that led to the chasm.

This night it was closed.

She set the candle down and attempted to open it. Her efforts were in vain. It was not only closed, it was locked.

"Dorrie?" she called softly. There was no answer. But the girl was hiding there, she felt sure of it. Disturbed by her suspicions, she picked up her candle and returned to the kitchens, placing the bottle and candle on the table as she searched for a corkscrew. Her hand felt sticky. She started to wipe it against her skirt. Instinct stopped her.

Holding it close to the candle flame, she saw that it was stained with red.

Blood!

Had her hand started bleeding again? She inspected it. The wound she had received from the splintered boulder had healed nicely. Then where had this stain come from? Frowning, she lifted the candlestick. The bottom of it, too, was coated with a foreign substance. Whatever it was, it had been picked up at the time she put the light down to open the trapdoor —

Wine! Of course, it was wine. Someone had spilled some, perhaps broken a bottle. And the puddle had evaporated, becoming thick and viscous.

Adria dipped water from a bucket into a basin, washing the holder, first, then her hands. Though she had put a name to the sticky substance, her earlier impression still stuck in her mind.

'Tis the house, she thought. *The way it cries tonight. And the walls.* It was eerie the way the water collected on the stone, like tears. A house that breathed, a house that sighed — and wept.

She opened the wine and carried it up to the table in the great hall. Seating herself, she found she was unable to eat. The thought that Dorrie might be locked in the chasm by mistake was too much to bear. Finally, during a lull in the conversation, she broke in, timidly.

"I had a thought about where Dorrie might have got to, milord. I wonder —"

Anthony's fist slammed down. "I do not wish to hear the girl's name mentioned again!" he thundered. "She's a troublemaker, and we're well rid of her! Is that clear, milady?" Before Adria could answer, he stood up, tossing his napkin to the table. "Mark," he said, abruptly, "I have some business to discuss with you. So, if you ladies will excuse us —?"

The ladies did, but they were disgruntled at his abrupt departure. They went to their rooms, followed by Edwin Osmund.

Adria left the table, unfastened a ring of keys from her waist, and headed for the wine cellar. Putting her candle down, she tried several keys, finally coming upon one that turned in the lock. At last, she managed to tug the door open. Down one step. Two.

"Dorrie?" she called.

There was no answer.

Had Dorrie done the thing she had threatened to do the night Adria gave her the charm? She could not imagine Dorrie throwing herself into the sea.

Adria looked fearfully down at the waters that lapped at the entrance, white froth moon-silvered where it touched the steps. Moving down the stone stairs, candle flickering in her hand, an icy finger of fear touched the back of her neck. She jumped as something moved along the wall. It was only a pattern of light and shadow, made by the moon on the waters below.

When she reached the place where the chasm hollowed inward to make a room, she stopped, grateful for the torch that burned here constantly, keeping watch over a king's treasure.

Dorrie was not here. And there was no other place to hide. Unless —!

Adria's eyes turned toward the boat, drawn up in its usual place. Her heart throbbed as she saw that it was covered with a canvas like that other time. She stood for a moment, mouth dry, wings of fear fluttering in her brain, wanting only to turn and flee.

Of course the boat was covered, to keep the interior dry! And below the boat, on the other side, would be a perfect place for a frightened girl to hide.

Carefully, she inched her way down the slippery stairs. "Dorrie," she coaxed, somehow reassured by the sound of her own voice, "Dorrie? Answer me! I won't hurt you. I didn't mean what I said last night."

She reached the dory and her heart sank. The girl was not here. To be certain, she went down a few more steps, stopping only when a wave purled in, wetting her to the ankles. Holding the candle high, she peered around the small craft, into the corner between the vessel and the stone wall, where a figure might crouch in the shadows.

And then she saw it. The limp hand, trailing in the water. It lifted in a helpless gesture on the next incoming wave.

Water dragged at Adria's skirts as she stood frozen. *Emma! Dear God, the body of Emma, still here!* Mark had lied. Lied!

No, he had not. For this had been the boat that brought their guests ashore.

Adria stood rigid for a long time, fearing that her knees would give way beneath her. At last, taking a deep breath, she moved. White-faced, she reached for an edge of the canvas with reluctant fingers, pulling it back —

The dead eyes of Dorrie reflected back the candle flame.

CHAPTER 22

The candle slipped from Adria's nervous fingers. It bounded, still burning, to the dark waters below where it was extinguished with a sizzling sound. For a moment, the girl did not miss its light. Blind with fear, she stared toward the thing in the boat, its image indelible in her mind. A picture of Dorrie's face, mouth open, twisted in a silent scream. The coarse hair disheveled and bloody.

Then, sensing, rather than seeing the darkness that closed in about her, Adria retreated upward toward the torch-lit cavern, hand pressed against her lips. At length the full horror of what she had seen overwhelmed her. She turned to run.

At the top of the stairs she ran full speed into a figure that emerged from the shadows. Arms closed about her. An unknown hand sought her mouth, cutting off the shriek that had only begun, half-smothering her. She fought back, unable to breathe, until she finally lay limp in her attacker's arms. As he dragged her, unresisting, down the steps she was sick with the certainty that she too was going to her death.

Instead, there was an impression of light through her closed lids. Flickering light. She had been carried into the cavern where the torch burned. Her face was being lifted, turned —

"God's teeth!"

She looked into Mark's amazed eyes and, with a little whimpering sound, went into his arms, shivering, unable to stop.

"Adria!" he choked. "Adria! What are you doing down here?" Then, after a pause, "You — found her?"

She couldn't speak, but she moved her head against his chest in silent assent.

"I'm sorry," he said, somberly. "I had hoped you would continue to believe she ran away. I came down here tonight to — to —"

He didn't need to finish. She knew the nature of his grisly errand. Dorrie was to follow her mistress, Emma, in death.

"How?" she asked, finally. "Who —?"

He shook his head. "We don't know," he said, his voice bleak. "Mistress Murchison found her this morning, near the stairs that lead down to the kitchens. That's how she injured her ankle, hurrying to rouse me. She needn't have rushed so. The girl had been dead some hours then."

At the foot of the stairs! The steps where Adria had met her the night before! Where the girl had knelt, clinging to Adria's cloak, pleading for her attention! What was it she had said? *"I know summat, see? Summat bad, wot's goin' to 'appen. You 'ave to stop 'im —"*

Stop *who*? Who had reason to kill Dorrie?

"Vincente!" The word escaped Adria's trembling lips before she could stop it. Vincente had every reason to hate Dorrie after what she had done to Prudence Shanks. She looked up at Mark, her face white as she waited for his affirmation.

"Not Vincente, lass." His voice was kind. "Vincente is gone, remember? He cannot possibly have returned so soon."

"Petro, then," she said, stubbornly. "Or Rico. Vincente could have made arrangements —"

"The rear door was locked. They could not have got in."

"You 'ave to stop 'im," Dorrie had said. *Him!* Vincente gone, the others barred from the house! That left Mark — Mark, who held her now in comforting arms — Anthony, and Edwin

Osmund. She could not see the artist as capable of murder. And Anthony? Anthony was blind! A blind man could not —

Dully, she remembered the shadow in the parlor as she had gone upstairs. Anthony needed no light to move by. And his other senses were alert. He could catch a whisper of movement, the rustle of a dress, the turning of a page.

And he had reason to hate Dorrie.

"She's a troublemaker, and we're well rid of her!" he had said.

Well rid of her.

As if he sensed her thoughts, Mark said, "Say nothing to Anthony regarding this, lass."

"But he knows of it, surely! You've told him!"

"The subject has not been mentioned, yet I would say he knows."

She was rigid in his arms. "What are you saying, Mark? Surely you don't think that Anthony —?"

"I think that Anthony is mad. Given to violent tempers and vengeful toward anything that threatens him, his desires, or his house. And I think you are in danger, milady."

"I cannot believe Anthony would hurt Dorrie!" Her voice was thin and she was near to crying. "Or that he would injure me in any way. Besides, how would he —?" She stopped short. She had been about to ask how Anthony knew Dorrie would be there, on the steps to the kitchens at that particular time, when it dawned on her that her husband might have heard Adria's footsteps along the balcony and followed. Was it possible that Dorrie was not the intended victim, but Adria herself?

She drew back from Mark's comforting arms and looked up at him, her hands pressed to her cheeks. "Nay," she whispered. "Nay —"

"I've stood beside Anthony for a long time," Mark said, "but the bounds of friendship can be only stretched so far. He has all he needs now. Wyndspelle, where he can be lord of the manor; the Lady Jane. He needs me no longer." He led Adria toward the steps, pointing toward the waters. "Three days hence, the ship out there will weigh anchor and set sail. I shall be aboard her, and I do not desire to return."

Adria made a little cry of disbelief. Surely he did not intend to desert her!

"I want you to come with me," he said.

She looked up into the handsome face, haloed with gold in the torch light, the steady blue eyes that touched her own so lovingly. Mark, her protector. Mark, who had said, *"I love you."* Words that Anthony had never said, even when —

There was a sound from above. A pebble, bounding down from step to step. Dislodged by something that moved in the wine cellars overhead. Beyond the trapdoor.

Mark's face went ashen. For a moment, he stood absolutely still, his hand raised in a gesture of silence. Then he went up the stone stairs, silent as a shadow, leaving Adria alone in the chasm — except for the thing in the boat below.

She waited for a long time, not daring to breathe, and at last he reappeared, still shaken.

"No one there," he said, unsteadily. "Still, 'tis not safe to leave things undone." He gestured toward the boat with its gruesome burden. "I have work to do this night. Can you find your way to your rooms, lass?"

When she assured him that she could, he pulled her once more into the cavern, touching her trembling mouth with his lips. She didn't want to leave the shelter of his arms, to return to the silent house and face its night terrors, but he pushed her gently away.

"I must hurry now. There is a candle in the cellars to light your way. And, lass — think on what I said."

"I will," she whispered. "I will."

Climbing the steps, she flinched as she heard the splash of the boat's launching. Before she entered through the trapdoor, the splashing of oars began. Mark had already bent to the task ahead. Soon the body of Dorrie, too, would drift down silently, as Emma's had. Into the cold wet darkness of the sea.

Adria began to shiver again. Snatching up the candle, she ran upward to the kitchens where she stood for a moment, her knees too weak to carry her; hearing the sighing of the house, seeing the weeping stones that formed the walls.

She rushed up into the parlor and ran across the hall to the stairs that led to the balcony. But as she moved, the door to the study crashed open. Anthony stood there, a monstrous figure against the light.

"'Tis you, milady?" he asked. "I thought I heard the sound of your step."

He came toward her, and Adria shrank, her mouth dry with fear. Her eyes darted to the balcony above. No one there! The others had been long abed, and she and Anthony were alone in the vast, echoing hall.

"Where have you been?" he asked. "Why are you wandering the house at night? Do you still delude yourself that you will find the girl?"

"N — nay," Adria stammered. "'Tis only that I've caught a chill."

It was quite true. She could not control her shuddering body. Anthony, reaching out to take her arm, could not help but be aware of it. He lifted his hand, seeking her forehead.

"You are burning with fever," he said, "and your hands are like ice."

"I am quite all right," Adria said, through chattering teeth. "I beg your leave to retire." Without waiting for an answer, she hurried toward her room.

She found the cat waiting at her door. She removed her gown, tearing at it with trembling fingers, pulling her nightdress over her shivering body. Then she crawled beneath the covers, still quaking, holding the cat close for warmth.

Was it a chill, she wondered, or fear? Fear that had been with her since she entered this cursed house? Remembering the locket still pinned inside the bodice of her daytime gown, she forced herself to rise and remove it, fastening it inside her sleeping shift. Immediately, she felt warmer. It was a charm, she thought. It brought her comfort. But it had not brought comfort to Dorrie.

Dorrie —

Dorrie, dead, her coarse hair matted with blood, her face grotesque with fear, bulging eyes reflecting a candle flame —

She drew in her breath, raggedly, then bit her lip to suppress the sound. As if it had been a cue for someone, there was a tapping at her door.

She sat up, a wild hope rising in her breast. Mark! He had returned. But no, there had not been time. "Yes?" she whispered. Then louder, "Yes?"

"Open the door," Anthony's voice came from the hallway. "I have something for you."

"But — I am abed."

"Then I will bring it in." He sounded exasperated.

Leaping from her bed, Adria snatched at a cloak, pulling it around her. She went to the door that led onto the balcony and opened it a crack. Anthony stood there, a goblet of wine in hand.

"I need nothing," she told him. "Though I thank you —"

"Nonsense!" His face was a dark, saturnine mask in the glow of her candle, his blind eyes unreadable. "You are still shaking, milady. I hear it in your voice. You will drink this."

She took it from him, flinching at the touch of his fingers on hers, and closed the door against him. How easily her doubts were aroused, she thought. And how quickly they were allayed. One moment she was terrified of her husband, the next, ready to weep with gratitude at a small kindness.

She was confused. So confused.

Taking a sip from the goblet, she shuddered again, this time with distaste. She liked not the taste of spirits. This, warmed, was even worse. And the color — it made her think of blood, of the stickiness from the candlestick that had stained her hand earlier in the evening. Even now, she could feel it!

Putting the goblet on the table beside the bed, she went to the basin and washed her hands in the cold water, scrubbing at them. They still did not feel clean, she thought as she wiped them dry. They might never feel clean again! Turning, she discovered the cat had leaped to the table where he licked at the ruby liquid with a long pink tongue, his green eyes daring her to interfere.

"Nay!" she scolded. "Nay!" But as she reached for him, he emitted a low growl. She considered the animal for a while, then shrugged. After all, he was accustomed to such imbibing. If it pleasured him, she would let it be. Besides, something, perhaps the memory of blood upon her hands, was making her feel quite ill. Strange that she should be so warm now, after feeling so cold a short time before. She had a smothery sensation and it was difficult to breathe. Perhaps if she opened the window the air in the room might freshen.

She parted the drapes and fought the glass open, breathing in great gulps of the night air. In a little while, her vision cleared.

She could see a tiny light bobbing on the dark sea — a light that marked the little boat, and Mark Welles on his tragic errand.

She turned back to the room — and the cat.

The wine in the glass was low and the cat was nowhere to be seen. Rounding the bed, she found him on the floor, writhing, his black fur flecked with foam from his open mouth. For a moment she watched him uneasily. Was this drunkenness? Had she allowed him to take too much? Her eyes went, stricken, to the goblet. Surely he'd taken no more than he was given at dinner the other night. Then he did not behave in such fashion.

Reaching for the animal, she jerked her hand back, staring in dismay at the scratch that bled from elbow to wrist. The cat was ill! Crazed with pain!

The thought that he might have come into contact with some rabid creature flickered in her mind with a brief fear. He seemed to be suffering. She stood, at a loss as she debated the best course of action. Should she call Anthony? Or run for Mistress Murchison?

"Kitty," she said softly. "Kitty!" And as she spoke, the black cat endured one final convulsion and stiffened, mouth open, revealing his white teeth.

Adria dropped to her knees beside him. He was dead! Dead! Dear God, did everything that entered this house have to die?

He had been all right only a few moments before. He had purred in her arms! What kind of feline disease could strike so suddenly? What had done this to him?

Her eyes went to the goblet of wine, its contents red and winking in the candlelight. The cat had been all right until he drank the wine that was meant for her. She took a few steps toward it, tentatively, her hand stretched toward the glass.

Then, a pain doubling her, a wave of nausea blinding her, she rushed to the basin where she was dreadfully, wretchedly ill.

Poison, she thought when it was over. Poison! Just a sip of it had made her ill. The wine had been poisoned!

Dorrie's death had been a mistake. A blind man's mistake. It was Adria Anthony wanted dead.

CHAPTER 23

Adria came to a decision during that night. As frightened as she was, she could still not leave with Mark and live with her conscience.

Her marriage to Anthony had been forced upon her, but it was consummated with her willing participation. Therefore, it was a binding one. If Anthony was at the root of the dreadful things that had happened, then he was mad. She had taken him in sickness and in health, therefore she must stand by him. She hated him and feared him, but she would stay.

There was a gentle tap at the door. She climbed down from her bed, trembling with weariness, and opened it a crack. Petro with her tray. Food she dared not touch and dared not send away. Taking it from him, she carried it to the table.

The goblet was gone! And with it, her proof of poison. She dropped to her knees, peering under the bed. Her proof was not all gone, though she wished it were. The body of the little cat was still there where she had wrapped him in a shawl and hidden him. She must ask Mark to help her spirit him away —

If Mark was in any mood to do her favors when he heard what she had to tell him! But he would do it, if he loved her —

The sight of the little animal, strangely shrunken in death, made her feel faint. Either she was still a bit feverish or it had turned unseasonably warm. There was a still, sullen feeling in the atmosphere.

Crossing to the window, she looked out. The sea was calm, an almost greasy look to it, like a pot that has not yet begun to boil, yet underneath the beginning turbulence presses up.

At the thought of what lay beneath those waters, Adria turned to the tray. She had no intention of joining Emma and Dorrie, not if she could help it.

But how would she manage to stay alive? Meals taken in company should be safe if she ate only what the others ate. She must manage a pot of tea for herself in the kitchens. Perhaps an egg cooked in its shell would be impervious to poisons. In the meantime, she must dispose of this food in some fashion.

She emptied the solids into a heavy wool cape, thrusting that also beneath the bed. The tea, she poured into the slops. For the present, she must rely on Mark to dispose of these discards. But what would she do when he was gone?

Her eyes filled with tears. She wished she had not come to Wyndspelle. If only she had been a quiet, submissive girl, obedient to Reverend Potts' admonitions! She would have married Joseph Shanks and lived peacefully for the rest of her life. Not knowing the fire of Anthony's love, or the warm affection of Mark Welles, but — peacefully.

A vision of Joseph came into her mind: his weak chin stubbled with beard, his bony, age-spotted hands. She shivered.

The house was already astir when she came downstairs. Anthony and Edwin Osmund were in the upper room, the artist proclaiming that he was suffering from an attack of inspiration. Mark, Lady Elizabeth, and Jane were at work in the chasm.

Adria wondered at the urgency that led them to be up and about so early this day. Surely they could not know of Mark's intentions. Or could he have told them, and enlisted their aid, in order to leave nothing undone when he went? There seemed to be a friendliness between them.

And with Mark gone, they would be completely in charge here. If he hinted that he was taking Adria, they would be delighted. Jane would be especially happy. The Lady Jane, with her fair white skin —

A skin that kept its fashionable pallor through the use of powders. Powders that could be fatal if taken in the wrong proportions. Powders that might be slipped into a glass of warm wine!

Adria stood bemused with her thoughts until she felt Mistress Murchison's questioning gaze. "Did you want something, mum?" the housekeeper asked.

"Nay, I — what may I do to help this morning?"

"There is naught. My ankle is better. I'm quite capable of handling the household now."

"But I insist," Adria said firmly. "You should be off your foot as much as possible."

"You don't look well yourself," the woman grumbled.

"I am quite all right," Adria lied. Though she was tense with nerves and lack of sleep, she knew she wouldn't rest until she saw Mark. She could not go down into the chasm since the ladies were there and she wished to talk to him alone. But she intended to wait here in the kitchens until he passed through. Since they couldn't speak before the housekeeper, they must arrange a time and place to meet.

She remembered the warmth of Mark's arms, the expression in his eyes as he said, *"I love you."* With Mark, there would be freedom. Here, only the consolation of knowing she was fulfilling her duty. And fear. Fear, with every step she took, with each bite of food.

Her attempts to speak to Mark were unsuccessful. He came through the kitchens only twice, both times careful to keep his eyes averted from hers.

Had Mark guessed at Adria's decision to remain? It seemed to the girl that his normal merriment was dimmed. His face looked tired and there were dark circles beneath his eyes. Remembering Dorrie's death and how he'd had to manage her burial in the night, she could understand his fatigue. She longed to comfort him, put her arms about him...

But she was Anthony's wife. Soon Mark would be gone from Wyndspelle. It would be better that way.

When the group came up from below, to ready themselves for the evening meal, Adria was at the churn before the fire. Her bare arms glistened in the firelight as she worked the dasher up and down. Her first knowledge that they had emerged from the chasm came at the sound of Jane's voice.

"What a charming picture! The country wife! Portrait of a dairy maid. Edwin must see this, I vow!"

"Indeed," Lady Elizabeth put in. "He has been longing to do some rural colonial scenes. And here he has a perfect model. They would adore this at Court!"

As the two women discussed her as if she were not present, Adria lifted stricken eyes to Mark. He stood, his face averted, slapping a pair of gloves against the palm of his hand.

"Speaking of portraits," he said, "how is Anthony's coming along? Do you know?"

"Splendidly," Jane enthused. "'Tis a marvelous likeness!"

According to the artist, no one was allowed to view the portrait until it was completed. "You have seen it, then?" Adria asked, her voice tight in her throat.

"But of course," the girl purred. "Edwin has consulted me from the very beginning. He prides himself on revealing the inner being. And, after all, I believe I know Anthony better than most —" *Better than you, his wife*, her voice implied.

Adria bit her lip, then looked down at the churn, feeling the change that indicated the butter had gathered. "'Tis ready," she said to the housekeeper. "I will leave the rest to you. I must dress for dinner."

She hurried to her room. There she changed into a fresh gown, thinking of the evening ahead. There was much to concern her. Her nerves were ragged, and she must hold her tongue against Jane's malicious barbs. In addition, she need be alert, eating only what appeared to be safe to swallow. And some way, some time, she had to get Mark alone. Tell him of her decision. Ask him to remove the small dead animal from beneath the bed, else she would not sleep…

In the kitchens Mistress Murchison limped about her duties.

"Let us serve colonial style," Adria suggested.

The housekeeper wouldn't hear of it. She, herself, would set the table and one of the men would handle the serving. Her manner conveyed a subtle reproach for the way in which Adria managed things while the woman was confined to her room. Adria watched as Mistress Murchison mounted the stairs, then turned at a cackle from Mother Moseby.

"Puts a store on class, she does! Come from a great 'ouse, real posh like, 'er leddyship did. *Scullery maid,* 'er was!" The old woman spat contemptuously into the hearth to prove her disdain for the housekeeper.

"How did she come here?" Adria asked.

The old woman, garrulous for once, spun much the tale Dorrie had told. Sir Anthony had taken Emma from gaol and married her. At the same time, he purchased the freedom of Dorrie and Mother Moseby. At Emma's request, they brought her sister, Amanda Murchison, along with them when they set out to sea.

"Eee, 'er's a wrong un," the old woman added with relish. "'Er's a bad un. I can tell you things about 'er, I can! And 'er so 'oity-toity! An eye for the men, 'er 'as!"

Adria blinked, startled at her words and her vehemence. "You mean — *Mistress Murchison?*"

The crone laid a crooked finger alongside of her nose and nodded wisely. "A word to the wise," she said. "Summat to think on. Like 'oo done poor Emma in?"

Was she insinuating the housekeeper had done it? Murdered her own sister? Such a possibility was beyond belief! Before Adria could question her further, she heard Mistress Murchison's limping footsteps on the stairs. Mother Moseby gave her a wall-eyed look of warning and turned to stir at a pot as the woman re-entered the room.

"'Tis all done, mum," she said, panting a little. "We won't be needing your help here."

Dismissed, Adria climbed the stairs. Mother Moseby had been trying to tell her something, but what? The conversation was only that of an old gossip. The idea of Mistress Murchison having an eye for men — it was ridiculous! While she was not unattractive, in a stern, unbending way, it would be difficult to imagine her in a man's arms.

When she reached the great hall, the others were waiting. They seated themselves at table amid a spate of desultory conversation. Due to the warmth of the evening, the fire on the hearth had not been lighted. There seemed to be a heaviness in the air. The furniture felt sticky to the touch and the house seemed dead and still. The faces around the table were wan and fretful under the pressure of the atmosphere.

"This will bring a storm," Anthony said, moodily. "I sense it, Mark. I must get out to the ship, tomorrow."

"There is no need for haste —"

"But there is. Captain Faulkes must pick up that load of lumber down the coast and be on his way before he's weathered in. Then he is to trade for rum in Barbados and on to England in the spring —"

"I have conveyed your orders," Mark said quickly. "Captain Faulkes will follow the best course. You need not concern yourself."

Anthony slammed his fist on the table. "Damn it, man! That's not the problem. You of all people, should understand my plight. I *want* to go on board! To feel the ship beneath my feet again, to feel like a man instead of a coddled, useless hulk! And I intend to stand upon my own deck tomorrow at the latest."

"The morrow would be difficult," Mark said in a strange, muffled voice. "Perhaps the next day. It has the feeling that weather is making up, but it will be some while yet. Trust me, Anthony. Have I not always looked to your interests?"

"I have always put faith in your word," Anthony said, "but —"

"Then do so now."

"Damme," Edwin Osmund put in, peevishly. "Such a to-do over nothing! And over boarding a vessel that heaves and rolls and makes one want to puke! 'Tis not for me!"

"Nor I," Jane shuddered.

"Besides," the small artist continued, "I will not hear of you leaving on such an expedition!" He raised his soft little hands, flexing his fingers. "You will sit for me until the portrait is completed. The magic is with me now. It is going well, and I shall not be cheated, sir. In the name of art, I ask for one more day!"

Adria joined, dutifully, in the ripple of laughter that ran around the table at the man's fierce words, then raised her eyes to meet those of the servant who had entered bearing the main course.

Vincente!

Vincente was back, his presence a reminder of Prudence Shanks and her ordeal beneath Adria's window. An ordeal that might not have taken place, had it not been for Adria's conversation with Dorrie. She wondered, again, if he might have plotted Dorrie's death, working with Anthony or one of his Portuguese companions. If he'd had anything to do with the attempt on her own life.

He served the remainder of the dinner, moving quietly, his face expressionless and his eyes unfathomable.

When the meal was ended, Mark stated that he planned to return to his preparations for the voyage. Adria opened her mouth, intending to offer to help him. It would be an excuse to talk to him alone. But he had already turned to Jane and to Lady Elizabeth, who were viewing him with indecision.

"Like Osmund," Mark smiled, "I believe in finishing a job when I feel inspired. Ladies?"

They trailed off after him, the artist trotting along to his room, leaving Adria and Anthony at table, Vincente clearing away.

Anthony stood. "Let this go for now," he told Vincente abruptly. "I must see you in the study at once. I want a full report on your journey and to talk of the matters we discussed before you left." Then, turning to Adria, "You will excuse us, milady, since our conversation concerns your welfare."

Then Adria was left alone.

She cleared the table, stacking the dishes for Vincente to carry down when his conference with Anthony was done. Anthony's last words had left her confused and a little frightened. It was understandable that Anthony would wish to hear the results of Vincente's trip down the coast, but why should Anthony discuss her own well-being with a servant?

Unless they were deciding her fate behind that closed door. And what had they conferred about before Vincente went away? Dorrie's impending murder? Or an attempt upon Adria's life? Since the wine had failed to do its job properly, were they now hatching a more foolproof plan?

The door was shut against her and she could hear nothing. The candles above her had burned low. The room smelled of dampness and hot wax. Behind her, the great hearth gaped blackly in the shadows, like an open mouth exhaling a scent of dead ashes.

Adria's head throbbed and she put a hand to it. She was a little feverish still. Perhaps that was why her imagination was running wild. She had done enough here tonight, and a night's rest might help her put things into a clearer perspective. Certainly, there would be no way of seeing Mark alone until morning. Leaving the soiled dishes stacked neatly, she returned to her room.

There, she changed into her nightdress and went to the window, drawing the draperies back to let the fresh air in. But there was not even a hint of breeze this night. Below, the waves came in lazily under the bright moon, black except for shreds of foam that coiled around the rock-strewn shore like snakes, and a light that bobbed and flickered on the waters.

Mark's boat. Moving steadily toward the ship. Did he go there nightly? Slipping away like a thief —?

A thief? What a name to call Mark! But once it was there, it would not go away. Mark's nightly trips to the ship, his access to the gems in the cavern. It did look suspicious. But he would not steal from Anthony's stores. Mark was the man's most trusted friend.

Perhaps he had his own possessions cached below and was slipping them away, a few at a time. Certainly, Jane and Lady

Elizabeth would not allow the jewels to leave the premises, not unless they went with them!

She shied away from the preposterous notion. Mark would never enter into a pact that would hurt Anthony. He could not desert him, leaving him blind, destitute on these shores. Had Mark not said, *"We will go away, just the two of us"*?

The ladies would not welcome Adria's presence if there were such plans afoot!

For a moment, she almost wished it were true. That they would all go and leave her here with Anthony. If he were mad, as Mark suggested, it was something that might heal with time.

Dreaming again, she thought bitterly. A dream that was as fragile as the idea that she and Anthony might have a little house together. Children. Or walk on warm sands under blue, smiling skies. A dream.

She had to face reality, now, and reality was a nightmare. A dreadful waking dream in which witches walked and fires were set. A nightmare that included poison administered by Anthony's own hand.

She was tired. So tired! The battle with her conscience that persuaded her to stay at Wyndspelle had left her emotionally exhausted, drained, sapped of strength.

Wearily, she turned toward her bed and threw back the coverlet. The blood drained from her face. Her hand went to her lips to suppress a strangled cry as she backed away, her eyes wide with horror.

For there, beneath the spread, back arched and stiffened in death, was the body of the cat.

What fiendish hand had placed him in her bed?

CHAPTER 24

Adria stood dazed with shock. Who would do a thing like this? Only someone who was mad — or who wanted to drive *her* mad! She backed away, unable to take her eyes from the dead creature on the bed.

Poor animal, she thought, pulling herself together, her eyes blurring with tears. Poor little thing, to be used in such a way! The horror lay not in the pitiful little body, but in the intent of the person who placed it there.

She could not stay in this room! Wrapping a cloak about her shoulders, she stepped out into the hall, then realized there was no place to go. She could not go to Mark. He was on his way to the vessel. And the ladies would be of little comfort in her situation. Anthony and Vincente would still be in the study below, and she would not go to them in any case. Mistress Murchison? Mother Moseby?

She would wait for Mark. But she could not wait here. Nor in her room. Uneasily, she gazed up and down the shadowed hall, then ran silently, on bare feet, the length of the balcony. Opening the door, she slipped inside, grateful that a candle burned on his bedside table. She had not thought of bringing light.

Mark's room was a lovely one, she realized, and suited him. It was done in strange shades: peacock blues, pale greens, touches of gold here and there. It was neat and orderly and now almost empty of Mark's possessions, pointing up his imminent departure, making it seem final.

The thought of his leaving struck her like a blow. Within the week, there would be nothing here of Mark. Nothing at all. And there would be no one to rely upon, save herself. Drearily, she thought of trying to return to her room. She could not bring herself to take the first step. How was she going to survive?

Sinking into a high-backed chair before the dead fire, she waited. And at last, she fell asleep.

"God's teeth!"

Adria jerked awake at Mark's outburst. Before she could speak, he had grasped her shoulders. "What are you doing here, lass? How long have you been here? Did anyone see you come?" His face was white and pinched with fatigue; his lips looked blue.

"Nay," she said. And, to her dismay, burst into tears, gasping out her story of poisoning in such confusion that he had to make her repeat it. She finished with the tale of the thing in her bed.

He looked as stricken as she felt. "I was afraid of this," he kept saying. "Afraid! Adria, we will slip away the day after tomorrow. Can you manage until then? Taking care with what you eat, and —"

"I am not going. I cannot."

"Don't be a fool, lass," he said, roughly. "You must! Can't you see you're in danger?"

"He is my husband," she said, forlornly.

He stared down at her. "You fool," he said. "You little Puritan fool!" Then he threw back his head and began to laugh. "You are no more wedded to Anthony Mordelle than you are to me! Think you that was a marriage? I am a ship's captain, lass — empowered to marry you to someone at sea. Wyndspelle is on the land!"

Adria shrank, her body turning to ice as her heart contracted at his words. "You cannot mean this!" As the expression on his face declared that he did, she asked, numbly, "Did — does Anthony know this?"

"Whether he does or not, I do not know. After all, it would make no difference. The marriage was only a convenience."

"Convenience," Adria repeated in a dull voice. "A convenience."

"Be that as it may, you are free, lass. Or you will be, as soon as I can steal you away from here. Now, I'm devilishly tired and have only an hour or two for rest. So, with your permission, I'll remove the offensive object from your room." He waved a staying hand as she attempted to rise. "Wait here," he said. "Shield the candle, so I will not be seen as I open the door."

Adria heard the door close softly behind him, then nothing more as he moved down the hall on silent feet. She was listening with her ears, but her mind was still on what Mark had told her.

"Convenience," she said to herself. "Convenience."

Convenience for Anthony, perhaps, and for Adria at the beginning, but now she had another word for it. An ugly word. *Adultery.*

The image of Reverend Potts appeared behind her lids. Reverend Potts, her own angel of vengeance, with his ranting voice that spoke of evil, his pointing finger and fanatic eyes.

"The wages of sin is death!" his words echoed in her mind. *"The wages of sin is death! The wages of —"*

The door opened and Mark entered. He looked at Adria for a moment, a strange expression in his eyes. Finally, he said, "There is nothing there, lass. It is gone."

She sprang to her feet. "But it was there!" she cried. "The — the cat was there, in my bed, beneath the coverlet! It was there! Dear God!" She burst into tears. "Believe me, Mark! You've got to believe me!"

"I do! I do!" He put his hands on her shoulders. They were cold. She could feel them even through her cloak. Like ice. And that expression in his eyes was of fear.

"I believe you, Adria. The thing that concerns me is this. Whoever put the animal there has taken it away. And that person knew you were not in your own room. That person knew you were here! They may think there's something going on between us, and I can't afford to let anything jeopardize my plans. God's teeth! I've waited so long —" His face was pallid, filmed with perspiration; his teeth clenched. Then he relaxed. "We'll have to take things as they come," he said. "Right now, the important thing is to get you back to your room. Perhaps I can make one more trip before dawn. You will go with me, lass?"

Why not? she thought, dully. There was naught to gain by staying. Nothing sinful in breaking the vows of what had not been a marriage, but a mockery. She had enough sin on her soul to last a lifetime, anyway.

"Yes," she said, "I will go."

Mark's face was triumphant as he pulled her to him and kissed her mouth. "'Twas the right decision, lass," he murmured. "I love you, and I will care for you always."

Her heart went out to him in an ache of affection as she closed her eyes against the memory of Anthony's blind, haunted features. Perhaps this was what true love should be. Not the blaze that had burned within her the night her husband came to her bed.

The husband who was not a husband, with his love that was not love, but a need. She had merely been a substitute for the woman he could not have; the wife of the brother he had slain. A convenience.

Adultery.

She stiffened in Mark's arms. Perhaps he would not want her now. "I have much to confess," she whispered. "There are things I must tell you —"

"I, too." He smiled down at her. "I have much to confess. Yet, with love, all can be forgiven. Let us say that it is even, and this is to be a new beginning."

His face blurred through her tears and she went into his arms again, this time of her own free will.

At last, he put her from him. "I must work a little faster," he said, "now that I have such a goal. We will try to leave at midnight, the day after tomorrow. And we must be very careful. Say nothing to anyone in this house. Lady Elizabeth, Jane, Osmund, Mistress Murchison. Tell no one. Can you find your way to your room in the darkness?"

"Yes, but —"

He put a finger to her lips. "No more questions tonight. We must hurry." With a final kiss, he opened the door for her, closing it behind her, and she hurried down the hall.

To get to her own room, she had to run the gamut of all the doors along the balcony. After Mark's door was Edwin Osmund's. Then the stair room fitted into the ell. As she turned, the door to the stair room opened and she flinched, blinded momentarily, by the candle flame the intruder held.

At last she was able to make out his face. The dark, expressionless features of Vincente who stood silent, observing her gravely.

She was frozen for a moment, unable to move. Then, gathering her cloak about her, she fled to her room. Safely inside, face flaming, she wondered what the man had thought. She could only have come from Mark's room — or the artist's. Barefoot, disheveled from sleeping in a chair, her hair down! How must it have appeared to the man?

Then she thought, drearily, that it didn't make much difference. She had looked like what she was! What Anthony had helped her to become. A harlot.

The word hammered away at her, and she turned her thoughts to Mark. Mark, whose loyalty to Anthony had kept him tied here until he had done all that was humanly possible for his friend.

But why was he slipping away under cover of darkness? Why did he not just go to Anthony and tell him he intended to leave Wyndspelle? Was it possible that Anthony, in his possessiveness, would refuse to let him go? That he would fly into a rage that might end in one or the other being hurt?

She had sensed fear in Mark tonight. Possibly that was the reason. Mark feared he might have to do harm to his blind friend in order to protect himself.

It was all too confusing. She asked herself questions she wished she had put to Mark before she left his room. Why had their guests been working with him in the chasm? It was almost as if the portrait painting had been a diversion to keep Anthony out of the way. What part did the newcomers play? Had Mark told them he was going? And if he had, why had he counseled her to be so secretive about his plans?

Her head throbbed. She felt depressed. She should be overjoyed, knowing she would soon be away from this cursed house; safe from the forces that seemed determined to destroy her; from the vengeance of the Puritans below — and with Mark, who loved her.

But why could they not leave now? What was this work he must attend to? Those frequent trips to the vessel? Stores for the voyage? Casks of water, perhaps, and food for their journey?

Over and over, the thoughts milled through her mind. Anthony's perfidy, Mark's love, the poisoned wine, Dorrie's dead face. Lady Elizabeth, Jane, Edwin Osmund. Vincente. When she finally slept, to wake in a tumble of garments, she was still exhausted and almost too stiff to move.

She had come a long way from the girl who had always slept on a pallet of straw. A long way.

But with the dawn, she was able to face her plight in a colder, more objective light. Anthony was not her husband. She owed him nothing. As far as Mark was concerned, she need not question his motives. It was enough to know he was going to help her to escape.

She must get through this waiting period safely. And to start with, she would go down to the kitchens before her tray was brought, and prepare her own breakfast.

She donned a morning gown and stepped out onto the balcony, glancing down into the great shadowed hall below. Her senses were alerted to the sound of movement. But where—?

Then she saw Edwin Osmund. The little artist was on his hands and knees, peering into the ashes of the dead fireplace, his stretched breeches bobbing like a pale moon beneath his parted coattails as he crept about, making a mewing sound.

What in the name of heaven—?

Hurrying down the stairs, she walked up behind him. "Sir Edwin?"

The little man jumped, attempted to sit back on his heels and lost his balance. He looked for a moment, like a choleric, red-faced beetle turned upon its back and helpless. Adria had to fight back a desire to laugh as she extended a helping hand.

"Damme," the man muttered. "'Tisn't wise to come upon a fellow from behind like that!" He glared at her, but with his wig awry and a smudge upon his nose, it did not have quite the desired effect.

Adria giggled, then was instantly sorry that she had offended his dignity. "Forgive me," she said, penitently. "But what *were* you doing there?"

"I was searching for the cat," he said, shamefacedly. "Not that I like the confounded creature. I detest it! But I was growing accustomed to the beast. I should not like to see anything happen to it."

"But what makes you think something might have?" she asked, carefully.

"I have no idea," he said, testily, "Except that this is a veritable madhouse! The Puritan witch-girl, a disappearing serving wench... Artists are sensitive, milady. And I can tell you —" he shook his be-ringed finger in her face — "I can smell intrigue, danger! The air is thick with it! Plotting, conniving —"

Was he trying to tell her he knew of her plans to leave with Mark?

"I hardly think so," she said faintly.

"'Tis true, and I must warn you to take care." He studied her face with round blue eyes, seeming to brace himself before he went on. "I know what you think me," he said quietly. "But I am not quite the fool I appear to be. I was not born with the physique of Anthony Mordelle, nor the good looks of Mark Welles. The fates dealt with me cruelly, giving me this body," he looked down at it, resentfully, "when I should have been a veritable giant! Yet, within this breast," Edwin pounded at it with a clenched fist, "beats a brave heart. And it is at your service, madam, should you require protection."

He bowed, pompously, and headed for the stairs on his way to the upper room, swaggering a little. Then he turned to Adria once more.

"If you see that nasty little beast, pray let me know," he said, crossly. And then he was gone.

Adria no longer had a desire to laugh. For the first time, she had seen into the heart of the small comic artist. Edwin Osmund was a sad and lonely fellow, trading on his talent and his wit. And just now, despite his pomposity, he had been sincere.

He had been sincere and he was trying to tell her something, to warn her against someone. But whom?

Making her way down to the kitchens, she discovered Mistress Murchison fixing a tray for Anthony. The ladies had already breakfasted and were at work in the caverns with Mark.

"Can I do anything to help?" Adria asked the housekeeper.

The woman tossed her a silken gown. "If you are set on working, you can mend this. 'Tis the Lady Jane's. And it must be mended *now*. Though why, I do not know."

Another job, Adria thought, gloomily, that she would prefer not to do.

By the time Adria had finished mending the gown, Mistress Murchison came limping downstairs, a tapping accompanying her footsteps. The woman was using one of Anthony's canes and her face was drawn with pain.

Adria decided to take the gown up to Jane's room. She would hang it in the wardrobe for her. The girl need not know it was Adria, rather than Mistress Murchison, who entered her room. As long as her precious dress was mended, she probably would not care. It had been such a small tear. One she might have mended for herself.

I should have stitched the sleeves shut, Adria thought, climbing the stairs. Then she remembered that she had no right to criticize the other girl. It was she, Adria, who was the intruder in this household.

Adria entered Jane's room, crossed to the wardrobe and threw it open.

It was empty.

Then she saw the trunk, lid open, Jane's things carefully packed. Across the room was another trunk, closed, strapped, ready for removal. Surely, Jane was not planning to leave?

A dreadful suspicion was beginning to ferment in her mind. She closed the wardrobe and spread the dress carefully on Jane's bed. Then she hurried to Lady Elizabeth's room. Here, conditions were the same.

What were Mark's words when he told her he was leaving? *"He has all he needs now — Wyndspelle ... the Lady Jane. He needs me no longer."*

Yet the ladies were packed and ready to leave. And there could be only one possible means of transportation: Anthony's vessel. The ship that was to carry her and Mark away.

Had she misunderstood Mark? Were they to be included in the party? No! He had cautioned her to keep his secret and he had mentioned their names. But apparently the ladies were making their own plans. Why? How could Jane leave Anthony who loved her, who could offer her the wealth she craved?

Jane might leave Anthony, Adria thought with certainty, but not his riches. That was what the ladies had been doing below: collecting the things they intended to take. But if that were true, Mark was involved with them. It would be Mark who

245

must move their ill-gotten gains to the ship, a small amount at a time.

"I can smell intrigue," Edwin Osmund had said. *"Danger! The air is thick with it! Plotting, conniving —!"*

Suddenly she realized she sensed it too. A thick suffocating cloud of fear that wrapped itself about her, weighting her down.

Dazed, she left Lady Elizabeth's room and went back to the kitchens, praying to find a moment alone with Mark. A moment that did not come.

CHAPTER 25

That night, dressed for dinner, Adria still hesitated. She had not seen Anthony all day. If she went downstairs he would be there, seated in his place at the head of the table. She would have to look at him with the knowledge of the past and the future in her mind. The memory of the night she spent in his arms, anticipation of the time, a day hence, when she and Mark would slip away together. Unless, of course, the things she was beginning to suspect were true. And that she could not bear.

She considered remaining in her room, feigning illness. It was close enough to the truth to be believed. Her nerves were shattered; all day, tears had come unbidden to her eyes when there had been no reason for them. But someone might come to check on her. Anthony, bearing a glass of warm wine...

Nay, there was no help for it. She must go down to dinner.

She opened her door a crack and heard a rustle of silk. Jane passed her doorway, clad in her newly mended gown, and around her neck the ruby necklace blazed. The necklace she had taken from Adria, telling her Anthony said she might have whatever she wished.

Adria stepped out on the balcony again. Peeping over the railing, she saw Jane cross the hall to Anthony, saw him smile and reach out to touch the ruby necklace, then draw back, as if in surprise.

He needn't have looked so shocked, Adria thought, stormily. He had told her she could have it! He was bowing, now, paying the girl a pretty compliment, no doubt!

So absorbed was she in watching Jane and Anthony, that she didn't hear the footsteps behind her until two hands grabbed her around the waist.

"Damme," Edwin Osmund crowed, "I've caught meself a spy!" Moving in beside her, he, too, peered down into the hall, his face avaricious. "Damme," he said in disappointment, "Methought something scandalous was afoot!"

"I was checking to see if the table was in order," Adria said, stiffly.

"Like a good little wife," the artist said, bowing. "Damme, but Anthony has found himself a gem."

Not a wife, Adria thought as he offered her his arm, *but a convenience.*

They went down to dinner together.

It was a miserable meal. Lady Elizabeth was cold and silent; Jane, simpering and coy. Mark looked tired beyond belief, and he was quieter than usual. Anthony, as he was the night before, worried about the weather.

"'Tis the warmest I have ever seen it for this time of year," he said. "There is foul weather coming. I can smell it! Tomorrow, Mark —"

"Tomorrow will be your last sitting for the portrait," Edwin Osmund said stuffily. "I shall insist upon completing it while the light holds. 'Tis by far the best that I have ever done."

"And the portrait is being painted for me," Lady Elizabeth broke in. "I insist that it be finished. I have not often commanded you, Anthony, but I shall in this. You have told me my every wish is to be granted. This is my wish, that you will sit for the painting until it is completed. Agreed?"

"Agreed." Anthony did not look too happy, but he smiled at her.

Again Adria thought of her earlier suspicion, that the artist and his work were being used as a blind to keep Anthony occupied, unaware of what was taking place below stairs. Her reverie was shattered as Jane spoke.

"'Tis truly a marvelous portrait, Anthony. It really is. Your friends in London will flock to see it! They will come in droves —" The girl's voice faltered and her face paled. She looked around the table, her eyes like saucers, as if for help. In answer to her signal, Mark's hand shot out, upsetting his goblet of wine.

"So clumsy of me," he said. "God's teeth! You will think me a barbarous colonial! My apologies, Lady Elizabeth, Jane," then belatedly to Adria, "Milady." He sopped his soaked trousers with his napkin. To Mistress Murchison, hobbling about the table with her cane, he said, "We will need more wine."

Adria was on her feet. "I will get it," she said. Before anyone could demur, she was on her way. She had a plan at last.

Leaving the parlor door open, she descended to the wine cellars below the kitchens. Selecting a bottle from the dusty shelves, she carried it up with her. Then, just at the foot of the stairs that led upward into the parlor, she dropped the bottle on the stone floor. She prayed that the sound would carry. And she waited, certain Mark would come to see what had occurred.

It was unlikely that either of the women would care enough to check. Anthony would not, or could not. He would send Mark, and there would be a few moments of privacy together. Moments in which questions could be asked — and answered.

For Adria was certain, now, that Mark had left much unsaid. The ladies were all packed, ready to leave without Anthony's knowledge. And Jane's remark at the table tonight, her reaction to her own words, had given her away. They were planning to go, and with them would go a portion of Anthony's treasure. They could not manage it without Mark's help. Yet Mark was Anthony's faithful friend!

Turning at the sound of a step on the stair, Adria looked up into the face of Edwin Osmund. Her heart sank. Her ruse had failed after all.

"Damme," the little man said, "What a racket! And you have made a mess here! Such a waste of good spirits, milady!"

"I will bring another bottle," Adria said, dully.

Leaving the artist shaking his head over the spilled wine, she descended to the cellars once more, returning with a bottle and placing it in Edwin's hand.

"Would you be kind enough to take this to the table? I must clear this up." She gestured toward the pool of wine that spread across the floor like blood.

"I would be happy to, milady." Then, "I volunteered to lend you my services through design, madam." He cleared his throat. "I trust my warning was sufficient this morning? You are aware there is dirty work afoot?"

Should she confide in him? Tell him what she suspected? Discover what, exactly, it was that the man knew or guessed? No, it would be unfair to Mark. She must face him with it. "Thank you for your concern," she said quietly.

The rotund artist stared at her for a moment, his round eyes expressionless. "You have but to call on me, milady," he said with dignity. Then he looked ruefully at the spilled liquid. "Damme," he said, "You should have the cat to aid you here. The little beast. One would think he had died and gone to heaven!"

Adria shivered. He had struck too close to the truth. Scrubbing up the mess, she made herself return to the table. There she sat numb to the conversation that flowed about her.

It was clear Mark intended to leave, and that Jane and Lady Elizabeth would return to London.

Anthony would be left alone.

Nay, not alone, for Adria would stay. But Mark could not know that as yet. He had said they would run away, just the two of them, and Anthony would have Jane to console him.

Mark could not know of the ladies' plans! Grimly she clung to that thought.

At last, Anthony pushed back his chair. "We have dined well, have we not? I must remember to compliment Mistress Murchison."

"And your little wife," Jane interposed. "'Tis a shame she is mistress of a great house. She has such talents in the kitchens, and here they are wasted."

"She has many talents, I can assure you."

Adria's face reddened. Did Anthony mean those words as a compliment or otherwise?

"And speaking of talents," Anthony went on, smoothly, "Will you sing for us tonight, Jane?"

"I think not," Mark broke in. "The ladies are most weary, having aided me in the chasm most of the day. I have heard them both express a desire to make an early night of it."

"Indeed," Jane rose. "So, if you will excuse us this once, Anthony?" She gave him a fatigued smile and headed for the stairs, followed by Lady Elizabeth who made her own apologies. Edwin Osmund also scuttled up the stairs.

Adria remained with the excuse of clearing the table as Anthony, too, turned away. Then she went to her own room. There, from her window, she saw a bobbing light at sea. Mark had certainly wasted no time. And when he returned, she would be waiting for him. There had been enough of dallying.

She had been as weak as Reverend Potts' wife, a shadow person, moving like a leaf with the wind.

She went openly, carrying a candle. If she met anyone, she would say she was going to make herself a pot of tea. Only when she descended to the wine cellars would that alibi fail. She prayed that she would meet no one and that Mark was at last alone.

Adria walked firmly down the stairs and through the great hall. Into the parlor. Down the steps that led to the kitchens. Reaching the wine cellars, she found the trapdoor that opened into the chasm. She trembled as she set her candle down to open it, thinking of that other time she had set a candle there and found the base of it sticky with a dead girl's blood.

Even now, she wiped her hand against her skirts, feeling the sense of revulsion that had plagued her since. Then she moved down the stone steps, reaching up to pull the door shut behind her before she turned.

Her gaze went first to the lower steps where the small boat usually lay. It was gone, with Mark having taken it out to Anthony's vessel. For that, she could be grateful. She did not believe she could make herself descend those steps in any other case. The memories of those other times were still too vivid in her mind.

Candle in one hand, she felt her way with the other, sliding her fingers along the damp walls of the chasm so that she would not slip and fall. At last she reached the spot where it widened, where there was light from the torches that were kept burning so that the cavern would remain dry. The treasure room.

She stopped, almost missing a step in her shock at the sight before her.

The flaring torches illuminated a room that was nearly empty. Save for a few small chests drawn up near the entrance, the place was a dark, shadowed hole. The jewels that had spilled over everything were missing.

The work done here had not been that of sorting and evaluating, but of packing things neatly so that they might be spirited away.

Mark was stealing from Anthony. He was a thief. And the others were his confederates. There could be no other explanation.

A sob caught in her throat as she searched for any clue that would deny the conclusions forming in her brain. Perhaps the removal had been accomplished at Anthony's orders. The treasures might be part of the ship's cargo, to be shipped somewhere, sold or traded for other commodities.

But she knew in her heart that it could not be. Still, there had to be another reason and she owed it to Mark to listen, to hear him out. Sick inside, she seated herself on one of the chests, and waited.

She was still sitting there, hands twisted in her lap, when he returned. She watched as he stepped from the boat, ankle-deep in water, and dragged it to its resting place. Watched as he came up the steps, head down, shoulders bowed with fatigue. She saw the expression in his face as he lifted his eyes with a dawning surprise that turned to anger.

"God's teeth!" he gritted. "What are you doing here, lass? You'll get me caught yet, with your meddling!"

"Caught? 'Tis a strange word to use. Then are you doing something wrong? Unlawful?" Adria's voice was steady. He stared at her for a moment, then his teeth flashed in an irresistible smile.

"And if I were, lass? If I were? Could you not love a thief?"

"I do not think so," she said quietly, though her hands clenched in her lap.

"Then," he asked in a coaxing tone, "what of a thief who steals from a thief?"

Raising saddened, puzzled eyes to his, Adria said, "I do not understand —"

"Then listen to me. Perhaps I can explain." Straddling the chest beside her, he took her hands in his, rubbing them gently as if to restore warmth to her icy fingers. "You recall the tale I told you? How Anthony and I went with Bolingbroke in an attempt to set what we considered the rightful king on the throne of England?"

"Yes — I remember."

"And I returned to find my father in prison, his property confiscated. Anthony, to discover he had been declared dead, his stepbrother made heir, and wedded to Jane, the girl Anthony was to marry?"

Adria nodded.

"As I explained, Anthony killed his brother, was imprisoned, then released through the offices of his friends. He recovered his wealth, but turned it back to his stepmother and Jane, his brother's widow. There my story ended, did it not?"

Without waiting for an answer, he continued. "So you see, this raises a question. A question you have not asked as yet. Remember, Anthony, except for his vessel, was then a poor man. The wealth you saw here — where do you think it came from?"

"Why — I believe you said trade, did you not? Until he was set upon by pirates —"

Mark threw back his head with a shout of laughter. "It is I who had forgotten our conversation," he said. "I worded it rather well, did I not? God's teeth, lass! Anthony *was* a pirate!

One of the bloodiest! Have you heard of Bartholomew Roberts?"

Adria shook her head, dazed at this new information. Anthony — a pirate himself? Dear God, no!

"First we joined with him," Mark went on. "Then we set out to loot upon our own. That's when they began to call Anthony *The Black Devil*. He was, in truth. You should have seen him—"

As Mark talked, his descriptions were vivid. Adria could see Anthony standing on a quarterdeck, his shirt opened to the waist, feet wide apart, sword swinging. Or laughing, his dark hair blowing in the wind, a smoking pistol in each hand as he fought and plundered his way across the seas. The ship's deck stained with blood, innocent blood...

Now she understood the meaning of the ship's model in the great hall. The little vessel with its pirate's flag.

"Nay," she said in an agonized whisper, holding her hand to silence Mark. "Nay!" She could bear to hear no more. Mark studied her face, his own serious now.

"Then Anthony was injured," he said. "Blinded. And we heard of this place from a new man who joined us. Some years ago, another pirate, Captain Avery, bribed the governor of Massachusetts to allow him and his crew to come ashore and dispose of their plunder. Our lad had been a member of his crew and knew of this promontory and the chasm that ran through it. It seemed a natural place. The treasure could be hidden here, a great house built. A perfect place for Anthony to retire and heal his wounds. Especially for a blind man with his conscience eating away at him, driving him to madness."

It had been a tale of horror. Adria was sickened. But it did not explain Mark's taking of the jewels, nor how the ladies, Jane and Elizabeth, were involved.

"You said you could go now," she said in a low voice, "since Anthony had Jane to comfort him — and his wealth. Yet you are planning to take those things away with you. 'Tis wrong—"

"But Jane and the others are not going." He smiled at Adria. "They but believe they are. I was forced to take them into my plans in order to keep what I was doing from Anthony."

"They are packed and ready —"

Mark began to laugh. "They will wake, ready to leave with the dawn, and the ship will have disappeared over the horizon. Can you imagine Jane's face? What a pity to have to miss it! And so far as Anthony's wealth is concerned, what do you take me for, milady? Both stair rooms are stuffed with the more valuable objects, locked away from the ladies' prying eyes, so that they would not insist upon taking them to the ship. I will take only the lesser things. Enough to buy back my lands — for you and for me — upon our return to England. Is that so wrong? He owes me that much."

Two wrongs do not make a right, she thought, dully. Seeing her obdurate expression, Mark rose, moved in front of her, and dropped to his knees.

"I know 'tis hard to understand," he whispered. "Your Puritan conscience has not had to stand against worldly things. True, Anthony saved my life. I have repaid him for it with long and faithful service. But lass, do you demand I remain loyal to a man through pillage and murder? The gems were not his. There was blood upon them. Is it wrong to put it to good use — to want a home for my wife — our children?"

A little house, Adria thought, dazedly, *and a man who loves me. A new beginning.* Seeing her face soften, Mark drew her close.

"You do understand," he said. "After all, 'tis money owed me. Gems in lieu of salary." His eyes pleaded for an affirmative answer.

"Yes, I — I understand. But the others. Lady Elizabeth, Jane, Sir Edwin — are you not cheating them?"

"They would rob Anthony," he said grimly. "And the women made Anthony what he is today. As for Osmund, he is a conniving little blackguard; an opportunist, for all his talent. Happy as long as he has a roof over his head and his belly's full. Waste no pity on them, love!"

Raising her to her feet, he said, "Go now. There is no time for distraction, lovely as this one is. The ship will be ready to sail at midnight on the morrow. I have given Captain Faulkes his orders, though he believes they are relayed from Anthony. Now I must tell him we will have another passenger aboard." He looked at Adria, anxiously. "I can say that truthfully, may I not? That you are going with me?"

It was wrong, Adria thought, but then — what was right? What was there for her here? The Puritans waiting at Wyndspelle's perimeter; a mock marriage to a madman who had made the seas run red with blood; the hatred of Jane and Lady Elizabeth and Vincente. At Wyndspelle she would dwell in mortal fear.

Though it did not seem fair for Mark to make false promises to the others, or to take from the wealth in the caverns, it was as he said, a thief taking from thieves. The treasure was not Anthony's, after all. It was pirate's loot, stained and tainted. And Mark was leaving much of it behind.

"Yes," she said, finally, "I will go with you." Her head ached and she felt dizzy and confused, but there was not much time left. She had to make a decision and stand by it.

"I knew it," Mark exulted. "I knew you would! Now get some rest. You will need it on the morrow. And you might pray to your Puritan God for a calm sea until we board, and then a fair wind." He paused, laughing. "Or to the witch of Wyndspelle, whichever you think will hear you out."

As Mark guided her up the steps, his hand firm on her arm, Adria feared she knew who would listen to her prayers.

God had never seemed so far away.

CHAPTER 26

Adria was still awake when the dawn came. The last dawn she would see at Wyndspelle. Tomorrow, when the sun came up, she would be at sea with Mark. And Anthony would be free of her. The man's dark face rose before her eyes, and she wondered if Jane would know how to care for him when his headaches came upon him.

But Anthony was none of her affair. She must remember he was a dangerous man, that he had killed and would kill again, that she had almost lost her life at his hands, and that he had taken her as wife when he had no right.

She looked out of the window. Below her the waters heaved in soundless swells, a greasy look to them. She thought of a pot just beginning to simmer below the surface. A witch's cauldron. The air had a feeling of tension and the sill was sticky to the touch. She could see the cairn of stones marking the place where Elizabeth Miller had stood, disarranged and scattered when Prudence Shanks was freed from that same spot. If the spirit of the witch still remained to haunt Wyndspelle, had it been angered at the desecration?

Adria stood at the window a long time, while below her the sea sulked and fretted.

At last, she turned with a sigh. She would make her preparations for leaving now. No trunks for her, no chests of silks and satins. She had come into this house with nothing; she would take only the bare necessities. Three dresses for the long voyage. A cloak. A dead woman's clothes.

Adria Anne Turner, witch, running from a murderer, accompanied by a thief. Wearing a gown that belonged to a corpse that would be performing a macabre dance beneath the very seas the vessel sailed upon.

She selected the plainest gowns, the warmest cloak, made a bundle of them, and stowed it beneath her bed. She had just risen from her knees when a tap sounded at the door.

She opened it to face Vincente with her breakfast tray. "So — early?" she asked, in confusion, seeing his eyes go beyond her and gaze at the gowns she had taken down and rejected, which were still in disarray upon her bed.

"The master's orders, *senhora*. He will see you in the upper room when you have eaten."

"Do you know what he wants?" Had Vincente told him he had seen her coming from Mark's room? Had Anthony, in some way, got wind of Mark's plans for departure?

"I do not know, *senhora*," Vincente said. He turned to go, his shoulders stiff and straight.

"Vincente —"

"*Senhora?*"

"I just wanted to say — I am sorry about Prudence. I hope she's well and happy —" Her voice trailed off and the man answered only with an inclination of his head. Then he was gone.

She looked at the tray. There was nothing on it she dared eat. Though she had no appetite, there was a hollow feeling in her stomach. When she knew she could delay no longer, she steeled herself for the coming interview and climbed to the upper room.

Anthony, for once, was not standing at a window, his sightless eyes fixed upon either land or sea. He sat at a small table, his head in his hands, his shoulders slouched. Before him was an untouched tray. At her entrance, he straightened, the old look of haughty command returning to his face.

"Ah, milady! You are prompt indeed! Did you take time to enjoy your breakfast?"

"I — I ate little. I have had little appetite of late."

"Then you might take a cup of tea with me. There is another cup." He gestured toward the tray. Adria filled his cup and hers, waited until he had raised his to his lips then sipped her own, savoring it. This, at least, could hold no poison.

"The weather," he said. "What think you? Does it breed a storm?"

"It is very still." Adria's hands shook as she set her cup down. This might well be a normal conversation betwixt a husband and wife at breakfast. Had he called her here for companionship? Or was he toying with her?

"I had hoped to go to the ship today," he said, "but the portrait will be completed at last. Osmund plans to display it in the afternoon. Yet, I feel if I do not board the vessel this day, it will be too late."

Too late? Adria froze, the blood running cold in her veins. There was a moment of silence. Then Anthony raised his head and smiled at her. "I know this coast," he said. "And I sense this is only the calm before a storm. Let us say it is an intuition."

Adria relaxed. He was only referring to the weather after all.

"Now let us talk about you, milady. Do you have anything to tell me?"

"To — tell you?" Again a cold fear.

"Are you too unhappy here? I know the ladies, Jane and Elizabeth, are not easy to live with. I must take some responsibility for their actions, since I owe them both a great debt. I requested they consider this their home. I did note that

Jane was wearing the ruby necklace. Did you give it to her willingly?"

Adria flushed, recalling how the girl had taken the jewels from her. "It suits her far better than it does me," she said, evasively.

"I had wondered. She can be somewhat high-handed at times. As I am. I have regretted speaking to you so harshly the day we found the Puritan lass tied to the stake below. But you have not answered my question. Are you happy here?"

Happy? How happy could one be in a dark, brooding house filled with secrets, death, and destruction? "I — I do not belong here," she faltered.

"Where do you belong? What *are* you, milady?" There was agony in his dark face. "On the one hand you are kind and gentle — but it does not fit with other things I know. Things I do not wish to believe! I thought perhaps we could meet like this, talk things out —"

Adria's body pressed back against her chair as she stared at him with frightened eyes. "I know not what you mean!"

He sighed. "I had hoped you would speak of your own free will. If not, I will make no accusations. I will ask you, though, to explain this."

From somewhere, he had produced something he held in his closed fist. Turning his hand, he opened it, palm upward, disclosing the remains of the ruby pendant. "Vincente brought this to me. He found it in your room."

So it had been Vincente! Prowling, spying, entering her room where he had no right to be! Her first reaction was a flash of anger. Then she remembered, drearily, that the pendant should not have been in her room — in her possession.

"I took it," she said in a dead voice, "though I didn't mean to." She went on to explain how she had found the stored treasure and tried on the pendant, liking the feel of it since it replaced the locket Dorrie had burned.

"She burned your locket? Was that your reason, then? Or because she had informed the Puritans as to your whereabouts? It seems small reason to take a life —"

Adria stared at him, dumbfounded. "What are you saying?" she cried. "What are you saying? Dear God!"

The blind eyes gazed at her steadily. "And what are *you* saying? That you did not?"

She was weeping, now, tears of shock and anger. "You are mad!" she sobbed. "Mad! I killed no one. And I stole nothing! I had the pendant around my neck and Mark came upon me, surprising me, telling me I should not be in that room. And I forgot. Forgot! It was only when I had returned to my room that I remembered!"

"Mark, you say?" he interrupted. She did not answer, but rushed on.

"Then it was broken when someone tried to burn me in my bed. It was stepped upon. And someone took it from my room—"

His face was white, a mask of horror as she babbled. "Why did you not tell me of the fire?" he asked. "Could you not trust me?"

"The guests," she sobbed. "Dorrie — the poisoned wine you brought me —"

He was still, his blind eyes dark caverns, his hand reaching out to her as she shrank away. "Tell me," he said, his voice hoarse. "Tell me —"

"Whatever it is, 'twill have to wait." Sir Edwin Osmund spoke in a pettish tone as he emerged from the opening in the center of the floor. "Damme, what a climb! I, for one, will be glad to see the end of it! You will excuse us, madam?" He scowled at Adria. "Your domestic problems will keep, will they not?"

Anthony pulled himself together with apparent effort. "I will talk with you later," he said to Adria. "There is too much that has been left unsaid." Then, painfully, he extended the hand with the pendant toward her. "If you like the chain, then take it. It is of no value, a thing of paste and glass."

A thing of paste and glass? But she had taken it from the room where the true valuables were stored — the greater treasures that Mark intended to leave behind!

Adria stood dumb as Anthony dropped the chain into her chilled fingers. Still warm from his hand, it seemed to burn into hers. Wordless, she turned and made her way down the ship's ladder and to her room.

She could not stay here! Her head ached, whirling with what she had gained from the morning's conversation. The smell of food on the untouched tray made her feel ill. Snatching up her cloak, she went downstairs and out through the door that led from the kitchens to the grounds of Wyndspelle.

The hope that clean air would refresh her mind was a vain one. There was no breeze, and the air seemed thick with the smell of death — rotting kelp, small shellfish cast up by the earlier storm, now simmering in the unseasonable warmth. A scent of decay. Perhaps even a body, caught in among the rocks offshore —

No! She would not let herself think of it.

A corpse. Dorrie! Anthony had accused her of killing Dorrie. Had someone in this house hinted to him of such a thing? Had his harshness when the girl's name was mentioned been a way of protecting Adria? Or was the accusation a new type of refined cruelty? Knowing he had done the deed himself, he was getting some kind of perverted pleasure from blaming it on her.

If this were true, then he was mad. As mad as Mark had claimed him to be.

Yet, when she had spoken of the fire in her room, of the burned locket, of the poisoned wine, he had seemed to be startled, shocked — but he had given her the wine with his own hands.

And the pendant! How could a fake jewel be found in a store of expensive gems? She recalled how she wondered at its dullness next to the ruby necklace, at the way it had broken so easily.

If there was one false bauble in a chest, would there be more? If there were, then that meant Mark... No, she would not believe that of him. He would surely not leave Anthony blind and penniless.

The remark about the ship — Anthony's intuitive feeling that it might be forced to sail before he could board the vessel. Had he been referring to the storm that was sure to come, or did he have some notion that something was going to happen, that he was being robbed of something or someone? And did he know she was involved?

"Where do you belong?" he had asked. *"What are you, milady?"*

"I don't know where I belong," she cried aloud, looking up at the sky, tears streaking her face. "And I don't know what I am!"

For she had reached the end of the laid-out path, had climbed the trail that led upward, and now leaned against the big stone that was scarred by musket-fire from the cliff above her. On that day, she had called down a curse upon her attackers and a fire had streaked from the heavens. *"A scent of brimstone and of evil —"*

With a whimpering sound, she turned and pressed her face against the stone. It should have been cool against her fevered face, but instead it only felt sticky and clammy in the brooding atmosphere.

It was a pity that the aim of the musket had been so poor, she thought, fingering the marred stone. A pity.

Sinking down beside the stone, she cried. Cried for herself, for Prudence, for Dorrie, for the poor dead cat; cried until she could weep no more.

Getting to her feet, she finally started resolutely toward the house. And, as she had on that other day, she saw Mark coming toward her. Mark, who was there when she needed him! Her heart lifted as she ran to meet him, then sank as she saw the anger on his face, his gesture that brought her up short as effectively as a wall.

"We're being watched," he hissed, jerking his head back toward the kitchen doorway where Adria could see Mistress Murchison standing. "What the devil are you doing out here, lass? Trying to get yourself fired upon again?"

"Just walking."

"Well, Osmund saw you from the upper room and casually mentioned it to Anthony. Anthony got stirred up and sent him down to send someone after you. Mistress Murchison had no desire to face a musket, so she came to get me. You've got the whole place in an uproar."

"I'm sorry." Her face contrite, she reached out a hand toward him, drawing it back at his expression. "I had to get somewhere I could think, Mark. Anthony had a conversation with me this morning."

His eyes were bright and wary now. "What did he say?"

"He — accused me of murdering Dorrie."

A moment's silence, then, "I told you he was mad."

"But that isn't all. I think he may suspect something. He said he had a feeling that the vessel might sail before he had a chance to go aboard."

"He told me to give the captain orders to sail before a storm. And this weather," he lifted his face to the oppressive sky, "this weather is certain to breed one. You imagine things, milady."

"There's something else. Something that troubles me. Remember the day you found me in the treasure room below the stairs? I had placed a pendant around my neck..." She continued, telling him the tale of how the jewel came to be in her possession, what had happened to it the night of the fire, and how Vincente had taken it.

Mark paled a little. "I'm certain you did no harm in taking it. Anthony has jewels to spare. Did he accuse you of stealing it? What did he say?" He had stopped, his blue eyes fixed on hers with an intensity that made her nervous.

"Only that the pendant was a forgery, the gem false."

Mark jerked as though she had struck him. "He said just that? In those words? Did you tell him where you got it?"

"Yes. Did I do wrong?" A shrill note of fear entered her voice. "Mark, was there any reason I shouldn't? The other jewels — they are real, aren't they? What was this one doing among them?"

"I have no idea." Mark paused to kick a stone off the path, his brows knitted in thought. "I suppose it might have been through an error in judgment. I'm not infallible, you know. There may have been some trade stuff among the loot from a ship — bound for trade among the natives, no doubt. I may have made an error in sorting. 'Tis dim there in the chasm, you know. You do believe me?"

"Yes," Adria said. She wanted to believe him. She had to believe him.

Reaching the house, they entered the kitchens and Mark left Adria there with a friendly admonition to wander about the premises no more, words obviously for the ears of the housekeeper. After he had left them, Mistress Murchison added her own scolding to his, telling Adria how poor Sir Edwin had to climb up and down all those stairs, just for her sake, and Sir Anthony had been so upset.

"I'm sorry," Adria said, mechanically. It seemed she was doing nothing but apologize all the time these last days. "The ladies are having a light lunch in the parlor," Mistress Murchison went on. "I suppose you'll want to join them. The master and Sir Edwin requested trays in the upper room, since the portrait is so nearly done. Master Welles had a bite here in the kitchen, earlier, so if you wish to eat, there's a place set for you."

Adria had no desire to join Lady Elizabeth and Jane, but she must eat to keep up her strength and the food would be safe. Thanking the housekeeper, she climbed to the parlor where a small collation was laid out upon a little table. Both ladies looked happier than they had since their arrival. When Adria entered, they exchanged little secret smiles.

"There you are," Jane cried. "From all the furor that ensued when you were seen out on the grounds, one would think Anthony believed you to be running away!"

"I was but taking the air," Adria said. "'Tis so still in the house."

Lady Elizabeth poured a cup of tea for Adria, handing it to her most graciously. "It is oppressive," the woman said.

"And with a choice of this house or those dreadful grounds...!" Lady Jane shuddered. "I don't know how you bear it, Adria. If I thought I should have to spend the rest of my life here, I would die! 'Tis like a tomb!"

Jane would have to spend some of her life here, Adria thought. Tomorrow at dawn she would rise to discover Anthony's vessel gone without her. Instinctively, Adria knew the girl would take it badly. It would be difficult for Anthony. She thought of him ill, at the mercy of two angry women. The fact that part of Anthony's treasure would be gone would not help matters, either.

"I shall be glad when this portrait is done," Adria said, changing the subject. "I fear such prolonged sittings may bring on one of Anthony's attacks. The only thing that seems to ease them is…" She described the treatment she had used to ease his almost unbearable pain, hoping that Jane, if she loved him at all, would listen.

"Illness bores me," the girl said, selecting a piece of fruit from the bowl in the center of the table. "I cannot bear to be around sick people."

"Nor I," said Lady Elizabeth. "Even when my late husband, Anthony's father lay dying, I could not bring myself to enter his room. Anthony is so lucky to have *you*."

But he will not have me, Adria thought. The bite she had taken stuck in her throat and she could not swallow it. *Anthony will not have me*. Instead he would have Jane, who would be cold comfort when he was ill, who would wear away at him in her unhappiness at being left behind.

Excusing herself, she left the table and went to her room. There, she lay on her bed, her mind in a turmoil over the step she was about to take. After all, she had no choice. Anthony did not want her, she was certain of that. She had brought nothing but trouble to Wyndspelle. If she could only stop thinking of him as the husband he was not.

Instead, she must think of Mark, of his blue eyes that could be warm and merry, his arms that were strong and protective. Mark, who had said, *"I love you."* Words Anthony could not say.

At last she willed herself to sleep, and she dreamed. In her dream, she was a barefoot girl in a drab gown, standing alone at the spring. Around her, the forest smelled fresh, and a few late leaves fluttered like banners above her where a bird sang. She filled the pails, a soft shade of gray from long usage, at the moss-edged spring and attached them to the yoke, lifting it over her shoulders, and turned —

Turned to face the pointing fingers of the elders in Meeting. *"She is a witch!"* the people cried in unison. *"Witch!"* And the Reverend Potts' voice sounded with the deep intonation of a bell.

"Evil! Evil! Evil!"

He pounded on the lectern and Adria knew her sentence was about to be pronounced. Then she awoke. She sat up, face damp with perspiration, dark hair plastered against one cheek. For a space, she could only stare, dazedly, wondering where she was and how she came here. Then the world righted and settled into place.

She was at Wyndspelle, and the sound she heard was a knocking at her door.

"Yes," she said in a trembling voice.

"'Tis I, milady." It was Edwin Osmund. "The portrait is done! We are all to meet in the great hall for the viewing."

"Thank you," she said, "I shall be right down." Then she put a hand to her cheek. It was wet. Wet with tears for a Puritan maid who was as dead as Emma, as dead as Dorrie. Weeping for her own young self.

CHAPTER 27

When Adria ventured out on the balcony, she could see that the others had all assembled before her. It had grown late as she slept, and the chandelier below glittered with a surfeit of candles, illuminating the great hall. The portrait had been placed above the mantel, and the other members of the household stood back to survey it, uttering little murmurs of appreciation that rose like a chorus to Adria's ears.

From where she stood, she could not see the painting. Only the faces and the expressions as they looked at the portrait, evaluating it. The artist looked on with unholy glee mingled with pride, as though he had perpetrated a monstrous joke and it had come off well.

And the women! They wore the look of those who had watched Goody Tillie Frame at her ducking. A smug expression of self-righteousness.

Descending the stairs, Adria joined the group, maneuvering her way until she could see the painted features. The flickering of the candles from above and the flames below gave it a dark mobility.

Adria's breath caught in her throat. It was so like him. So like him! It was a pirate's face, arrogant and satanic. Yet Osmund had caught the gentleness she had known several times, and some of the agony of a tortured mind. The painted scar from forehead to cheekbone seemed to pulse in the fire's reflection—

But there was something wrong. Something wrong with the painting that she could not put her finger on.

"'Tis my best work," Osmund said, proudly. The others agreed in a jumble of voices as Adria stood silent.

"Do you not agree, milady? You are my eyes, you know." It was Anthony beside her. She jumped a little.

"How did you know I was here?"

"A lucky guess." He smiled, then his face grew grim. "We must continue our conversation of the morning. There is much I wish to know. Dinner is to be served soon. But afterward — will you come to the upper room."

It was not a question, it was an order. Adria trembled. The last dinner at Wyndspelle. The time for leaving so near. Hours, now. What if Anthony had guessed? What if he asked her point blank? Could she bring herself to lie for Mark's sake?

"Will not the morrow be a better time?" She tried to sound casual, though this, too, was a form of falsehood. On the morrow she would be gone.

"Tonight," he said. Then, turning to the others, he said, "Enough admiration of Osmund's work for now. I suggest we retire to ready ourselves for dinner. After all, you will be forced to look upon that painting every day hereafter. Is that not true, milady?"

His fingers bit into Adria's arm, a little cruelly. "Yes, milord," she said. But the words were faint and unconvincing.

Still rubbing her arm, she watched the others mount the stairs to their rooms, the small artist spouting happily about his accomplishment. No one noticed she had remained behind. Moving to the center of the great hall, she stood with her hands clasped behind her, studying the portrait. *Something wrong,* her mind kept saying. *It is a perfect likeness but there is something wrong.*

Then all at once it struck her. She had found the flaw in the picture. The haunted eyes that seemed to follow her, moving

272

with her movement, were blind. Edwin Osmund had painted him blind. And he was not.

He was not!

Her breath caught and held as she realized and trembled on the edge of a new awareness. Dear God, was it possible? Yet there had been signs all along —

"Why, you are wearing the rubies!" he had said.

And that day in the gardens, when his face had become a demon's mask of brooding horror. *"Damn you!"* he had snarled. *"Damn you! Do as I tell you! Leave me to my own private hell!"*

And the morning in the upper room, when he said, *"Tell me what you see —"*

There had been something in his eyes at those times, something like burning embers. Was it possible that his sight was returning in flashes? That his first true picture was of the bitter, blighted land of Wyndspelle — where he had expected a garden to be? No wonder he'd thought himself damned. No wonder he'd struck out at her!

And his ramblings when he was ill. *"Everything I touch dies —"*

How much more had he seen? The revulsion of Jane and his stepmother to his scarred face? The avarice in their eyes as they discussed the treasure below? Mark's false friendship? Even — dear God — the guilt on her own face?

It was even possible that Anthony had guessed what was going on. That he knew Adria planned to go away with Mark. Conspired with Mark to rob him.

As if in answer to her thought, the flames in the fireplace flared high. By its light, the features of the portrait seemed to writhe as the awful eyes looked at her in a kind of agonized pleading.

And, as though it had been a signal, the house began to breathe.

Adria fled to her room, numbed with a sick feeling of horror mingled with pity.

Anthony Mordelle. Man or demon? Saint or Satan? A man who believed in nothing, and who had been given no reason for belief. A man no one would really ever know, even a wife.

But a man she loved! And for one night she had been his wife in the eyes of God...

Leaving her room, Adria went out onto the balcony. All along its length, doors were closed, the occupants dressing for dinner. But there was only one of them she wished to see: Mark Welles. She wanted to tell him of her new revelation. Beg him to let the others go, taking what they would. She and Mark would stay behind.

Tapping at his door, she entered as he called out, "Yes?"

He was standing beside his bed, shirtless, his body golden in the candlelight, his face a mask of surprise and shock. "God's teeth, lass! What are you doing here? Are you out of your mind? Are you trying, deliberately, to ruin me? Can no woman be trusted? Get out. Out! And try not to be seen!"

"I have to talk to you, Mark. I am not sailing with you."

With a muffled curse, he dropped the shirt he held in his hand and came toward her. "Adria! Please!" He erased the scowl he was wearing, turning it into an affectionate smile. "You're frightened, aren't you?" he whispered. "Well, you need not be. I will take great care of my little Puritan love. The only danger is in being found out. In getting away. All is aboard except the ladies' belongings, which they believe me to be taking to the ship tonight. Instead," he smiled and touched a finger to her cheek, "I shall be taking you."

"I cannot go." She said numbly, seeing the anger that began to flicker in his eyes again. "I cannot leave Anthony."

"God's teeth!" he said with a harsh laugh. "You are a glutton for punishment. I've told you the man is a killer. He's not sane. Your life is in danger as long as you remain here. And you owe him nothing. He doesn't even want you. I'm beginning to believe you to be as mad as he is!"

"But he has a reason," she whispered. "Mark, he isn't blind. He can *see!*"

Mark looked at her oddly for a moment, then said, in a gruff voice, "You are mad! You're being a sentimental fool!"

"No, just honest with myself. What you plan to do, stealing from him, 'tis wrong. Let the others go. They are not happy here, and they will only hurt him, but he trusts you, Mark —"

"But I am going. And you will come, too. Because you love me."

It was a statement, not a question. And Mark's face was not that of the merry gentleman she had met near the spring. It was hard, now. Cold. Ice-chiseled. His eyes like splinters of stone. Lowering her gaze, she saw his hands, clenching and unclenching as if he would like to close them about her neck.

Trembling, she backed away from the danger she felt in the man.

"I suppose you've talked this over with Anthony? That you've told him what I intend to do?"

She shook her head, trapped by the power in him, like a small bird hypnotized by a snake.

"And are you going to tell him?"

"Nay, 'tis your affair."

Mark began to laugh, a ringing mirthless laugh. "'Tis I who have been mad. To think I would consider taking a pious, prudish Puritan lass to set up as a great lady in London. You are a witch, indeed! And I have been bemused for a time, but now the spell is gone. 'Tis ended. If one wants a lady-wife, one should begin with a lady! And Jane is willing. She indicated that she was before she had been here two days. A lovely armful!"

His words triggered a memory in Adria's mind. Two cloaked figures in the great hall below the balcony; the lady's hood falling back to reveal Jane's blonde hair. It was Mark who had taken Jane into his arms. Mark! And she had believed it to be Anthony. She couldn't suppress a low moaning sound.

Mark misunderstood, thinking he had hurt her by his own unfaithfulness, enjoying the fact. "All along," he said, cruelly, "I have had a choice. I was still thinking on it when you came to my room. I was angered when you came, but now I thank you. God's teeth, a maid like you in London? You have saved me from being a fool."

Adria backed to the door, unable to take her disbelieving eyes from his mocking face. Feeling the knob beneath her fingers, she fumbled at it until the door opened. Then she ran, his ugly laughter still ringing in her ears.

Back in her room, she sat in one of the high-backed chairs, a small huddle of misery, her face burning with humiliation at Mark's words. Then, remembering it was Mark she had seen with Jane that night, not Anthony, recalling Anthony's seeming surprise when she mentioned the fire in her room, the poisoned wine, she began to feel a small dawning hope. And Dorrie! Anthony had accused her of being responsible for the girl's death when Mark had insinuated it was Anthony. Could it have been Mark? The suspicion trembled in her mind for an instant, but was then dismissed.

Mark had not set the fire in Adria's room. He had not brought her the poisoned wine.

Hearing the footsteps of the others going down to dinner, she sighed and prepared to join them. This would not be her last meal here, as she had planned. Tomorrow, Mark would be gone, the guests would be gone, and Adria would remain. She would be careful to sleep lightly and select the food she ate, living with fear as long as whoever or whatever hated her in this house allowed her to live.

Dinner was a miserable affair. Anthony was preoccupied and silent. The ladies and the artist seemed nervous, jumpy.

"'Tis this infernal house," Edwin Osmund said, pouting like a child. "Damme! The place is breathing again! What d'you think, Mark? Are we in for a blow?"

"Not until after midnight," Mark said.

They then turned to discussing the portrait. Adria's eyes scanned each of them in turn. The pompous little artist. Was he involved in the conspiracy? Lady Elizabeth, with her hard sophistication. Jane, eyeing Mark in a manner that said they shared a lovely secret. Jane, wearing the ruby necklace to dinner for this last occasion. The ruby necklace that she was certain to take with her when she left this house, leaving only the jewels in the rooms that held the stairs, in the storage beneath the steps.

Adria thought of the pendant with its false stone. A cheap gee-gaw for trade purposes. How had it found its way into the select company of priceless gems? Then a new thought came to her, making her shake and drop a spoon with a clang. It brought attention to Adria, and for once, she did not blush. Her mind was too shocked at the notion that had struck her.

What if none of the jewels in the storage spaces were real?

What if Mark was planning to abscond with all that Anthony owned? Ill-gotten though it was, it still represented the blind man's livelihood. Dear God! Mark could not. Would not!

Drearily, she had to admit that she did not know Mark. To her, he had been her laughing, merry protector. Anthony's true and loyal friend. But the man she had seen in his room this night was not the Mark she knew. She thought of his hard face, the granite eyes, his cruel laughter.

Anthony had taken Mark into his employ when Mark had nothing. And he had brought these others here through a troubled conscience, giving them shelter, wealth. And now they were stealing away, taking from him, leaving him in his loneliness. Perhaps taking everything.

Her chin set firmly. She would get her keys, go to those storage places beneath the stairs. And if she discovered her suspicions to be true, she would stop them. She wasn't quite certain as to how it might be done, but she would stop them!

"Milady?" It was Anthony from his place at the head of the table. And he was talking to Adria. "My head is paining me somewhat," he told her. "I shall beg leave to excuse myself. I will lie down for a few moments." He stood, swaying a little. "I will, however, see you in the upper room as we had planned. Tap on my door as you pass, and I will join you." Then, turning to the housekeeper who had entered, he said, "Mistress Murchison, I will be obliged if you would send Vincente to me—"

"And a glass of warm wine," Lady Elizabeth said. "I, myself, will prepare it for you, Anthony. I recall how much it helped your dear father."

Adria bristled at the fawning note in Anthony's stepmother's voice, frowning at Lady Elizabeth's retreating back as she turned toward the kitchens. Then, with a shock, she noted that Anthony, too, had gone, and that Mark was scowling at her.

"I fear Anthony is unwell," he said. "I'm sure, milady, that you understand how dangerous it would be to upset him. Perhaps *fatal.*"

Adria felt a tingle of fear along her spine. "I will not upset my husband in any way. That is something you can depend upon," she said, slowly.

"I was sure of that." He smiled, his eyes steely slits, then, raising his goblet, he said, "To a fair wind."

Lady Jane echoed his toast.

When dinner was over, the ladies retired to their rooms, Mark disappearing below. Adria assisted Mistress Murchison and Mother Moseby in clearing the table, half-irritated, half-amused at the antics of Edwin Osmund. The silly little man had transferred himself to Anthony's chair, stubby legs straight out, his head a full foot below its bejeweled back.

"I shall sit here," he announced, "in regal splendor, and meditate!"

He was obviously clowning, but when he jumped at a sound, his eyes alert as his head swiveled toward the parlor door at Vincente's entry, Adria understood the reason for his posturings. Edwin, too, knew that something was afoot tonight. And, either for her sake or his own, he did not intend to miss out on anything.

When they were alone at last, he beckoned to her, speaking in an exaggerated whisper to indicate the need for secrecy. "Do not fear, milady," he said. "Your household is in good hands this night! Sleep well."

"I shall," she whispered in reply. Then, for no reason except an impulse, she bent and kissed the little man's plump cheek. To her surprise, his eyes brimmed.

"Well — damme," he stammered, blinking rapidly. "Damme!"

The Puritan and the painter, an odd pair of friends, thought Adria, as she hurried away and up to her room. There, she took up her ring of keys and fastened them at her waist, finally lighting a candle at the fire. She would need it to see in the darkened storage room.

Ready at last, she tapped at Anthony's door, then ran without awaiting an answer. Though Anthony was familiar with his surroundings, it would take him a little while to feel his way along the hall, tapping with his cane. Unless he moved faster by night, when there was no one to see?

By the time he reached the stair room, she could be inside the storage area beneath the stairs. She would check out the rest of the gems and see if they were real or false.

If they were truly valuable, then let Mark and the others take what they had stolen — and God bless them! But if they were fakes, merely trade goods stored here to cover the stealing going on down below, then Adria would have to think of a course of action.

Let them be real, she prayed as she fumbled with the key in the lock. *Please God, let them be real.*

Once inside the narrow space, a smothery feeling of fear came over her as she thought of Mark's tales of spiders and snakes from exotic climes. She could not bear to close the door behind her, thus shutting herself in with some fearsome creature. She would leave it open, just a crack, shielding the candle with her body.

Shivering a little, she advanced into the darkness, so deep that it seemed to blot up the candle's small flame. She bumped her head on a low spot before she remembered to bend down. And here was the chest that had contained the pendant. A king's ransom, glittering before her. She searched, and found another pendant, a large blue gem on a silver strand.

Placing the jewel on the floor of the storage space, she summoned her courage and stepped upon it — hard.

The jewel crunched beneath her foot and her heart sank. *A thing of paste and glass.* A forgery. Another. The same.

Sick at heart, she moved to another chest. More trade goods, but worse, this chest had a false bottom. The space beneath the tray was empty. The next chest —

Adria stopped short, hearing the tapping of a cane, slow, halting footsteps. Anthony! She was very still, crouching in the shadows. She had assured Mark she would not inform upon him, and she would not. How could Anthony help in this, blind as he was? And — she had to admit to herself that this was the most important factor — Anthony might be injured, perhaps killed. While Mark did not have the courage to steal from Anthony openly, it might be different if he were trapped. He might stop at nothing.

The steps had halted. They seemed to have stopped just outside of the door to the space in which she was hiding. It was possible that Anthony could see her small light. She blew the candle out. She would need it no longer; she had found what she. wished to learn. She waited, holding her breath in the silence. Then the door closed against her.

The door closed, leaving her trapped in a small space that was said to be crawling with horrid poisonous creatures. And as she stood, frozen with shock, she heard a grating sound as someone removed the keys she had left hanging in the lock. Then there was a tapping as that person moved away. The tapping of a cane.

"Anthony," she called. "Anthony, it is I, Adria. I am here — in the storage room!" Her voice was thin with fear. Surely he could hear her! She called again.

There was no answer. Only the sound of footsteps, a tapping cane, and then — nothing.

CHAPTER 28

The only sound Adria could hear was that of her own uneven breathing. Anthony had locked her here in this room. But why? Could it possibly have been an accident? He might have brushed against the keys hanging from the lock, noted that the door was open and closed it, not knowing there was nothing valuable left to safeguard.

But she had called out to him! Had heard the sound of the keys and his breathing. Surely her voice would have carried to his ears. He knew she had called out to him, and he had left her.

She was trapped, and in a few more hours, Mark would be leaving, taking all that Anthony owned. Now there was no way to stop him, unless — She went cold as a new thought entered her mind. Perhaps Anthony was aware of what was happening. He may have imprisoned her here for safekeeping while he went to confront Mark, not guessing at his danger.

Groping her way to the door, Adria pounded on it, calling until she was hoarse. Calling for Anthony, for Mistress Murchison. Finally, hopelessly, for Mark.

At last, she turned back into the darkness, feeling her way, hoping to find some object she might use as a lever to pry at the door, or to smash away at the lock. As she moved, something trailed across her cheek. Raising a hand to brush it away, she shuddered back. A spider's web.

For the first time, she forgot the intrigues among the people in the house, remembering only what Mark had told her of this place —

"These things come from the Orient or the Indies, 'Tis not uncommon to find poisonous creatures among them. Spiders that have hatched out upon being kept in a warm dark place. Small snakes —"

With a little moan, Adria staggered back against one of the chests. Something slithered from it to wrap around her ankle and lie against it — cold and reptilian.

She froze. Then, when the object failed to move, she reached down slowly. Her fingers recognized the thing as metal. A heavy braid of fine chain.

Returning to the door, she pounded against it with both fists until she sank to her knees and leaned against it, sobbing with fatigue and terror.

Hours passed. How many, Adria had no way of knowing. Here, in this room beneath the stairs, it was always night. Possibly Mark and the others were leaving even now, filing down through the dark chasm like shadows, leaving her here to face a madman's anger. His revenge. For Anthony would not have shut her into this room were he not mad.

Her own mind, rebelling at the horrors it had endured, was numb, drugged, and she fought against sleep. The small room was airless, and she feared that if she slept, it would be forever. Still, she was in an almost dreamlike state when she heard the footsteps. Soft footfalls, as if the owner were moving quietly so that he would not be heard.

"Please," she called in the voice of a tearful child, "Please! Help me!"

The sound stopped. When it began again, it was moving away. *I am to be left here,* she thought, numbly. *Left here to die —*

And then the steps returned. A key grated in the lock and the door swung open.

Vincente! Vincente, with a candle in hand. Never had a light been so welcome, though his face was shadowed and sinister above it.

"Vincente!" His name was uttered on a sob.

"*Senhora!*" The man was stunned with surprise. "*Senhora!* What are you doing there? Who has locked you in?"

She looked at him, wide-eyed. Anthony's faithful servant. What would his reaction be to the truth? For a moment, she felt the temptation to hedge, to explain that it had been an accident, but she set her jaw in resolution.

"Anthony did," she said. "I know 'twas Anthony. I heard his cane."

"But the master sleeps. I have not left his side. He was sleeping when you tapped at the door and I could not wake him. At last, I remembered you were expected to be in the tower room and came to get you. When I heard your voice, I went back for the keys. Someone had dropped them on the balcony —"

"If it were not Anthony, then who —?" She stopped short. Anthony was sleeping. Vincente could not wake him. "You took him the warm wine?"

"*Si, senhora,* but —"

Adria was past Vincente and gone, running through the stair room door, down the balcony, bursting into Anthony's room. The memory of warm wine was in her mind. The poisoned wine! The poor black cat. Anthony! Dear God! Anthony!

At the door to her husband's room, she paused, fearful of what she would find. Then forcing herself to enter, she approached Anthony's bed.

He was sleeping. Thank God, he was only sleeping. But it was not a natural sleep. His breathing was labored, but steady, his face serene.

Then he had not been poisoned.

Taking her eyes from the recumbent figure, Adria moved around the bed. There, near a window, a tray was placed upon a small table. A half-empty beaker of wine, two cups, one unused. Someone had planned for Vincente to have the opportunity to join in his master's libation.

Tipping a bit of wine into the clean cup, Adria smelled it, tasted it, recognizing it. It was what she had been given, though much stronger. Taking Anthony's wrist in her fingers, she felt for his pulse. It was strong and steady. He would be all right, but there would be no waking him until the morning.

The morning, when he would rise to find himself a poor man. Robbed. Left stranded on an unfriendly shore. Her heart wrenched as she studied his face in the firelight. Sleeping, he looked young, innocent, trusting —

There was a sound of footsteps outside the door. Dear God, *Anthony's footsteps!* She could hear his tapping cane. And the door was opening.

Falling to her knees beside the bed, she crouched in its shadow, eyes wide in the darkness as the intruder entered. *Mistress Murchison!* She had forgotten the woman's sprained ankle, and that she was using one of Anthony's canes. A wave of relief washed over her. She started to rise, only to remember the footsteps outside the storage room door. It was the housekeeper who had locked her in! But what part did she play in this? She was surely not included in Mark's schemes. Mark had been very explicit about that in their conversations. But there was something about the woman now that was frightening, an aura of evil —

And the woman's shadow as she crossed the room was reminiscent of the figure Adria had seen through the draperies the night of the fire on the night of the witch — Had she come to harm Anthony? Adria's heart was in her throat as she braced herself, preparing to defend him. At least she would have surprise on her side.

But the woman went to the far wall, reaching upward, taking down the dueling pistols. When she turned, the firelight touched her face. The housekeeper looked mad, crazed in her anger. Was it possible that she was faithful to Anthony? That she had discovered what was to take place tonight and intended to stop it?

Again Adria almost rose, wanting to blurt out that she knew what was happening and wanted to help. But something held her back. She sank down again, taking Anthony's limp dangling hand in hers, pressing it against her cheek. She would remain where she was until the housekeeper had left the room, and then she would follow her.

But in order to do that, she would have to leave the sleeping Anthony alone and unprotected. Where was Vincente? Why had he not appeared? She had expected him to follow her. Was it possible that he, too, was involved in some way? That he had only returned to release her at the last moment before they went out to the vessel?

She held her breath until she heard the door open and close behind the housekeeper. Then, touching her lips to the sleeping man's forehead, she said a prayer for his safety and followed, waiting a moment at the door. She stepped out onto the balcony. Below her, the shadow of Mistress Murchison moved crab-like across the floor. When the woman disappeared into the parlor, Adria took a deep breath and descended the stairs.

Pausing at the foot of the steps, she could hear the wind beating at the great door, a scattering of sleet against the tinted glass set into the arch above. The fire in the hearth had gone out, and there were candles at either end of the long table.

So like the night she arrived that she looked down at herself, half expecting to see the shreds of a Puritan gown. Her hands clenched at her sides as the house gasped and breathed in agonized, measured spaces. In. Out. In. And she had an eerie sensation that she was not alone. That someone was watching her.

As she crossed toward the parlor, the feeling was so strong that she stopped, scanning the room, flinching in spite of herself as the firelight glinted on a pair of eyes fixed upon her from the depths of Anthony's chair.

Sir Edwin, of course! Keeping watch as he had promised. She was no longer alone.

She went toward him, weak with relief. "Milord," she said. Then, "Milord?"

For he was looking at her in such a strange way, his blue eyes popping a little as if he'd just come into possession of a tidbit of gossip, his mouth open in a rather silly grin. He didn't answer, yet he was not sleeping. Perhaps he had imbibed too freely.

She reached out a hand to him, a vague chill of alarm beginning to crawl along the network of her nerves. "Sir Edwin," she said as she touched his shoulder. "Milord —"

The word seemed to hang in space as he toppled forward, his eyes straight ahead, unblinking, wig sliding askew to reveal a shiny balding head. And as he rested his forehead on the table in a puddle of spilled wine, she saw the thing between his shoulder blades. The jeweled blade that had severed Sir Edwin Osmund from his life.

Tears streaming, Adria tugged at the knife, murmuring little broken consoling syllables, the artist's blood streaking her small brown hands, until at last she had to admit defeat. Still, she could not bring herself to leave him as he was, hunched forward in a ludicrous manner, his smooth scalp exposed.

Pulling and tugging at the limp body, she managed to move it back into position, the knife protruding through the rungs of the chair. Then, with bloodied fingers, she contrived to set the wig back in place, sobs tearing at her throat as she finished. She reeled a little, catching the back of Anthony's chair to steady herself —

Anthony's chair, which once had been studded with precious gems. Now, only gouged, scarred wood remained. The stones had been pried away. Even these Mark and his crew would not leave behind. Even these!

And even in death, Sir Edwin had been denied his right to sit in regal splendor.

Adria was no longer afraid. Her terror of the dark house, her shock at finding Sir Edwin in such case, had all been wiped away with a chilling flame of rage that turned her heart to ice, her spine to steel.

Picking up the poker that leaned against the hearth, Adria descended the dark steps, her face set as she stood at the top of the steps leading to the wine cellar. Her mind was cold and calculating, set upon one objective.

Sir Edwin would be avenged!

There was the sound of Mistress Murchison's cane upon the rocky floor below; a creak as the trapdoor that led into the chasm was lifted. It was time to follow. Moving cautiously downward, Adria found the wine room empty. One of the chests from the ladies' rooms sat near the opening in the floor, a burning candle atop it. So those allied in theft and murder had not yet gone aboard the ship. But Mistress Murchison was out of sight. She evidently had joined the others in the chasm.

Adria stepped forward, cautiously, looking down. The housekeeper stood just below her, blotting out much of the scene, but it was clear that the base of the rift, at the water's edge, was a beehive of activity. Lady Elizabeth and Jane, their skirts pinned up like serving women, were attempting to wrestle with one end of a heavy chest, while Mark heaved at the other. They were too intent upon what they were doing to see Mistress Murchison who stood, grim and silent, the leveled pistols in her hands. The cavern seemed filled with sound: the scraping of the chest, the booming sea.

"Mark! Mark Welles!"

Mistress Murchison's voice cut through the noise like a thin blade. Mark jumped, dropping his end of the burden and the chest slid a few steps, carrying two indignant ladies with it. Mark stared upward, his face white in the torchlight. He moved, raising a hand uncertainly.

"Stay still!" the housekeeper cried, her tone ringing with hatred. "Stay where you are!"

So the woman was loyal to Anthony! Adria, seeing how the dueling pistols trembled in the woman's hands, stepped down into the rift to stand behind her. Mark's eyes flicked to Adria's for one startled second, narrowing with implacable fury, then moved back to Mistress Murchison's. He lifted his hand placatingly.

"Put those guns away, Amanda," he said to the housekeeper. "Come on, love. Put them away." He had summoned his winning smile, and looked like a young prince as he gazed up at them; the torch burnishing his fair head, turning it into a crown of gold. He took another step forward. "Amanda?" he said, coaxingly.

The woman tensed. Adria could see the tendons standing out on the hands that held the pistols. "'Tis over, Mark," the housekeeper said in a dead voice. "'Tis ended. You have lied to me enough. Now I am going to kill you."

"Amanda! When have I been false to you? This — this is not what it seems. I can explain!" Mark had taken another step, still holding the woman's eyes with his own.

"This is not what it seems," she repeated, mocking him. "You can 'explain'! I suppose you will tell me the master does not lie drugged in his room; that you have not slain that little fool of an artist; that you are not, at this moment, planning to sail, leaving me behind —!"

"Nay," he said. "Amanda, listen —"

"I have listened too long!" The woman laughed wildly. "As I recall, the first plan was to get Emma out of the way. I would wed the master and we would share his wealth between us. Then you took up with that chit from the settlement. It was no accident she came here. I have eyes. But she wasn't good enough for you, was she? You set your sights on her ladyship! Miss High-and-Mighty! A ruse, you said. Let them think they were going, then you and I would slip away —!"

"Amanda, we can still —"

"We cannot." Her voice was weary, but definite. "I've done all you asked. Even to Emma. Stopped Dorrie from talking when she found you out —"

"And a few things I have not asked," Mark mocked. "Did I tell you to set Adria's bedding afire? Or to put the poison in her wine? It was you who convinced Dorrie the girl was a witch, then informed Anthony you saw Adria push the girl to her death. You took too much upon yourself, mistress!"

"I did it for you, Mark. For us." The woman swayed, her voice weakening. "Until tonight, I believed you were taking her in my place. I have her locked away in the stair room now."

"Indeed? I would say she stood behind you!"

The startled housekeeper whirled around and stared at Adria who stood, transfixed by what she had heard, the poker raised as if to strike. The pistols in Mistress Murchison's hands wavered as she lost her balance momentarily.

With one leap, Mark reached the housekeeper's side, slamming her against the rough wall of the chasm as her bad ankle twisted beneath her. Then, lifting her, he hurled her outward with all his might. The black-clad body seemed to soar for a space before it crashed to the stone steps near the ladies waiting below.

No one moved for what seemed an eternity as they all stared at the broken, crumpled body; at the pool of blood that formed beneath the housekeeper's head and began to run, snake-like, down the damp steps and into the sea.

Jane screamed. The poker fell from Adria's nerveless fingers, clattering down the stairs.

CHAPTER 29

The scream that rang through the chasm was like an electric shock; an awakening from a horror-filled dream. Except the nightmare had not gone away. Mistress Murchison's body lay huddled below, a twisted thing of black rags, the head tilted at an impossible angle.

And the man responsible for the housekeeper's death had turned his attention to Adria. He looked up at her, his boyish, winsome smile back on his lips.

"I see you have changed your mind, lass. You are going to join us?" It was the same beguiling tone he'd used on Mistress Murchison.

She could only look at him, her face bleak, hating. Once before, he had stood below her looking up in much the same way.

"I love you," he had said.

Now, seeing his flat, killer's eyes, she sensed that Mark Welles had never known the meaning of love. He was the true obscenity. A perfect body, a perfect face, and an imperfect soul.

"I would rather die," she said, her words falling into the chasm like a tinkle of ice.

Mark shrugged. "You do pose a problem, you know," he admitted. "You should have stayed where Amanda put you."

It was not a threat, but a statement. With it, he sentenced her to death.

"We've waited overlong now," he said, moving up a step. "The vessel may have moved to sea to ride out the storm. If 'tis true, we must hold here until it calms again. And we cannot have you running to Anthony, or his men in the quarters."

Her eyes went past him, fastening on the pistol that had fallen from Mistress Murchison's hand to lie halfway down the granite steps. If she could keep Mark talking, evade him as he reached her —

But she could not kill a man!

"I'm sure Anthony knows," she said coldly, returning her gaze to his face. "I believe he intended to let you go freely. But not now! Sir Edwin. Mistress Murchison. You have too much to answer for. You cannot conceal what you have done."

"Then I will deal with Anthony, also. It should be easy to lull the suspicions of his lads for a day or two. Tell them he wishes them to remain in their quarters. 'Twill not be difficult."

Dear God! He intended to murder Anthony. Anthony, now drugged and helpless. "You cannot," she said, in a voice thick with revulsion, "You cannot —!"

"But I can." He was smiling again, coming toward her, step by step, elbows bent as he flexed his fingers. A murderer's hands. He was planning to strangle her! For a moment, she stood frozen, seeing only his eyes fixed upon hers, growing larger as he moved upward, filling her world. Yet, strangely, she was not afraid. At least for herself. It was concern for Anthony that beat at her brain.

Surely the women below would intercede on his behalf. Elizabeth, Anthony's stepmother; Jane, who had once loved him.

With an effort, she managed to tear her eyes from Mark's hypnotic gaze, lifting a pleading hand to the women at the base of the rift.

They misunderstood her gesture. The Lady Jane's voice rose high in a taunting laugh. "You had best hurry, Mark, before she puts a curse on us. Remember, the girl's a witch!"

Adria's eyes returned to Mark's in time to catch a glimpse of something. A flicker of doubt? An instant's hesitation on his part? She recalled his words. *'Pray to your Puritan God for a calm sea … and a fair wind. Or to the witch of Wyndspelle, whichever you think will hear you out —"*

"Go on, Mark," came the voice of Jane above the booming sea. "Or are you afraid?"

Was he? It was worth trying!

Adria looked at her extended hand, seeing it crook into a witch's claw. God had not heard her prayers. Perhaps the spirit of Elizabeth Miller would. Had she not helped her that day when the Puritans had fired upon her from the cliff's rim? A strange sense of power surged through the girl's body. Her voice rang clear and true, like a sounding bell.

"He is afraid," she cried, "And he is right to be! I curse you! Thieves! Murderers! I curse you all! I consign you to hell, where you belong!"

Her last words were blotted out on a roar of wind. The sky over the frothing sea was riven by a brilliant flash as lightning descended, striking the brass-bound chest in the boat below, setting it aflame, blinding the occupants of the chasm temporarily, stunning and deafening them.

Adria recovered her senses first. She still stood, hand outstretched, Mark, dazed and white-faced just below. The others had been flung clear of the small boat which had burst into flame, a holocaust that illuminated the dark mouth of the chasm, pointing up the dreadful thing beyond it —

The thing that was coming from the sea —

A wall of water, as high as the promontory on which Wyndspelle stood. A great wave that would strike at the chasm with the force of a hammer. That would —

Adria found her voice and screamed. A thin, knife-like scream that rose above the roar of the wind. Mark shook his head as if to clear it, looked at Adria, then turned to follow the direction of her horrified gaze.

"God's teeth!"

Mark turned, plunged down a few steps, stopped and turned again. Now his face had lost its youthful charm. It was a thing of ugliness, lips curled back over his teeth in a snarl, eyes mad with hatred and frustration.

"You!" he choked. *"You —!"* He came toward her.

But Adria had scrambled up the stone steps, her breath tearing in her throat. As she reached the top with Mark at her heels, an arm reached downward, jerking her through the opening, throwing her to one side upon the floor of the wine cellar. She heard the crash as the trapdoor was slammed down.

And then Mark's muffled screaming. The frantic scrabbling from beyond the door. While all around her, the stone-walled room beat in her ears like a drum.

She looked toward her rescuer. Vincente. He stared at the closed door and then at Adria. He would open it, she knew, if she ordered him to. His face was impassive as he waited.

"Nay," she said in a sick voice. "Nay."

Without a word, Vincente seized her arm and rushed her up the steps into the kitchen. They had just reached its safety when the house was struck by a giant blow that set it shaking. It screamed in agony. A long, shrill shriek that rent the air and hung there, trembling, afterward. A death cry.

Adria shuddered against a weeping wall, watching in horrified fascination as water ran from beneath the door that led to the cellars from the kitchen, forming a pool on the stone floor.

Like a pool of tears.

She could hear the words of Reverend Potts above the sound of the mourning house. *"She called out to the spirits of the wind and the sea. A wind came, and a great wave. And when it was gone, it had taken her and those who stood on the sand."*

A story of a thing that had happened, and a prophecy of a deed to come. For Adria, too, had called, and the wind and the sea had answered.

And Adria had been given a chance to save her soul. The opening of a door might have saved Mark Welles.

She put her hands to her ashen face, hearing Reverend Potts say, *"You are evil, girl! Evil! The devil is in you."* Was it she who had brought the wind and the wave? Or would they have come in any case? Was it possible that she, Adria, was truly a witch — or possessed by one?

Whether she was or not, she thought dully, made no difference. For her list of sins had stretched to include the one God would not forgive.

Murder.

She looked at her hands, still smeared with the blood of Edwin Osmund. But in her mind, it was Mark's blood. Lady Elizabeth's. Lady Jane's.

Stains that would never wash away.

CHAPTER 30

Adria was awakened from her horrifying nightmare as an apparition appeared in the door of one of the cubbyholes leading off the kitchens. It was Mother Moseby, her scanty white hair flying, her bony frame clad in a ragged nightdress.

Candle held high, the old woman peered at Adria and Vincente, suspiciously. "Wot's this ruckus?" she wanted to know. "Fit to wake the dead, it was! Be you the one wot screamed out, mum? I 'eard it, I did." She frowned at Vincente. "You be 'urtin' the lydy? Eee! The master will 'ave yer ears, 'e will!"

Vincente's face blackened beneath her accusing stare. "Silence, old woman! You heard only the storm. We — we are checking to see if things are secured."

He strode to the back door, unlocked it and looked out, stiffening in surprise. Adria, remembering the building behind the house where Petro and Rico would be sleeping, followed him, fear catching at her heart.

The outbuilding still stood, but it was plain that the floors were flooded. The lightning that flashed from time to time illuminated the scene below, glinting on black waters that had surged into the cup formed by the horseshoe cliff.

Except for one dead twisted tree that clawed at the sky, the storm touching its wet branches with ghost-fire, there was nothing else to see. Wyndspelle stood isolated on its promontory, cut off on all sides by the sea.

As they watched, too shaken to speak, the waters seemed to lift, moving back toward them. The tree went down, and they saw it strike against the building below them. The structure stood against the onslaught of wind, water, and debris, though it shuddered and seemed to move for a brief moment. Then the waters parted as they reached higher ground, pouring down both sides of the rock on which Wyndspelle stood anchored, flowing in a rushing torrent back to the sea.

Only a pool was left. An inky lake at the lowest point of Wyndspelle lands, reflecting back the fury of the storm. The paths were washed away, gone from the sterile grounds that Anthony had thought to be a garden...

Anthony!

It was as if she and Vincente were of a single mind and did not need words. "Go to him," the man said. "I must see to my friends." He gestured toward the building at the rear. Then, as she turned away, he spoke again. *"Senhora —!"*

"Yes?"

"Closing the door against them — it was not your doing but mine. Do not let it cause you pain."

Adria's eyes blurred with tears. "Thank you, Vincente. And — Vincente — the little artist, Sir Edwin, he — he —!"

"I know, *senhora*. My friends and I — we will make the arrangements. Do you wish me to escort you to the master's room?"

"Nay," she said wearily. "Nay."

She climbed the stairs to the parlor and entered the great hall. Edwin Osmund still sat as she had left him. Such a strange little man he had been. Gregarious and lonely; malicious and kindly; cowardly but brave.

Eyes brimming, she bent and kissed his cheek as she did that other time. But this time, it was a kiss of farewell.

She went to the stairs that led upward. Clinging to the railing with blood-stained hands, she dragged herself, wearily, to the balcony and then to Anthony's room.

He was still sleeping. His breathing was not so heavy now, but it might be hours before he woke up. And in those hours, she must decide exactly what to tell him.

The truth? She imagined it in her mind as it would be told.

"You were drugged by those you love most. And Mistress Murchison locked me in the stair room. Edwin Osmund sits below, in your chair at table, Mark's knife in his back. And Mistress Murchison is also dead at Mark's hand, as I would be, as you would be, had I not called down a curse upon them, bringing the great wave again to Wyndspelle —! Therefore, Mark is dead, Lady Elizabeth is dead, and Jane is dead. We closed the door against them — Vincente and I — but their blood is upon my hands —"

It sounded insane, even to her! How would it sound to Anthony, who loved Jane, trusted Mark, felt a responsibility toward his stepmother —

And who did not believe in witchcraft.

Even now, Adria could not convince herself it had all happened. Dear God, if it could only be a dream!

She went to the window. Here, it looked over the land, still shuddering in the grip of the raging storm. She could not see the waters from here. Only the pool that was left where the land dipped down.

After a quick glance at Anthony who seemed to be resting comfortably, she stepped into the hall and entered her own room. Going to her window, she drew back the heavy drapes with a wild hope that Mark and the others might have escaped, that she would see a light bobbing against the dark ocean. A light that meant the boat had been salvaged and those trapped in the chasm had survived.

A flash of lightning slit across the sky, and she could see there was no longer cause to hope. If through some trick of fate, they had missed being swept out to sea, no boat could have survived in those waters. They boiled and churned, sending waves of spume high into the air in their relentless fury.

Like those waters, her mind could know no peace.

She went to the connecting door between her room and Anthony's, lifting the tapestry, sliding back the bolt. There was something symbolic about the action.

The man who lay in the great bed before her was a pirate and a murderer. But he was no worse than she.

There was a rumble of thunder as she pulled a chair close to his bedside. He tossed restlessly, mumbling something. A jumbled sentence that contained Mark's name. And soon he would wake to learn Mark was dead. And to the double shock, that those he loved had plotted to rob him, and to kill him.

She touched her hand to his, tentatively, and his own curled around it, tightening. "I love you," he murmured in a slurred voice.

Loved whom? Perhaps he thought that she was Jane!

Putting her cheek against his hand, the hand that had caressed her in love and struck out at her in anger, she wet it with her tears.

When morning came, Adria struggled upright. She had fallen asleep in her chair, her head pillowed on Anthony's bed, her fingers still clasped in his. The room was gray with the morning light; the wind no longer beating its wings against the windows.

Anthony's eyes were open, embers glowing in their depths. She could swear they were watching her — seeing her!

"It — it is I, Adria," she stammered.

"I rather assumed that it was." His voice was dry, amused. "I recall we were to have a conversation, milady. Did you dread it so much you would meddle with my wine?"

"Nay, I did not —"

"But someone did. I recall drinking it, then nothing more. I must have slept like the dead."

Adria trembled. All night, she had been planning what to say to him when he woke up, and ways to say it. Now, face to face with him, her mind was a mass of confusion. She needed time. Time to become fully alert. Her head felt the strain and exhaustion of the horror-filled night, her brain fogged with it. She could not think!

"You will need a cup of tea, milord," she said, jumping to her feet. "Then we will talk. I will go prepare it." She hastened to the door, stopping with her hand on the knob as he said her name.

"Adria."

"Y — Yes, milord."

"Send Mark to me, will you? I have something to say to him, also. It can no longer be postponed."

Adria fled without answering. Mark's name on Anthony's lips made her shrink, bringing to mind all of the hideous events of the night. As she crossed the great hall, she stopped at the memory of Edwin Osmund's glittering eyes. She forced herself to turn.

He was gone. The great chair at the head of the table was marred, but it was empty. Only an overturned wine glass remained to show the artist had been seated there; his monument, a portrait of a blind man staring down from above a lintel that had been a stake from a witch's burning.

And the house was breathing —

In Adria's mind it was suddenly the breathing of the dead, absorbed by this dreadful house, that would go on — and on —!

Clapping her hands over her ears, she descended to the kitchens. Water still stood pooled on the uneven floor. Adria looked fearfully at the door that led to the cellars, Mark's face seeming to float before her as she had last seen it, lips curled, hatred in his eyes. What if he had survived somehow, and was just at the other side of that closed door — waiting?

"The 'ousekeeper don't be down, yet, if 'tis 'er you be 'untin' for."

Mother Moseby's voice made Adria jump in fright.

"Eeee," the old woman cackled, "guv you a fright, I did. You w'ite, you are!"

"I didn't see you," Adria whispered.

"Course you didn't. You was a-lookin' at that door like you was expectin' the devil, like. Now, I wants to know oo's to 'elp me fix them trays for them upstairs." She glowered toward the ceiling. "Mistress Murchison sick abed?"

"No one's well this morning," Adria said through stiff lips, her mind racing. "There will be only Sir Anthony. I'll fix his tray and something for myself. You were disturbed so last night. Why don't you get some rest? We don't want you ill, too." Her attempt at a laugh sounded false in her own ears.

"Wot's wrong?" Mother Moseby glowered at her. "Be they faultin' me kitchens? No bad food 'ere, mum!"

"'Tis only that the storm kept everyone awake," Adria said. "And we are all chilled. Later, perhaps." Her voice sounded nervous and she was talking too much. At last, she said, "Oh, go back to bed!"

Grumbling, the woman complied. Adria fixed a pot of hot tea, placed it on a tray with two cups, and carried it back to Anthony's room, still uncertain of what she intended to say. As she approached the door, it opened. Vincente came out.

Adria stopped dead, the cups on the tray jangling in her shaking grip. Vincente's face was, as usual, inscrutable. "Vincente," she said, "You — you didn't —?"

"I told him, *senhora.*"

"That they were dead?" She saw the affirmation in his face. "But not *why*, Vincente? You didn't tell him what they were doing in the chasm?"

Again that expression that told her her fears were realized.

"I would not have told him everything," she faltered. "I see no point in destroying his belief —"

"*Senhora*, you should have more belief in your husband. Perhaps he knew more than you think."

He was suggesting that Anthony was aware of what was happening. How *much* had he known? That Adria, herself, had planned to leave with Mark to almost this last day?

She recalled the way he'd shown her the broken pendant, asking what she knew of it. *"Who are you,"* he'd asked. *"What are you?"* He'd known of the false gems, and he had considered her to be part of Mark's plans. A thief in his house. A traitor! As she had been, though misguided. Vincente, too, knew of it. He had seen her leave Mark's room, and in a disheveled state. She could not raise her eyes to meet his.

Nor could she face Anthony.

"Would you give the master this?" she asked, shoving the tray toward the servant.

"But he wishes to see you, *senhora.*"

"I cannot — I cannot!" She flung her head back and looked at him, her eyes blurred with tears. The man only gestured toward Anthony's door. Numbly, she moved toward it, then turned with a final, delaying question. "Have you checked the cellars? Has the water gone down?"

"You wish to know what has happened below, *senhora?* If the bodies are still there?"

She nodded, swallowing. "All is gone. Swept clean."

"And Sir Edwin?" It was a whisper.

"The master has instructed me to bury him at the turning of the path where it rises to the cliff. I, myself, will carve his name upon the large stone that marks the turning."

Her eyes burned. Though Edwin Osmund would be laid to rest in blighted land, it would be a place of his own. She had had dreadful visions of a small boat covered with canvas, waiting for calm to settle on the sea.

"Vincente —"

"Yes, *senhora?*"

"Make the letters of his name large, if you will. Large and deep-cut, so they will remain clear."

"I will, *senhora.* And is there more you would like me to place below the name?"

"Just *Edwin Osmund*," she said. Then she added, *"Artist and Gentleman."*

His expression approving her words, Vincente bowed and left her. Bracing herself for the coming interview, Adria entered Anthony's room.

He was up, now, dressed, standing at the window, his hands clasped behind his back. He turned toward her, his face dark with some unknown emotion. As always, she felt the magnetism of his personality like a shock.

"Vincente told me," he said, somberly. "'Tis over and ended, is it not."

It was both a statement and a question. What kind of an answer did Anthony want? What were his feelings, now that he knew he had been betrayed; that the girl he loved was dead — and with Adria's cooperation? His features were harsh, intense. Anger? Grief? Pain?

"Put the tray down," he said, "and sit here." He gestured toward a chair. "I have much to tell you and I want no interruption." Passing his hand over his eyes, he said, "I must think where to begin. Suppose I tell it as a tale, such as you told me that day in the study, beginning with *Once upon a time.*"

It was the story that Mark had told her, save for a few small changes. But those seemed to make all the difference. Adria could see a young Anthony, motherless, idealistic, and lonely with Lady Elizabeth as stepmother. Elizabeth, who loved only the boy's half-brother, Charles. Her own son. She pictured Anthony growing up, as he talked: somewhat wild, a rebel, taking on causes since in working with others, he found companionship.

She could see the responsibility he felt toward his young friend Mark, who followed him into Bolingbroke's service only to meet defeat.

"And," Anthony was saying, his face grim, "when we returned to England, Mark was destitute. I, too, was dispossessed of all that was mine."

Then he told how his brother had confronted him in a public place. It was Charles who had issued the challenge, not Anthony. And it was Charles who lay dead on the field while Anthony went to prison.

The remainder of the story was as Adria had heard it from Mark. Anthony's marriage to Emma; the return of his father's wealth to his stepmother and his brother's widow — save for enough to outfit a ship.

Adria flinched and Anthony looked at her, knowing that she had been told of his past.

"Aye," he said, wearily. "I became a freebooter. A pirate, if you will. There is much blood on these hands." He studied them, scowling. "Yet, I did not think of it as piracy. Only a way to repay a grudge against a world that had treated me most unfairly; a continuation of Bolingbroke's campaign. When I was struck down and blinded, it was like the hand of God. Mark brought me here, where every day has been a penance! The vessel now engages in honest trade. Fish and lumber for hemp and rum. Sometimes a passenger —"

"Such as Lady Jane?" Adria spoke for the first time since he began his story. "You must have loved her very much to send for her."

Anthony started, his face blank with astonishment. "*Loved* her? Good God, no! After what she did to me and my half-brother, Charles? It was she who urged him on, praying I might be killed before I could prove my identity. Yet, I felt a guilt. I could not let the girl starve or go to debtor's prison. No more my stepmother, whom I robbed of a son. Bringing them here, giving them what I had amassed in a wrongful way, 'twas my way of easing a festering conscience. A payment for the wrongs I did them."

It was what Adria had wanted to hear, but there was more. "What of your wrongs to *me*?" she asked, in a voice that trembled with remembered hurt and anger. "Why was it necessary to wed me in the manner you did — through trickery?"

Printed in Dunstable, United Kingdom

Anthony bowed his head, passing his hand across his eyes again. "Another mistake," he said in a dead voice. "Another error to add to my list."

"'Tis an error which may be remedied should you wish."

'Nay, hear me out!" he ordered. "Jane had heard from someone, perhaps Mark, that I had wealth once more. I received a missive from her stating that she still loved me. That if I would rid myself of Emma, she would gladly become my wife. She and Lady Elizabeth were in dire straits, and wished to come to Wyndspelle. *Look at me, Adria!*"

Her head jerked up to meet the full force of his angry eyes.

"Hear this," he said. "Then call me coward, fool, whatever you will, but try to understand. After I learned they were coming, Emma died. Poor harmless creature. I knew that Jane and my stepmother would try to force me into a liaison I could not abide. I needed a wife. And you came. I was in a state of desperation, and I used you to my ends."

"Treating me with contempt, at times," Adria said, her color high. "Humiliating me —"

"What would you have of me? I could not see you. I did not know you. You could have been anyone — anything. I had begun to mistrust Mark already, and to have some doubts about Emma's death. And you appeared at a most propitious time. You seemed to be Mark's confidante. You brought the anger of the Puritan community down upon us in what could have been a contrived plan. Mistress Murchison implied you were involved with Mark, romantically. And you were, were you not?"

Had she been? Perhaps for a short time. She felt an ache now at the memory of his boyish face, his merry smile, blond hair gleaming like a halo. But the picture was displaced by one

of a man who stood on the chasm steps, looking up at her with a killer's eyes, threatening her and Anthony.

"Adria, you have not answered me!" Anthony's hand closed over her wrist, pulling her up to stand before him. "You are such a little thing," he said in an odd, broken voice. "Do you realize that with my one hand, I could snuff out your life, as if it were a candle? I have thought of doing so, you know. Are you not afraid?"

"I do not think you would hurt me," she whispered. "Not without reason."

"But you have given me reason." His grip tightened and then released, slowly. "You have given me good reason! You have made me believe in you, when I did not wish to believe. You made me love you. After I had taught myself to love no one, trust no one."

Adria dared not believe her ears. *"You made me love you,"* he had said. Yet this could be only one of his moods. A promise of something that would be torn cruelly away.

"Anthony!" Her voice was taut. "Milord —"

"Be still," he said, huskily. "Be still!" His hand moved upward, caressing her cheek. Embers smouldered in the eyes that looked deeply into hers.

"For a lass who has endured much while her husband slept, you are a pretty sight," he said.

Adria drew in a shuddering breath. "You see me! You do! You *see*!" She had been right in her assumptions when she had stood before the portrait. "But how long — how long —!" She stopped, overcome with excitement, unable to finish her statement.

"Long enough to recognize my friends — and my foes," he added bleakly. Then, his harsh face softening, "Long enough to

see sweetness and purity in a girl's eyes. To know that I want that girl and need her."

With a sob, she buried her face against his chest.

"But I am not finished," he said, soberly. "My sight has returned in flashes. The ruby necklace first. Remember? And again on the day we walked in the gardens. I saw your features for the first time, that day. And I saw something else. The desolation around me. A land of death and devastation where I had thought flowers would bloom. It was as if I were cursed. As if everything I touched turned to ugliness and ashes. For a while, I was half-demented, believing I was damned for my sins. I swore I would protect you from myself, even though I made you hate me —"

"Yet you came to my room —"

"A moment of weakness. I could not help myself."

"No more than I can help loving you." There, it was out! She had said it!

Anthony stared at her for a moment, a figure carved in stone. Then he put Adria from him. Turning on his heel, he walked to the window, where he stood, feet wide apart, hands braced at either side of the frame. An edge of sun slipped from behind a black cloud, rimming it with fire, touching on Anthony's face, delineating his rugged features as he breathed deeply.

"Thank God," he said, softly. Then, in a hoarse cry that carried above the sound of the surf and the wind, "I thank you, God! For being kinder to me than I deserve!" Then, turning to Adria, his face still blazing with a new hope, he asked, "Is it possible, my love? Is it possible to put the past behind us?"

The horrors of the night returned to her. The memory of Mark's cries, the closed door that a word from her might have opened. And she knew, given a second chance, her reaction

would be the same. She wanted to hide her face in her hands, but instead, she looked Anthony squarely in the eye.

"As long as there is a future," she said.

"Then, if the ship still floats, we will board her and sail away. We will go to the warm islands, as I once promised you. We will find a new home, a new beginning, with the help of God."

His arms closed around her and he held her gently as she wept. For the first time in her life, she knew what it was to shed tears of happiness. And she could not hear the breathing of the house over the throbbing of his heart.

CHAPTER 31

Five days later, Adria and Anthony stood at the rail of his vessel, their faces turned toward the structure they had left forever. They had seen the ship's sails at noontide, and Vincente had signaled with a mirror from the upper room, asking that a boat be sent ashore. But it was only when they were at last aboard that they dared believe their good fortune.

The vessel itself was sorely damaged, with splintered masts and ragged sails, but it would make it down the coast to a port where it might be repaired. There, Anthony would go ashore and convert some of his treasure into coin, or give it in trade for supplies to make their journey.

But first, something far more important was to take place. Without telling Anthony of her fear that their marriage was not valid, she requested that they say their vows again. And Anthony had agreed. It would be performed as soon as they were under way.

"'Tis almost time," he said, touching her cheek with a loving hand. "I will go in search of the captain. But I do not wish to leave you waiting here. Come away. 'Tis not good to look back—"

"I cannot explain it, but I must."

"Very well, then." He smiled at her and disappeared among the sailors who swarmed across the deck, busy at their duties.

Adria turned to gaze back toward Wyndspelle, the intensity of her concentration surrounding her like a glass bubble, cutting out the sound and movement behind her.

It was a still time of day. The fog had not yet crept in, though the waters were beginning to blue with the approaching night. The sun was setting behind Wyndspelle, its last rays touching the rippling waves with edges of brightness, but Wyndspelle itself loomed dark and gaunt against the crimsoning sky. It was empty, now, for Mother Moseby was aboard, and Vincente, Petro, and Rico had gone down the coast to their own village.

Empty? Or was it? From where Adria stood, she could see the promontory and the beach below and to one side, where the Druid stones cast shadows — shadows that crept into the sea at the water's edge. And on that beach, there was a cairn of stones where Elizabeth Miller once stood, calling to the spirits of the wind and the sea —

Just as Adria had called. And her cries had been answered. But there was nothing in witchcraft to be believed. Anthony had told her. Still, if Adria did not possess magical powers, she had *been* possessed! And if she were, was it by the spirit of the witch of Wyndspelle — or some ancient evil within the house itself?

She shivered, now, thinking of the rift in the rock, the old tales that it was a stairway used by demons of the deep. Supposing it were possible! Supposing *things* might rise from the depths of the sea, to enter the great hall and stand beneath the portrait that still hung there — the portrait of a man with blind eyes. They would be things of horror, trailing sea-slime. The unquiet dead. Elizabeth Miller, Emma, Dorrie, Mistress Murchison, Lady Elizabeth, Jane, Mark —

Perhaps even Edwin Osmund, entering from the back door, shaking the grave dust from the ruffles at his wrists. A black cat following at his heels —

Returning to a house that corrupted. A house that breathed. Adding to its aura of evil and hating —

Impulsively, she lifted her hand. "If I have any powers, let me leave a spell behind to protect the innocent. As long as this house shall stand, shall this blessing be invoked. To all women such as Elizabeth Miller, such as I, who come here for sanctuary, deliver them from evil."

She halted, dropping her hand to her side. She could feel the power no longer. It was gone.

She moved her gaze down the shore a little, lifting her eyes to look inland. There, against the late autumn sky, rose a single column of smoke. It would mark the Meeting House in the Puritan colony, she thought, since this was a Sabbath Day. A place to which she would never return. Another part of her life that was dead and fallen away. She had never known happiness there, but still the thought of leaving it left a dull ache in her heart.

As Adria scanned the horizon, she caught sight of the island. The island Anthony had shown her through the glass from the upper room. Where the gulls nested in spring, each with his own territory, no love or kindness between them — like the Puritans, the Portuguese, and the devils at Wyndspelle.

Behind her, someone shouted in a spate of foreign words. Rigging creaked and the darkening atmosphere was lighted as ship's lanterns were set burning. Behind her, there was life. But the empty windows of Wyndspelle reflected the light briefly.

Spirit candles in dead eyes. Eyes that flickered and were still.

"Adria?" Anthony's hand was on her arm, warm, compelling. She looked up into his face. Scarred, sinister, mysterious in the fading light, it was the face of a man a wife would never know completely. Yet there was a gentleness behind it that made her

heart turn over. She knew he held her happiness in the hollow of his hand.

"Are you ready, my love? The captain is here — and waiting."

She looked up at him with dazed eyes. "Ready? Yes. But wait a moment."

Returning to the rail, she reached inside the bosom of her dress and unpinned the burned locket she still wore there. Leaning forward, she dropped it into the sea.

Why had she done it? She did not know. Perhaps a desire to propitiate the troubled spirits that lay beneath these waters. Perhaps a wish to be reborn this moment; to leave behind all traces of a child born on a storm-ravaged night; a Puritan lass who could not conform to Reverend Potts' teachings; the sinner of Wyndspelle —

She drew in a startled breath as something rubbed against her ankles. A black cat! The ship's cat, so like the one that befriended her — and died in her stead.

A witch's familiar?

Adria picked up the animal and held it. It purred.

You cannot run from the past, she thought. *It is always with you.* She and Anthony were moving toward a new beginning, but there would always be scars. There would always be reminders.

Head high, she stood for a moment. Then, placing the cat on the deck, she moved toward Anthony. It was time to be joined in a true marriage.

As the captain read their marriage lines, the vessel heeled and was underway, a plume of white in its wake as it caught a fair wind in its broken wings.

And behind it, a single gull circled in the red sky above a house that stood waiting.

BIOGRAPHICAL NOTE

My mother, Aola Vandergriff, was an American author in the 1970s and 1980s, writing twenty New York Times bestselling gothic and historical romance novels under her own name and a pen name, Kitt Brown. Reviewers compared her deliciously eerie gothic romance *Wyndspelle* to *Wuthering Heights*. The second novel in her 'Daughters' series, *Daughters of the Wild Country*, was recommended along with a handful of books for accurately portraying Alaskan history. She was humbled to find her name "right up there with Jack London".

Mom was born Lola Aola Seery on a college campus in Le Mars, Iowa, in 1920. Her mother once described her as, "a merry little pixie of a child with magic in her fingers and her eyes". Perhaps this daughter of a blue-collar craftsman and a teenage mother absorbed her love of books in this very environment. By the age of five, her talents, interests and abilities began to separate her from her humble beginnings when she stood before classmates and parents and read from Edgar Allen Poe's *The Masque of the Red Death*. By the time we, her children, were old enough to appreciate her special gift, she was our walking dictionary/thesaurus and our very own Scrabble queen.

As the Seery family followed my grandfather's work across the Bible Belt, they struggled through the Great Depression and eventually settled in Oklahoma. During these years, Mom earned small prizes in the Denver Post poetry contests. She was a voracious reader and prolific poet by the time she was twelve. She launched her writing career at seventeen with the publication of a book of poems, *Golden Harvest*, which she also

illustrated. The book earned her the title of 'Oklahoma's Baby Poet'. Fresh out of high school, she received her own radio program where she read her poetry to a large audience.

In the early 1940s, Mom became protégé to Jennie Harris Oliver, Oklahoma's Poet Laureate. Impressed with Mom's artwork, Ms. Harris chose her to illustrate her book, *Pen Alchemy*. About this time America entered WWII and Mom married a young soldier, Bill Vandergriff, and saw him off to England when my older sister was only two months old. He returned to civilian life when my sister was two years old, eventually becoming a New Mexico State senator. Dad's post-war jobs took them through several states while Mom focused on raising six children. I was number three.

I have great memories of a woman other people never knew. She would chase us, screaming and giggling through the house, with cold cream on her face. She loved rock hounding and was fascinated with "Pecos Diamonds". We always kept an eye on her as she drifted from one desert ant hill to another where the little residents had discarded these worthless pieces of quartz from their homes. She loved to watch the dust devils spinning in the distance, and when she said she wished to be cremated, my youngest brother said, "And when we see a dust devil, we'll say there goes Mama." I still say that.

In the evenings, Mom would sit in a chair or on her bed, kids circled around, and read a novel, or perhaps it was back to Poe, but she just never stopped reading, and she never stopped writing poetry. It is the hundreds of poems she left us that warm my heart and bring her close to me. When I picture her, I see her with a book in one hand and a cucumber sandwich in the other on her way to a hot bath. It may have been the end of our day, but it was not the end of hers. We could hear her typing late into the night, using the only time she had to herself

to craft her stories straight into the typewriter in near final form, seldom changing anything beyond the first page.

Mom did not make a leap from poetry to fiction, she just sailed into it. She used to say that when her children were nearly grown, she was leaning on a broom one day and thinking life is supposed to begin at 40. That thought spurred her to take a $3 creative writing course. Her novelist teacher, Ms. Ethel Bangert, immediately recognized her potential and pushed her forward. She began by writing "true" confessions and other short stories and articles. I hope I haven't spoiled the illusion that confessions are true. Eventually Mom published over 2500 of these stories. Now her long suppressed desire to write really caught fire. She sold the first novel she ever wrote, *Sisters of Sorrow*. It was so rich with exciting cliffhangers, Ms. Bangert suggested, "My dear, you must let the reader rest sometimes."

Mom paid the support and encouragement forward that she received from family, Ms. Oliver, and Ms. Bangert. She spoke at schools and various organizations and taught writing at American River College in Sacramento, California. She was also an associate editor for *Writer's Digest*. Mom was interviewed many times, including on a renowned nationwide television talk show where she was introduced, along with a racy novelist, as "Hot Blooded Writers of Lusty Novels". That was a misnomer for Mom to say the least and an affront to her genteel nature and passionate, but classy novels.

The unexpected reward of her career was when the woman who inspected every ant hill she saw in the desert and every dust devil whirling across the horizon now got to see the world with her husband and dive deep into history books so her novels would be as authentic as possible. Sometimes she had to come home and write, of course, and that is when she and Dad

built an adobe hacienda in a haunted New Mexico canyon where they finished out their days, perpetually in love.

Rebecca Williams
Daughter of Aola Vandergriff

A NOTE TO THE READER

If you have enjoyed this novel enough to leave a review on **Amazon** and **Goodreads**, then we would be truly grateful.
Sapere Books

Sapere Books is an exciting new publisher of brilliant fiction and popular history.

To find out more about our latest releases and our monthly bargain books visit our website:
saperebooks.com